The Girl
in the
Green Glass
Mirror

Also by Elizabeth McGregor

A ROAD THROUGH THE MOUNTAINS

The Girl
in the
Green Glass
Mirror

Elizabeth McGregor

BANTAM BOOKS

THE GIRL IN THE GREEN GLASS MIRROR
A Bantam Book / August 2005

Published by Bantam Dell
A Division of Random House, Inc.
New York, New York

This is a work of fiction. Names, characters, places, and incidents
either are the product of the author's imagination or are used
fictitiously. Any resemblance to actual persons, living or dead,
events, or locales is entirely coincidental.

Book design by Virginia Norey

Bantam Books is a registered trademark of Random House, Inc.,
and the colophon is a trademark of Random House, Inc.

LIBRARY OF CONGRESS CATALOGING-IN-PUBLICATION DATA

McGregor, Elizabeth.
The girl in the green glass mirror / Elizabeth McGregor.
        p.   cm.
        ISBN 0-553-80359-X
1. Dadd, Richard, 1817–1886—Appreciation—Fiction.   2. Art—
Collectors and collecting—Fiction.   3. Divorced women—
        Fiction.   4. Auctioneers—Fiction.   5. Architects—
                Fiction.   I. Title.
                PR6063.C485G57 2005
                813'.6—dc22   2004065585

Printed in the United States of America
Published simultaneously in Canada

www.bantamdell.com

BVG   10 9 8 7 6 5 4 3 2 1

For Roger, with love

The Girl
in the
Green Glass
Mirror

Prologue

He held up the magnifying glass to the light.

It was smaller than a crown piece and had a thick ebony edge, rubbed smooth, as smooth as the glass itself. He looked at it for a moment, at the grain within the wood, at the silky rim. He lifted it to his face and saw the world change again inside the glass, reducing down to flurries of shade.

Richard Dadd leaned against Bedlam's upper window.

This part of London's greatest lunatic asylum, in 1844, was a long corridor, filled with people, and there were only two windows, one at each end. Between lay a hundred feet of squalling darkness, a storm of indistinct faces. There must have been one hundred and twenty men crammed into the space. A hundred and twenty in the dark, and only two windows. A place of madness and fright. Someone close to him was sitting on the floor, his possessions huddled into his side, his arm sheltering himself against the shuffling feet of the crowd.

Dadd looked at the face.

It was a boy of perhaps fourteen. His skin was dirty close to the roots of his hair, but he had been washed by one of the attendants, a flannel taken swiftly round his face, leaving the tidemark of grime. Dadd looked down on this stranger, seeing the bone, the eye socket, the mouth, the eyes. Most of all the eyes. The hand without the magnifying glass twitched, the second finger and thumb pressing together. He needed a pencil in his *grasp, or a piece of charcoal. But not color. There was no color in these eyes, nor in any eyes he saw any longer.*

He saw only an eye leached of pigment, with reflections hurrying within it. And deeper still, beyond the surface of the eye, the alternative landscape of thought. Inside the thought, instinct. Inside the instinct, creation. Here was God in the eye of a bewildered boy sitting on a filthy floor. Here was God, forcing the fuse into the explosive, priming the weapon. Here was God painting light on darkness, fashioning the stars, and breathing creation into ashes.

Dadd looked away from the boy.

He turned back to the window, to the crane fly caught against the bars.

He brought the magnifying glass to it, searching the dry, convulsing thorax, watching the brittle leg pulling in the web. The fly became a monster, but audaciously beautiful. Opaque segments formed its being, faint spindles of carbon. In the tissue, he could see mountains.

He could see open sky. He could see mouths and grasses and insects and instruments and folds of fabric and sailing ships and hands. He could see Bacchanalia and Diadonus, a vine seat, the blade of a knife, and bridges and moorland and clusters of ferns, and the magician with his arms outstretched.

He leaned back, gasping.

There was another world, and another world, and another world.

1

It was only a week after her husband had left her that Catherine Sergeant went to a wedding.

It was a cold and bright spring day, a blue sky, frost on the deep grain of the church door. She purposely arrived late, to avoid the conversations; but she couldn't avoid them afterward, when the congregation emerged.

The photographer took the bridal couple close to the trees, to be photographed in the sunlight under a thin veil of blackthorn blossom.

"Catherine," a voice said.

She turned. It was Amanda and Mark Pearson.

"Why didn't you tell us that you were invited?" they demanded. "Why didn't you mention it? We could have come together."

"I didn't decide until the last minute," she said.

Amanda had looked around her. "Where is Robert?" she asked.

"He's gone away."

"Working?"

There was a moment. "Yes," she said.

She moved from person to person, friends of friends. Fortunately, this was not a family wedding; Catherine was a peripheral guest.

There were some people whom she didn't know, and who asked her nothing.

She moved to the very edge of the crowd and leaned for a moment on the wall. She was wearing red, and she thought suddenly how very inappropriate it was, this celebratory color, this color of triumph. She felt anything but triumphant. She felt disoriented. It seemed incredible to her now that she had come at all; got dressed this morning—got in the car. Driven here, in a new red suit, wearing new shoes. Incredible that she had even gone out this week and bought the shoes. Sat in a shop, wrote a check. Incredible that she had gone through the motions.

The routine things. Working, driving, buying, eating, sleeping.

Had she slept? Four hours, perhaps. Never more each night in the last seven days.

Looking out over the valley, this country valley folded in with pasture, dissected only by one road, and that road passing through what seemed now to be a gray cloud of leafless beech on the hill, she felt excruciatingly tired.

She looked down at the wall.

The corrugated color, pale green and acid yellow and gray, of the lichen on the limestone; that was animation of sorts. She focused on the colors. Beyond the wall, the graves. The angle of the April light against the graves.

ALEXANDER SEELEY, BORN 18 NOVEMBER 1804,
HIS WIFE CLAUDIA ANNE.

The snowdrops forming a white square. The blackbird eyeing her from the neighboring plot, perched on a stone angel with great folded wings, feather upon feather.

A couple nearby had brought a hamper. They were coming through the crowd laughing, holding up the wicker basket. Setting it down again on the path. Unbuckling the straps, they brought out champagne and glasses.

Beyond them, Amanda was beckoning her, holding up a glass.

It's not difficult at all, Catherine told herself.

Your husband is away, working. It's a very simple explanation. Simple. Plausible. You've come on your own out of necessity. But tomorrow, or the next day, he'll come home.

This is just a piece of time with a wrinkle in it, like a sheet wrinkled from sleep. Time had wrinkled away from habit, from predictability, and had become—only for a while—unfathomable, like the experience of a dream, where days and weeks become mixed. Living through this was just a matter of coming to terms with the change. Hours that buck and race or slow to a crawl.

Tomorrow or the next day, he'll come home.

Repeat it, repeat it.

Saying it makes it so.

2

It was 8 a.m. when she got to the auction rooms on Monday morning.

Pearsons occupied a huge barn of a building in a country town that had been known for its silk weaving two centuries before. Now all that was left of the silk was the single row of cottages on the main street, lavishly embellished above the doors with a scroll bearing the initials of the old company, and the Pearsons hall behind them, with its pink-yellow brick.

Behind the town were the chalk hills; open downland with shadows of old hedges, even of medieval fields. Sometimes in the last light of a winter day, as she drove over the tops toward the town, she could see the ghosts of those old furrows.

Catherine passed now under the archway of the front door: Georgian columns, a tiled floor of white acanthus on blue. She took off her coat as she went, glad to be inside. It was still bitterly cold. Just as she draped it over her arm, she felt for the cell phone in the pocket. Took it out for a moment to check that it was turned on. No messages. No text. She put it back.

Beyond the acanthus floor, Pearsons was far more prosaic: two small offices to either side, and past them a vast ceilingless room, the timber joists of the roof revealed. The hall was packed this morning, with barely an inch of floor space showing. "Victorian and General" was the sale title, and it encompassed a vast variety of objects, the remains of scores of lives. Dealers were already in, eyeing the goods: she recognized the usual faces, the diehards already scribbling in their catalogues.

She paused here, looking around herself at the variety. Nearest the door was a metamorphic library chair of modest beauty, decorated with floral inlay, its steps stored beneath the seat; past it, by way of contrast, was a peeling chest of drawers that had never been beautiful even on the day it was made. She edged down the narrow aisle, past desks and porcelain, empty frames, Lloyd Loom chairs, ivory and silver locked in the one glass-fronted cabinet; the skeletons of clocks, the gray-on-sepia of faded watercolors. As she passed a cardboard box full of vinyl records, she glanced down at the cover of the first one. Tchaikovsky's second piano concerto. The illustration on the sleeve was a damask rose. She looked at the rose for a moment, then turned her head.

And it was then that she saw the painting.

The face of the girl was looking down at her. It was a familiar portrait of a young woman seated on a chair; a woman in a white dress, her left hand holding the edge of the seat of the chair, her right hand curled in her lap. Behind her, the draped curtains were yellow, and there was a suggestion of a street. Muted blues.

Catherine's eye ranged over it again. If you regarded it critically, not a great deal was anatomically correct. The right arm was foreshortened, the fingers only outlined. The left hand was almost bulky. Neither was the frame of the chair absolutely right; the back curved awkwardly, as if added by chance. And yet, when she stepped back, the picture was perfect. Something in the failings made it wonderful.

Mark Pearson was at the desk at the farthest end of the hall.

"Catherine," he called.

"It's here," she called, pointing at the painting. "Why is it here?"

He got up and walked toward her. "He brought it in himself."

"Mr. Williams?" she asked, astonished.

"Yes. On Saturday. I couldn't turn it down."

No one would. The portrait was by a Scottish colorist.

"It doesn't belong here," she said. "It belongs in the arts sale next month."

Mark waved his hand. "I told him, I told him," he said. "You know the obstreperous old coot."

"But he didn't want to sell. He told me so."

"I knew he would, though," Mark told her. "Calling you back to the house—what is it? Four or five times?"

She frowned. "I can't believe it," she murmured. "I don't understand. He loved this painting."

Mark smiled. "Maybe he fell out of love with it," he replied. "It happens."

She shook her head.

As she walked back to the office, a dealer saw her coming and gave her his leering smile. She good-humoredly raised her eyebrows at him. He was sixty. She guessed twenty stone. Gray hair combed over a bald spot.

"Hey, Catherine," he said, looking her up and down.

"Hello, Stuart. How are you?"

"Fine display you've got." And he started laughing.

She went into the office, threw her coat on a table. "Brad Pitt, eat your heart out," she murmured.

She sat down and stared at the door she had closed behind her. She pressed her hands to her face, and the roses bloomed suddenly back at her, roses from the record cover, with their velvet petals, so sensuous to the touch. A bank of red roses in a garden, long ago. A bouquet of red roses in a cellophane wrapper, not so very long ago. Forty-two red roses of overpowering scent, of asphyxiating luxury.

Why did you send these?

Because I've known you forty-two days.

The door opened.

She took down her hands.

"What's the matter?" Mark Pearson asked.

"Nothing," she said.

"What did Stuart say?"

"It wasn't Stuart. It wasn't anything," she said.

He came round the side of the desk. "Remind me what you look like when it is something."

She smiled, and opened her calendar.

He put down a cup of coffee in front of her. "Take note of the cup," he said. "Minton."

"Thanks. I'm touched. What's this?" she asked, pointing at a calendar entry for the next morning.

He perched himself on the edge of the desk. "A man who rang up yesterday."

"Bridle Lodge?"

"Somewhere near West Stratford." He peeled a yellow Post-it from the edge of the page. "I wrote the directions down."

"Don't you want me here?"

He drained his own coffee and looked her in the eye. "Not with a face like a wet weekend, thank you."

She looked back at him. Mark, fifteen years her senior, was one of the kindliest men she had ever met. Kindly—and not simply kind—in an old-fashioned way, with courtesy and sweetness.

"What is it, really?" he asked.

She ought to have been able to tell him, of all people.

But she couldn't.

That night, she phoned Robert's mother.

She hadn't seen her in over a year. She sat in the kitchen, the phone in her hand for some minutes.

All around there was still the evidence of him. His magazines piled in the basket on the edge of the counter; his notes on the memo board: the chiropractor's appointment, the dry cleaning receipt. The coffee cup that he had used last Saturday night stood by itself on the board by the sink, where he had left it. She was too superstitious to move it.

When she eventually summoned the courage to dial, it rang for ages. She was about to hang up when Eva at last answered.

"It's Catherine," she said.

There was a pause. "Hello, Catherine," said Robert's mother.

"How are you?"

"I'm well, I suppose."

Another pause. "I know that this seems like a strange question," Catherine said. "But is Robert with you?"

"Robert? I haven't seen Robert for months."

"He didn't ring you?" Catherine asked. "Any time in the last week?"

"Robert doesn't ring me," his mother said. "For that matter, neither do you."

Catherine pressed the fingertips of her left hand hard into her palm. "There's been no letter?" she persevered.

"Catherine," Eva Sergeant replied, "what exactly is going on?"

"I don't know," Catherine said. "He left home."

"Left home?" Eva echoed. She sounded amused. "Have you had an argument?"

"No," she told her. "Nothing."

"There must have been an argument."

"There was nothing at all," Catherine responded. "I woke up on Sunday morning and he had gone. His clothes were gone. His money, cards, checkbook. His phone. Everything."

"You've tried his number?"

"Of course," she said. "I've tried it fifty times a day for the last five days. I've left messages."

"There's no need to raise your voice to me."

Catherine took a breath. "I'm sorry," she said.

There was a long silence.

Catherine imagined her in the five-story house. She could see Eva now, sitting at the basement kitchen table, the cigarettes next to her, the lighter in her hand. The house was always shuttered and closed. The upper rooms were faded, as if the house itself had drained the color out of the furnishings. Robert's mother kept the blinds drawn to preserve the carpets and furniture that she and Robert's father had brought back from the Far East, but, despite that, they still had a bleached look.

The kitchen was a relic of the 1950s, yet she gravitated there, to the warmth. What time was it? Catherine glanced up at her own clock. Six fifty.

"What is he doing?" Eva asked.

"I'm sorry?"

"Robert. What is he doing?"

"He's not at work . . ."

"But it's still the same job?"

"Yes." How could it be otherwise? Robert was wedded to his work. He was an accountant for a national company, based in a regional office in Salisbury. He drove for an hour each way, every day. He would set off at seven in the morning, always wanting to be the first there. Regularly, she suspected, he was the last to leave. She scoured her memory for some fragment from the last few weeks. Some mention of a client. But there was nothing.

But perhaps it was otherwise. Perhaps he had left his job. This spectacular possibility had never even occurred to her until this moment. The firm had told her that he was on vacation, but they could be covering for him, she guessed.

"Well, at least he hasn't been spirited away," Eva commented.

"What do you mean?"

She heard the sound of Eva lighting the cigarette, the intake of breath. "If he took everything, he intended to leave," Eva replied.

Replacing the phone in its cradle, Catherine stood up and went upstairs.

Only when she got to the bedroom did the full weight of Eva's insouciance hit her. She took off her clothes with a kind of savagery, got into the shower and let the water pour over her, turning up the temperature. She scrubbed at her skin furiously, washed her hair. How could a mother not care where her son had gone? Eva had treated it as if it were a joke. And then the final insult, the hint that Robert's leaving must be no accident, but, rather, planned. Not a word of comfort for her, no trace of sympathy.

Soap got into Catherine's eyes, and she rubbed at them, knuckling her fist against her face. Eva's tone had suggested that such behavior was inconsequential, almost to be expected. But Robert did not do such things. Robert was ruled by time. He was utterly dependable. It was one of the things that had first attracted her to him, this air of complete security and reliability. Eva was wrong. But then Eva did not care. Eva and Edward—Robert's father, who had died some years ago of a stroke—had sent their son to boarding school when he was tiny. Eva had showed not a particle of emotion on Catherine and Robert's wedding day. Robert had considered it a minor miracle that she had even showed up at all.

Catherine got out of the shower and caught sight of herself in the mirror, flushed, hollow-eyed. Drying herself off, she walked into the bedroom, laid down on the bed, and pulled the covers over herself.

She did not cry. She was too angry to cry.

With her eyes closed, the truth rushed up at her.

This was how she had felt about Robert for at least a year.

3

Her life—what she thought of as real life—began in paintings.

It had been one day in the summer, an interminable summer when London was full of asphyxiating heat, when the Portland stone looked bleached, washed out, aching to the eye like faltering neon, that Catherine had discovered the galleries. Tired of touring Oxford Street with her friends, pushing through tourists, the first visit had been prompted by an argument with her best friend. They had fought on the corner of Millbank over something too trivial to remember, and Catherine had caught a bus, got off by the Tate, and walked in, up the Cinderella-sweep of steps, idly imagining herself in full ball-gown regalia. Thoughts turned inward, to herself, to all the obsessive circularity of being fourteen. She couldn't have been less interested in art.

And then it began. She had found herself in a wide empty space where the floor was cool. She sat down, right in the center, and looked up, dwarfed by the paintings, the Raphael cartoons. She looked at the figure of Christ, and the reflections in the Sea of Galilee, so cleverly made in negative to bring the correct perspective to the finished tapestries. A thrill—the thrill of the ingenuity of it.

Until that moment, Catherine had been following her parents into a scientific career. A chemist. She had this blueprint plan for herself, to research something, to get famous for some discovery. To astound the world. She had opted for science because it seemed like an inside route, a path, a fast track to the unknown. Putting her eye to a microscope lens, she liked the invisible detail, the silent explosion of life that carried on every day without any human witness. She liked the thought that she—that everything—was built on these indestructible threads, threads that reformed themselves after apparent annihilation. Life triumphant wriggling in a mirror, in a piece of glass.

But this was the day—the day of the dwarfing Raphaels—that she first saw Richard Dadd's painting.

She had come away from the giants and wandered into a smaller room. There, on a wall in the corner, tucked away almost out of sight, she found him.

Catherine had leaned forward and stared. The painting was small, perhaps only twelve inches by ten. It was intensely green. It was called *The Fairy Feller's Master-Stroke*. Just below the center of the picture was a man, his back to the viewer, with an axe raised over his shoulders. In front of him on the ground was a dark oval, and the blade of the axe formed a gold rectangle above it, one of the few bright patches in a complicated sea of green and brown.

All that Catherine noticed at first was the man, and the crowd around him, and the fact that he was in some sort of clearing; then it dawned on her that the man was, in fact, standing not between trees but between tall grasses, and that the crowds around him were not ordinary people but extraordinary ones.

There were pirates, and dwarves, and dragonflies. Misshapen faces and hands. Tiny feet above grossly distorted calves; wings folded behind backs. Satyrs crawled in the weedy undergrowth; an old man sat almost below the axe. Courtiers of all kinds—insects, humans—surrounded a crowned couple. Under them, crouching under a daisy bank, his arms extended left to right across the picture, was a robed magician, his finger raised as if commanding the moment of execution.

She looked again at the title. *The Fairy Feller's Master-Stroke.*

She wondered for a second if the old man were the victim of the axe; then she looked again at the dark shape on the ground. It was a hazel- or beechnut, stood on end to take the blow, and split in half. A master stroke, to cut the whole in one clean movement.

Leaning down still further, Catherine had a great temptation to touch the surface of the paint. It was thick—each tiny leaf, each petal exactly rendered. The grasses cut across the painting like cords, raised up from the paint. Every fraction of a millimeter—even the eyes, the fingernails, were accurate, tiny as they were. Each crease of clothing and fold of skin. The exacting, almost painful detail. Everything in the detail.

At last she walked away from it, out into the brilliant gaze of the Victorians and pre-Raphaelites of the main display. She walked on past Sargent, and out again to Frith's *Derby Day*, and, running her gaze over the crowds in Frith's painting, she saw echoes of the goblin faces of Dadd, and the vibration of color of the axe hanging in midair.

Several weeks later she had found out more about Dadd: that he had shown promise, been hailed as a genius. That he had gone to Syria and Egypt and fallen ill there. That he had come home in the first throes of schizophrenia. And that he had murdered his father, cutting the old man's throat with a pocketknife, and spent over forty years imprisoned, and that the painting that she couldn't put out of her mind—along with all the other paintings that had started to inhabit her waking moments—that *The Fairy Feller's Master-Stroke* had been painted in Bedlam, the hospital whose very name had become a password for fear.

Her parents couldn't understand her. They judged the obsession with art to be a passing phase. They made light of it; even laughed about it, as if indulging a childish whim.

Working abroad as they did, her parents only saw her every month or so. They were sociable people, generous people, working in Brussels for Médecin Libre. Their life was talk—they negotiated aid agency funding; they crossed frontiers. For two whole years when she had never seen them—lonely years of being nine and ten, and farmed out to friends and families at Christmas and the holidays—they were in Somalia. Each a scientist, each an administrator, each with two pragmatic feet firmly on the ground, they caught the Richard Dadd story only as a passing half-truth.

"Is that real?" her father had asked her, laughing, as he drove at a suicidal speed out of London. "A painter? Some crazy painter?" He'd looked over his shoulder, smiling.

"I'm going to change courses," she'd replied.

Her mother had then turned to look at her. "To do what?"

"Fine arts," she'd said.

"Heaven help us all," her mother had said, smiling, thinking that it was Catherine's joke.

"Not real, my love," her father had repeated. She could still see his tanned hands on the steering wheel. He was so glamorous, this loud-voiced man, almost a caricature of the ruddy-faced Englishman. He had a life planned for his daughter. A life of research and exploration, a factual life. That was it, that was it exactly: a life of fact, a life in fact.

"Fine art history," she'd told them. The headlights of the car were dancing through the hedgerows. Pale blue light was stretched on the sky even though the ground was dark. Threads and filaments of stars and clouds were inappropriately visible in the blue. Dadd was whispering in her ear, a nail scratching on glass, a burr in cloth pressed to her skin.

Her school was on the fringes of Hampstead. Each day, Catherine passed a white clapboard house on the Heath. It had a curved bay window facing the road directly, so that if you couldn't see over the white-painted wood gates you might think that the house was very narrow, like a white shoebox. One day not long after she had seen the Richard Dadd, she had stopped to look at the blue plaque on the wall of the clapboard house. George Romney, it said, 1734–1802.

When she looked him up in a textbook, she saw that Romney had been an artist who had tried to set up a little academy and been bankrupted for his trouble. She had sat back from the reference book in the school library and thought of magnified threads, and Dadd's cordlike grasses, and Romney's brush on the canvas in the narrow boarded house on the corner of the street, and the detail—all the complicated detail—of observation in Frith and Dadd.

Turning the page, she saw Constable's painting of Hampstead Heath: a rural idyll with a blue-shaded London far in the distance; and later still, his pencil and watercolor drawn two years after his wife died. It was so full of dancing light, sun pushing rain from the canvas, a huge overarching ceiling of white light pressing from the left of the picture. She found that he had kept a scientific diary of the sky: *September 21st 1822, looking south, Brisk wind to East . . . S.E. 5 O'clock Wind East.*

It was the pinpointing of light on a certain day, at a certain time, that bewitched her. The carefulness of it all, the way that art stopped time entirely, framing a moment on a canvas, or in rock, or bronze. Frith freezing a London train station to a single moment of the late nineteenth century. Constable scratching his observations to seal a few seconds of an afternoon that would otherwise be completely lost.

It was the *seeing*. The artists saw the world, but something else, too, a part of themselves, transmitted itself to the picture, the canvas.

That weekend with her parents. Spring, fifteen years ago. Her mother had a cold and was curled up on the window seat of the cottage, staring glumly at the rain. Her hands around the coffee cup were roughened with salt. They had been to a freshwater project, an estuary in Israel. They still had temporary tattoos on the backs of their hands that a kibbutz girl had given them. Catherine remembered looking at them, at the complicated circular patterns.

Her mother had reached out an arm, to include her in her embrace. Catherine had sat with her in the window seat, watching the rain run down the windows.

"Such a dismal country," her mother had whispered.

"Do you think so?" Catherine asked.

"Absolutely," she told her daughter. "That's why I always come back here." The broad smile faded slightly and she tilted her head. "Will you tell me what's the matter?"

Catherine had replaced her head in the crook of her mother's shoulder, running her finger over the tattoo patterns. "Take me with you when you go," she'd murmured.

Her mother sat upright, and moved her body so that it was angled to face Catherine. She put down her cup. Catherine had looked into her eyes and seen concern and everything else her mother was: clever and courageous and outrageous, and—to a teenager—insufferably calm.

"You do such interesting things," Catherine had complained.

"But you must finish school."

"I know," Catherine said. "But when I was little, I always went with you."

And so she had: preschool. Her early years had been full of color. She did often wonder in adulthood if the sight and senses of those years had fixed her future occupation. She had all kinds of countries in her head, and each one without a name. Too young to retain the exact location, she could remember nevertheless the taste of coffee, drunk from her father's cup, on a bare roof terrace; of white and near-white and cream houses and other roofs falling, a spilled pack of playing cards, down a long hill, allied curiously and indivisibly with the very sweet taste of tomatoes, more like a sugary fruit than the acidic ones she knew at home. And other random memories: the sound of ripe oranges hitting a tin roof, waking her first thing in the morning, at a farm they had stayed at once in Jamaica, and of the red soil creeping between her toes as she took a bucket and collected every fallen orange before anyone else was awake, and of lemons lying rotting on the ground because the old man who owned the farm was too arthritic to bend to retrieve them; the carpet of orange and yellow and red earth, and the smell of the flyblown acid pith and flesh under her heel.

"We'll be home for six months after this project's finished," her mother told her now, trying to reassure her. "All summer, all autumn. We'll go riding. We'll get a cottage in the Lakes. How about that? Would you like that?"

Catherine had felt a rush of guilt. All her life she had heard about the worthiness of what they did. But she had this feeling—she had had this feeling since seeing the Dadd—some premonition. Of things that needed to be captured rushing away from you, of the necessity of holding on to the unseen, the unspoken. She had gazed into her mother's light brown, hazel-flecked eyes, seen her open expression, the smile.

"We'll make the time," her mother had promised.

And when they were both gone, and Catherine was alone, she held them in her heart with the entire experience of that winter and spring, that had begun with the Raphaels and *The Fairy Feller's Master-Stroke*.

Walking alone, walking down the sudden grief, so violent it hurt her like the residue of a physical assault, she could soothe herself only with light: the way light refracted in water, in mirrors and windows, and the way it was diluted or pinpointed or subdued by oils and pastels and watercolors.

And she would find herself staring into the heart of a picture, into Ford Madox Brown's *An English Autumn Afternoon*, into the shadows, into the startling brilliance of detail, the trees, the inclination of a woman's face, the distance of a church tower, the scrupulous delicacy of hands or wings or leaves against the green of a garden, longing to blunt the blade of unhappiness that she felt was pressed against her throat, cutting off her air.

Saturday morning.

Catherine was still in her dressing gown, on her knees, looking through the drawers of the study desk. She hadn't slept until three or four in the morning, and when she had finally woken four hours later, this thought was in her head.

That there would be a clue. There would be something—there *must* be something—that she had overlooked. A light, she had added to herself. A detail that she had overlooked. Everything in the detail.

She had gone straight to the room where Robert had seemed to spend most of his time in the past month or so. Closeted in the study, accounts spread all around him. Once she had looked over his shoulder and seen that they were their own household accounts and not a client's, as she had supposed.

"Anything the matter?" she'd asked.

"No," he'd told her.

She had never queried it. Robert always liked to check. He was a meticulous person. She had once admired the fact that he was so careful.

"I'm your walking safety net," he had once joked when they were first together.

She opened the first drawer.

It was full of stationery: his business foolscap white envelopes; paper clips, staples, postcards. She took out the postcards and looked at them.

Mark Raven's postcards from Amsterdam, bought in the Van Gogh Museum shop. They had gone there last autumn for the weekend. It had been her idea. "It seems a lot of money for just a weekend away," he'd protested. "But it's only two hundred pounds," she'd replied. "It's a special offer." "Even so," he'd murmured. But they had gone.

She spread the images out on the floor. Robert had bought these. Raven's colors: black, white, gray, green. Subdued. Here was a lovely Ghirlandaio portrait of a young girl in profile, dressed in a gold embroidered gown. She looked beautifully calm and composed. She imagined Robert leafing through the postcards while she looked at the art books. Picking up anything. Nothing. Something of significance?

She looked again in the drawer.

Catalogues of the Pearsons sales. A dozen or more. One was folded back at a particular page. She glanced at it. *Lot 543, a Victorian-style yellow gold necklace in the shape of a dragonfly with stylized foliate panels* . . . Her eye ran down the page. A pendant, a pebble pin, an enamel chatelaine. An aquamarine butterfly brooch. She frowned at the list. She couldn't remember if this page had any significance to her. She didn't recall being asked to bid on behalf of a client. She had no interest in the items themselves; she never wore necklaces or brooches. She only had one bracelet.

She looked at the dragonfly, composed of cabochon rubies alternating with brilliant-cut diamonds; an expensive piece. She put her hand on the page and felt how it had been folded back for some time, how the small book resisted being turned back to show its cover.

Putting it to one side, she looked in the next drawer.

Discs for the computer, a roll of parcel tape, scissors, print cartridges.

And the next. The bank statements. She had looked at these first, the very first day he had gone, feeling absolutely sure that Robert would have left a reason hidden here, in the language he spoke most fluently. She had scanned the pages for the obvious: unusual debits, unusual amounts or places. Looked, too, at the credit card bills, only received last week. No hotels. No travel companies. Nothing out of place.

She dropped from her hunched position, half squatting, and lay down on the cards, the catalogues, and pressed her face into the floor, her hands to her head, her body curled in on itself.

"Where are you?" she whispered. "Where are you?"

By midday, she was driving to Bridle Lodge.

She hadn't intended to do so; she hadn't rung the owner to say that she was on her way. She had just snatched up the car keys and her coat, and slammed the door behind her. Only when she got to the edge of town and looked down at the map beside her did she realize that she was panting for breath, in the grip of panic.

She was only here, only at the wheel, to escape the waiting; the waiting that hung behind her in the house. It was impossible to focus on anything but this persistent circular thought: *I'm waiting for him.* It had assumed a presence, a body, a weight. After drinking her coffee—she couldn't eat, but she was thirsty, persistently thirsty—she had stood indeterminately in the hallway; she must have stood there for at least fifteen minutes, oppressed by indecision. What if he came back while she was out? What if he rang?

She had stared at the silent phone. Staying in the house would not bring him back. Better to occupy herself. She ought to drive over to Amanda and Mark's. Ask them, confess to them what was happening. It made no sense to keep this secret.

"Why on earth didn't you say anything?" they would ask. "Are you crazy? How long has he been gone? Nearly two weeks! Catherine . . ."

"I've been waiting," she would say.

And it sat next to her now in the car, the waiting, like an inanimate shadow that she couldn't understand or grasp or get a hold on, or lever against. And she felt a violent resentment toward him for doing this to her, for making her this way, for throwing her into this helplessness.

She sat at the junction of the road until a driver behind her leaned on his horn. It was a narrow lane, at traffic lights. No other car could get past her. Eventually, the driver got out and came and rapped on her window, frowning.

"What's up?" he yelled. She looked at him.

I can't help it, I'm sorry, she wanted to say. *I'm waiting.*

"Oh, God," she whispered.

She held up a hand, an apology.

She put the car into gear and her foot on the accelerator and sped out from the junction without even checking the road.

Flight Out of Egypt

∞

1849–59

All Dadd had been able to think of since they had brought him to Bedlam was flight.

At first it was simply the flight of escape; he had hardly recognized that he was truly imprisoned—the time lost shape, compressed or elongated into dreams—and he had entertained a notion that to change his landscape would be as easy as putting a brush to paper.

But he no longer thought that way.

Five years had passed in the cages, as if he were a species of carnivore at the Zoological Gardens. Sometimes Mr. Munro came, the physician in charge of his case. Munro had told him that he was not only the son of a doctor and a grandson of a doctor, but that all three—son, father, grandfather—had been the physicians to Bedlam, the monstrosity of an asylum in St. George's Fields. He had told Dadd one day, trying to elicit a response from the silence, that he had been brought up in a house where Turner and Hunt and Cotman were frequent visitors.

At the name Turner, Dadd had looked up at him.

"I am not indifferent to art," Mr. Munro had said.

And they had brought Dadd oils and a canvas.

At first he painted what he remembered of his trips to Syria and Egypt, before the time that Osiris had captured him and shown him the point in the throat above the ridge of collarbone, the place where life is breathed into the body by God himself and the place where the blade must be put to release life. When Adam was filled with breath, God had put his mouth to this very spot above the clavicle. Osiris showed him the place, in Egypt, in 1842, under a full moon, while the crew of the boat chanted in a circle on the sands.

When Dadd had seen his father standing before him in Cobham Park that fateful evening, he had known what it was that he had been sent to do. The voices urged it; it was his divine instruction. It was not to end life, but to free it. Not to defy God, but to confirm him and his creation. Only the few were brought this way. Only the few were shown the edge of life where creation and destruction trembled together and fought for dominance. Osiris had put the knife in his hand, the forearm on his father's shoulder, the blade against his father's throat.

Come Unto These Yellow Sands, he had called a painting that same year. His siren call. A journey back to the sand-filled Nile, the silt making whorls in the water, his hand scoured by sand if he dipped it into the current.

On the canvas, half-naked and naked figures streamed through a rocky arch at the edge of the sea, threading like music realized in flesh through the sky, clefts and chords uncurling into bodies.

Inside the bellowing cages, the ranting galleries of corridors and cells, in the half-light afforded by tiny windows high in the walls, Dadd had painted Syria and Luxor and Damascus. He had filled notebooks with them all. He tried to bring back the aching sunlight he had known; the heat, the intoxication of the senses.

My mind is full of wild vagaries, he had told himself.

Outside in the greater world, men moved across the globe. Livingstone crossed the Kalahari Desert and reached Lake Ngami; the English colonized India; Paganini was approaching the last virtuoso ascension of his life; revolutions crossed Europe; Chopin struggled in the long closing journey of consumption; the speed of light in air and water was first measured by Foucault and Fizeau. And when Munro allowed the easel to be put before Dadd, he painted flight and deserts of his own.

And so he came, in the fifth year, to this great living image. The canvas was forty inches by fifty, a blaze of red, gold, white, and green. The water carriers, the women, and the men seated on camels and horseback, and the blades: spears and curved scimitars; swords and daggers at the waist. The broadness about faces and foreheads was back, the emptiness of some eyes, the unfocused insignificance. Hands reached from the bottom left-hand side of the picture, devilish claws below the seemingly innocent image of a shawled girl bringing jars to the side of the stream. In the center a warrior stood drinking, a leopardskin around his shoulders. To the right, a boy whispered in an old man's ear. There were dancing girls and merchants and soldiers, and in the corner, at the foot of this bedlam, was the Christ child at his mother's knee.

Dadd went over the painting again and again. He couldn't make the spear points go away, or the reflections of metal from the armor. Light picked up the spouts of drinking vessels and coated them in silver. Anywhere the mouth touched. Anywhere God had put his mouth to man, breathing life through the color on the brush. They were created and ignited, all of them, all the girls, every child, all the women's faces, all the knowing broadness of the men, the strange ridged veins on the forearms, through the bleeding tip of the brush.

It exhausted him.

He had flown; he had disappeared for a while. He had vanished into a painted crowd.

4

Robert was coming through the airport when he saw Amanda.

He supposed that it had been ridiculous of him to imagine that he might get away with becoming invisible, and as soon as he saw Catherine's business partner standing at the departures gate—Amanda in all her full-blown finery, the white pashmina, the upraised arm as she waved to her retreating mother, the whole commanding Amanda—his heart did a lazy double-flip.

Well, so here it came.

"Robert!" she called.

He smiled and pushed the luggage trolley in her direction.

She reached out and kissed him. "Been away?"

"Yes." Did she know? Was it possible that she didn't know?

He stood and looked at her.

"Anywhere nice?"

A beat while he looked at the bland expression on her face. "Italy," he told her. "Rome."

"How lovely!" She was already shepherding him out of the flow of arriving passengers, hand under his elbow. "I must say, I approve of a company that sends one to Rome on business." She sighed. "I can't remember when Mark and I last went anywhere. The only time I see a bloody airport is when I bring Mother here."

They were getting to the exit. He listened to her objectively, politely, wondering if he would ever see her again.

"She says she's perfectly capable, but, you know, seventy-seven! I imagine her going around and around the M25 in some taxi, forgetting where she's meant to be."

"Is she well?" he asked. He didn't want to know. In fact, he didn't want to talk. He wanted to get away.

"Arthritis," Amanda said. "Mark will be breathing a prayer of thanks as we speak. She's awful to him. Awful."

They stopped. "Got your car here?" she asked.

"Yes."

"Don't want a lift?"

"No. Thanks."

There was the slightest of pauses. Amanda frowned a little. "Catherine will be glad to have you back," she said.

Was there anything in the phrase? *Catherine will be glad to have you back.* No. Amanda would not have kept her temper if Catherine had confided in her. He would have been met with a stream of invective and demands.

"Well," she said. "I'm off, before the M4 disappears under a tide of Range Rovers heading west."

"OK."

"See you at home," she told him, and kissed his cheek. "Why don't you come to supper on Sunday? You can tell us all about Rome."

He smiled. "Good-bye," he said.

And watched her thread her way through the crowd. She walked at a rapid pace. She drove the same way, he knew. She would be back in three hours or so. Perhaps three hours or four before she spoke to Catherine.

Is Robert home yet? I saw him at the airport.

"Good-bye," he murmured again to himself.

5

In the spring, the valley below Bridle Lodge had flooded.

John Brigham had walked his dog right down to the water meadows and seen the river break its banks. It had been a Sunday morning. The weather was bright and cold after the week's downpour of rain, but the force of the water from upstream had suddenly pushed the capacity too high. In a second, John saw the meadows, with their Victorian irrigation ditches that so rarely filled, turn from a vivid green plain, intersected by low hedgerows and trees, into a lake.

He'd just been coming down the path from Derry Woods; it was eight in the morning. Ahead of him, Frith was charging along the bridle path, the spaniel's tail whipping about. John had stopped at the intersection of three paths, one that led deeper into the woods, one that led back to the lane, and the third that came down into the village by the bridge. He had looked at the valley below him, with streams of mist pouring off the river and a faint wash of blue in the sky promising a sunny day. He had leaned on the stile for a long time.

At that point he had been back in the country for just two weeks; lived in Bridle Lodge for just ten days. Frith was still cold, shivering at English frost after the Andalusian sun. In Alora it would be mild now, the first heat coming to the mile upon mile of olive trees. There would be a curious opalescent haze along the coast, the harbinger of summer; the corrugated iron of the terrace roof would begin its spring percussion, cracking and expanding in the afternoon heat. They had lived in a farm near Alora, in the mountains, for the last seven years. In January he had rented it out, packed his bags, and come home.

Frith ran back to him as he leaned on the stile, one hand on his chest, knuckle pressing under the sternum. The dog watched with anticipation, a quizzical expression on its face.

John had got over the stile and walked on, and Frith kept close to his side along the narrower path, hedge on one side, field fence on the other. Sheep were on the pasture below the wood edge, on the slope of the remainder of the hill; they bunched in one corner as dog and man passed. Only as they rounded the hill did John see the sudden influx of water onto the meadows below. And the strip of tarmac lane, which barely allowed two cars to pass, suddenly vanished.

A man of fifty or so was standing outside his house as John and Frith emerged into the village. The bridge, a three-arched packhorse and four centuries old, was now just a brick strip with no road leading to it, and no road leading away from it. The well-trodden river paths were gone, as were the shallows where watercress grew impossibly thick in the summer. The river was a fantastic sight near the bridge: contorted, swirling. A writhing gray mass. Farther out, the grass had gone. The water flowed away almost serenely, in rippling shallows. Several other people had come out of their houses to watch.

"It just went like that," the man said to John, snapping his fingers. "There was a car coming along the lane," he added. "They had to go in reverse. Elderly driver, too."

"Where are they now?" John asked.

"Somebody come along behind them," the man replied. "They turned the car round for them."

John smiled. The man held out his hand. "Peter Luckham."

"John Brigham."

"You're the new man in Bridle Lodge?"

"That's right."

"You don't mind my saying . . ." Peter began.

"What?"

"Well, this might not happen if the weirs and channels were cleaned out at the Lodge."

John had frowned. "Weirs?" he said.

"Down below the house, where the rhododendrons are."

John knew the patch, of course. Even as the hasty prospective buyer he had been in the autumn, on a flying visit from Spain, he could hardly have missed the giant rhododendrons and camellia below the tiered walkways. The gardens close to the house were untidy and unloved; but where the lawn and box tree hedges ended, the garden fell away toward the stream in a series of zigzagged paths, the gravel of which had been full of leaves and weeds when John had given them a cursory look. The rhododendrons climbed up beyond them, forty feet high.

"A wonderful sight in the spring," the estate agent had commented.

And John had thought to himself, *A wonderful amount of work*, and speculated if he would see it done.

He looked back now at Peter Luckham. "There are weirs," he said, flatly stating it.

"There used to be, when my father worked the garden," Peter replied. "A whole series of gates. You could regulate the water."

"I haven't noticed anything," John told him.

"There isn't much to see with all that muck," Peter replied.

John had smiled. Muck was one way to look at it—a forest of uncut shrubs, the densely overhanging evergreens, the tangle of nettles and hellebores. A few days ago, he had glimpsed the first shoots of blue between the trees, and realized that the ground would soon be awash with bluebells flourishing in the dank shade.

But weirs on the stream? Weirs and irrigation gates? No. He hadn't seen them.

"Pettertons built the Lodge in 1880," Luckham continued. "Planted the gardens out. Put in the weirs to make a lake. More a pond now. Choked with water lily. All that stretch that looks like marsh."

"All of that is man-made," John mused, seeing how it made sense. All winter it had simply been swamped with mud. A thick bank of willows obscured what he had thought was a natural bank.

"Wants clearing out," Luckham said, hands in pockets, gazing at the bridge. "If you don't mind my saying so."

It was almost spring now. Or would be in another month.

John had begun the crazy task himself weeks ago, one evening in February. He had gone out just as the light was fading and walked down to the lower garden.

Dusk was ephemeral, barely fifteen minutes in that low, gray day. He had been sitting indoors and the oppression of the flat sky, threatening rain but never quite delivering, had got to him. He had to go out to get air.

Frith had been delirious, running in circles on the wet lawn, leaving muddy sprays where he skidded. John followed at a slow pace, feeling the immediate settling of damp on his clothes. The trees dripped moisture.

He had felt then, and the remainder of that week, that he should not have come back, let alone bought the Lodge. And yet it had been an overwhelming conviction to come home that had possessed him all that autumn. It wasn't that he felt the prognosis would be any better in England. He just wanted to be in England again, to be where he had grown up. And he had to remind himself of that as he had walked down through the trees to where the lakes had once been. This is what he had come back for, he told himself; England in its underwater gloom of January and February, as the endless Atlantic rain swept in across the Somerset levels.

He had stood under the laurels and camellias and looked at the water that threaded down the slope. He was thinking of the last design job in London before he had left for Andalusia. He had been forty then. It was two years since Claire had died. Even when he took the Hampstead job, he knew that it would be his last in England. It was his turning point, his new life. Everything he had touched was full of change.

He had made that last house full of light.

The client had seen the Daryl Jackson beach house in Bermagui and wanted something exactly the same, with full-length wood-framed windows and a loose informality of styles. He couldn't provide Bermagui, of course. Hardly, in Hampstead, in a row of Edwardian terraces. But they did take out the back wall to two stories, and extended the stone yard fifty feet, and put in an open passage that was almost like a cloister running through the center, with windows on either side opening out into the garden.

"It's so light," the couple kept saying. "So light."

And that's what he had given them: some of the light he could feel slowly filtering through himself after two years in the dark. Two years of sleepwalking through London from one project to another, fixated on stress structure and weight ratios and planning permissions; hunched over his drawing board until the early hours of the morning because he dreaded the empty bedroom. Marking time only, in a kind of painted forest.

That's what London—that's what everything—had been to him then. A kind of moving fresco projected onto walls. Silhouettes only, with very little sound. After Claire went, and he drowned himself in work, everything around him had possessed this two-dimensional quality. Plans in his head. Drawings of buildings. Renovations. The curious flat place where his life ground almost to a halt.

And when houses were finished and became three-dimensional, and the flat spaces were filled with people—with talking, moving people, and families, and animals, and colors—then he lost interest.

All the talking and animation seemed to disgust him. He didn't want noise. He didn't want families and color. He wanted to stay in the flat white world he had created.

But the last house, the Jackson-inspired house, was quite different. On the day they finished, he drank champagne with the owners and felt their thrill. They were beginning something. And so was he. He was going to Alora, in the Spanish mountains, to live in the light. He left his business in capable hands; he would keep on the office and the staff, returning only for the odd consultancy. He felt that the time had come at last. He was breaking away. His world was altering.

There had been a sudden flurry of movement. Frith had come hurtling out of the bushes. Preceding him, with a clockwork whirring of wings, was a pheasant. Surprised, John stopped. His thoughts of houses and light flashed past with the movement of the bird and the dog. He was suddenly back in the gray and dripping garden. The pheasant skirted the ground, hauling its body aboveground with obvious effort. Then, in the very next second, Frith was gone.

The dog simply vanished for a second, one moment on the edge of the path, the next nowhere. John had run forward. The next instant, Frith surfaced from under the mat of thick weed; spluttering and thrashing, he tried to get back to the path.

"Here, Frith," John called. He bent down. "Get out of there."

Frith, soaked to the skin, the liver-and-white coat plastered flat, looked at him with almost human eloquence. He was getting nowhere. Only his front half was visible; he started clawing at the surface. His mouth gaped open with effort and he started to whine. It was a noise John had not heard before: not the whine of excitement or impatience, but a kind of keening terror. Then, abruptly, he went under.

John sat down on the path. He hesitated a second, then he swung his legs over the side and into the slush of mud and weed. He felt about for purchase under the water and felt a gravel edge. He stepped forward, feeling about with his hands for the dog. There wasn't a hint to show where Frith had been. The water lilies, discolored by frost, leathery and tattered remnants of summer, and laid over with rotted leaves, obscured everything. He began to gasp with the cold. He could feel blanket weed clinging to his legs and fingers. He started to sink: mud had replaced the gravel underfoot. He tripped slightly on something heavy: a branch, lodged next to the bank. His boots filled with water.

"Frith," he muttered, hands splayed beneath the water, feeling for him.

The dog's whole body weight suddenly crashed into his leg. He could hardly get hold of the spaniel because, in panic, Frith was trying to lunge upward. John stooped in the water and got both arms around Frith's body. He pulled. Frith's head came out of the water and the dog's claws dug into his shoulders. But John couldn't pull him any further. He felt down the body and his fingers fastened on thick weed wrapped around Frith's back legs.

As Frith pulled, the weed tightened. John felt in his jacket for the pocketknife he sometimes carried. But it wasn't there. He sank a few inches deeper into the underfoot slime; Frith, seeing the bank and safety, tried to wriggle out of his grasp, over his shoulder. He had to grab the scruff of the dog's neck and shake it.

"Stop," he shouted in its face. "Keep still."

He felt in the other pocket. Miraculously, a pair of pruning shears. Underwater, he got them out and, holding Frith with his right hand, felt about for the weed, trying to get purchase in a left-hand grip. Frith flopped against his shoulder, the dog's head on his neck. John could hear water rattling in Frith's chest.

It seemed hours before he cut through the weed, but in reality it could not have been more than two or three minutes. But as soon as Frith felt himself released, he lurched for the path and John lost his footing. With a splash, kicking clumsily, he went underwater, and it closed over his head. He had a second to feel himself into the murky green world below; then he surfaced. He lost a boot, climbed out of the water without it, and lay on the path gasping.

There was absolutely no pain then or when he got up. He straightened, with mud and water streaming off his clothes. Frith stared up at him, slowly and apologetically wagging his tail. John turned round and went back to the water's edge, took hold of the nearest clump of lilies, and wrenched them out of the pond. With them came the matted weed; he dug his heels into the ground and tugged. The stuff came up with a rush of suction; he flung it behind him. He got back down on his knees and found the branch that he had tripped against; he pulled it to the side and yanked at it until it came free. Frith seized on it and dragged it away, enormously pleased at this unexpected prize.

On hands and knees, utterly soaked to the skin, John felt the breath scorch in his chest. He stopped and then stood up. He was beginning to shiver. Calling Frith, he set off for the house, and it was then, under the lavish greenery of the camellias, that the pain struck. John knew far better than to try and get to the house. He sat down while the garden tilted and his view of it compressed into a narrow line. He thought: *No one will be here for days. Maybe a week. Maybe more.*

Eventually he laid down on the gravel, on his back, while the pain cruised through him, a heavyweight pain, an out-of-control truck gathering speed down a highway.

"Shit," he muttered. Frith came to look down at him.

"You'll have to bury me," he told the dog, and started to laugh at himself, at the absurdity.

He waited, expecting the impact.

It didn't come.

Only when the last of the light had gone did he get up again, and felt his way to the house in the dark.

The men came up at the beginning of March and it was now four weeks since work had begun. A landscaper did the really heavy-duty stuff during the week, but on the weekend it was just John, and Peter Luckham and his two sons.

In the last month, the mesh of willow and reed had been taken away, and one of the willow trees itself, rotted beyond saving, had been cut down. Now, when John stood at the edge of the path, he could see right across the fields to the Sherborne Road.

They had found four little footbridges and discovered that the first two ponds were almost circular. At either end of each bridge was a stretch of brick in the ground, each shaped like a fan. In the center of each fan, lighter-colored brick described the intertwined letters *L* and *H*.

They had all stood round and looked at the design.

"Who were L and H?" John asked.

"I don't know," Peter told him. "The first owners, maybe?"

They worked their way along the banks. A trailer attached to John's four-wheel drive towed the debris away, plowing a furrow up the garden paths and across the lower part of the lawn.

It was Saturday morning and the sun was out. They had stopped to inspect the mechanism of an irrigation gate when Peter Luckham noticed the movement of a car turning off the road and beginning along the drive.

"You've got a visitor," he observed.

John looked up. The small red car disappeared between the trees.

"Expecting anyone?" Luckham asked.

"No."

They carried on with their work; two minutes later, John's cell phone rang. He fished it out of his coat, looked at the display, but didn't recognize the number.

"Hello?"

"Mr. Brigham?" A woman's voice.

"Yes."

"I'm Catherine Sergeant, from Pearsons. You asked us to call?"

"Is it you up at the house?" he asked. "Driving a red car?"

"Yes," she replied.

"You didn't make an appointment."

"I'm sorry," she said. It was a perfectly toneless reply.

He sighed with impatience, shook his head. "Wait there," he told her finally. "I'll be up in five minutes."

He turned to Peter Luckham apologetically.

"Selling something?" the man asked him.

"Yes," John replied. He shrugged his way out of the coat and threw down the heavy gloves.

"Hope it's worth something," Luckham said. "To pay for this lot."

She was sitting in a patch of sunlight on the porch, on one of the wooden seats. With the tip of her shoe, she was tracing the tile pattern on the floor. He couldn't see her face, only the light brown hair and the slenderness of her hands, folded in her lap. By her feet was a briefcase. She wore a pair of jeans and a sweater, not the usual business suit.

"Miss Sergeant?" he asked.

She looked up.

He stopped in his tracks. He knew her. This was the girl.

The shock of her face astounded him, took his breath away. He saw her unguarded expression for just a second: naked sorrow. She stood up and held out her hand. She seemed to pause, too, and hold his gaze. Then, "It's the same pattern," she said.

"I'm sorry?" he said. He tried to look away from her, in case she thought his expression was strange.

"The floor here," she said. "Exactly the same pattern as the entrance hall in Pearsons."

"Is it?" he asked. They looked down at the yellow-and-green floor together. "Acanthus," he said.

"That's right." And she smiled.

He released her hand. He had got something from her; some tremor, like extreme fatigue. She had a lovely face, but my God, he thought. He had never seen anyone so pale.

"I'm sorry if I disturbed you," she offered. "You're working in the garden? I saw the tree by the drive."

They had put the carcass of the willow there for collection. "Yes," he told her, getting the door key from his pocket. "We're clearing the waterway."

He opened the door leading into the shadowy hall. He wondered what her reaction would be. He hoped he wouldn't see her cast an insurance assessor's eye over the place. He hoped her attitude—what seemed to be a quiet, taciturn attitude—wouldn't change.

He ushered her inside. Their footsteps echoed a little.

Bridle Lodge had been built in 1880. From the first moment he had seen it, he was touched by its style, the upper windows framed by their decorative columns and pediments, as if trying to be classical; the lower windows and doors entirely Gothic, arched and pointed. Whoever had first designed the house had built a plain and substantial villa, a truly Victorian red sandstone pile. Then, it was as if the owners had suddenly come into money. They had poured the incredible embellishments all over the house, decorating every inch of stone so that it crawled with leaves and vines, putting elaborate ridge tiles on the roof, with shields and spearheads in the castellated pattern. But it was really inside the house that they had excelled themselves.

The estate agent had been apologetic. "It's been allowed to decay a bit," he'd said when they'd gone into this same hallway. And he'd stuck a finger in the paneling. "Got a bit of worm," he'd noted. "Might as well point it out to you. Not a great deal to put it right, but all the same . . ."

But by then, John hadn't been listening. He'd been staring up into the enormous stairwell.

All the way up the stairs, alternate treads were topped by painted panels. They had once been gold; now the paint flaked. Here and there, it had simply been painted black. But those that remained were beautiful faded icons of William Morris and Burne-Jones: each panel a picture of herbs or fruits. Variegated sage, a checkerboard of pale green and white; oranges and their fruit blossom; apricots, grapes, apples.

But the window. The amazing window.

Halfway up, the stairs divided, going from a single wide flight into two that took a dogleg turn and went up to the first story on left and right. And at this halfway point was an enormous stained-glass window. It was the most astonishing color. Pale sea green, the color of a tropical sea just where it touches the sand. Hundreds of small circular discs made up this section, discs varying from turquoise to yellow, and, combined, producing this watery effect. Right in the center of the window was a pre-Raphaelite figure: a girl, her fair hair braided modestly on her shoulders. She was holding the heavy fabric of her dress in deep folds.

He had walked straight up the stairs and gazed at her.

"Lovely feature," the estate agent had said. "Very rare."

John had been speechless. He'd been looking at the girl's face. She was the girl from Holman Hunt's *The Awakening Conscience*, the girl starting up from her lover's lap to gaze at the transforming light from the garden.

"Who did this window?" he'd asked.

"I couldn't say."

"Not a local artist."

"I really don't know . . ."

John had looked down at the house details in his hand. For the hallway, it simply said, "Paneled stair with stained-glass window."

He'd put his fingertips on the window. Some of the green glass discs were cracked. But the glass was thick, with very faint traces of air.

Now, as John brought Catherine Sergeant into the hall, she said nothing. She didn't seem to notice the window, which was behind her; she had walked ahead of him, her eyes on the floor. She stopped and waited for him, glancing in at the boxes in the nearest room and the alarm on the wall outside the drawing room.

"I haven't unpacked everything yet," he told her. "But the kitchen's habitable."

"Is the dresser in there?" she asked, naming the piece of furniture that he wanted valued.

"Yes," he said. He opened the kitchen door.

Catherine walked forward, glancing left and right. Then she turned back to look at him. "The Astons owned this house," she murmured.

"That's right," he said. "Did you know them?"

"Yes," she murmured. "Not Colonel Aston. He had died by the time I joined Pearsons."

"His wife lived alone, I believe."

"Yes," she told him. "For twenty years."

He smiled. "Nothing had been touched. There was even electrical wiring tacked to the plaster, running along the picture rails. When I lifted the floorboards"—he paused slightly—"some of it was the original, the 1920s stock, like telephone cable."

"I visited her in the nursing home, but only once or twice here."

"So you don't know the house?" he asked.

"Not really. It was always rather dark in here."

"I must show you one day," he said. "It's an Arts and Crafts museum."

She said nothing. He wondered again at her soft, compliant attitude that almost smacked of indifference. She was hardly the saleswoman he had expected.

"This is the dresser," he said.

She was already looking. She placed her hand on the satiny top, rubbed smooth by generations. "French," she said.

"Yes."

"A family piece?"

"My wife's family."

"It's lovely," she told him. "Why does she want to part with it?"

"She isn't here anymore," he told her. "And this, as you can see, is really too large for this room."

She looked directly into his eyes. "Even so," she said quietly. "It's a shame to part with it. I'm afraid you won't get what it deserves here. You would raise more for it in London."

"You don't want to take it on?"

"Oh, we'll take it, of course," she told him. "I only hope we can do it justice."

He smiled at her. "Would you like some tea?"

"Thank you," she said. And again she gave him a lingering look, a duplicate of the one when she had first taken his hand.

He indicated a chair. She sank into it. Just as she did so, he noticed that he had left the miniature—his favorite, the one that he had been looking at first thing this morning—on the dresser, on the lowest shelf. He reached up immediately and put it into his pocket, amazed at his forgetfulness, his carelessness.

Catherine Sergeant glanced at the movement and then back at the dresser, but said nothing. The moment passed and her gaze drifted off to the side, to the window.

She didn't even comment on the rest of the furniture: the large farmhouse table and bentwood chairs, which had also belonged to Claire's mother and had followed him to Spain, and the top of which he loved, scrubbed fiercely as it had been to the consistency and color of old ivory, scored by knife blades and stained here and there by faint coffee rings.

However, as he got out the cups, she stood up and walked over to the window. Next to it, hung on the wall, were the Wedgwood trials.

"What are these?" she asked.

He came over and stood next to her. "Jasper trial pieces," he said. "From the Wedgwood factory."

She looked very closely at the little tongues of clay lined up in rows under the glass. "What do the numbers mean?" she asked.

"Each one corresponds to an entry in the Experiment Book," he said. "They're test pieces, for colors, consistencies."

"I've never seen anything like it," she murmured admiringly. "How old are they?"

"Eighteenth century." He went over to the tea, poured it, and brought it back to the table. When he glanced up, he saw that she was watching him with what looked like fascination. A smile flickered.

"Are you involved with the porcelain industry?" she asked.

"No," he said.

"A collector?"

He paused. "Yes."

"And you're renovating the house?"

"I'm an architect."

She nodded. "Are you working on something now? Something else in this area?"

"No," he said. "Actually, I've retired."

She raised her eyebrows. "You're hardly retiring age."

"I'm fifty."

She sat down opposite him.

He smiled at her. "I lived in Spain until last year, I worked there. Before that, it was London."

"Did you work on anything in London that I would recognize?"

"Well . . . the Parbold house . . . Greens restaurant . . ."

She smiled back, a true smile. "I worked near Greens. At Bergens."

"As . . . ?"

"I specialized in nineteenth-century art."

He hesitated. "And why did you leave them?" He held up his finger. "Let me guess. You got married and you came looking for the country idyll."

She stopped speaking. The conversation, running so quickly until then, came to a resounding halt. She reddened.

"Oh, I'm sorry," he said.

She was opening the briefcase, taking out a pen and paper. She laid a Pearsons form on the table and began to fill it in. He watched his address being completed. She pushed a business card across the table, not looking at him, continuing to write. "I'll give you our estimate," she said. "I'm going to say the furniture sale, not the general. Early nineteenth-century French country dresser . . ." She glanced up. "Is that right?"

"Yes," he said.

"Early nineteenth . . . I would put a reserve on it . . ."

"All right," he said.

"Two thousand pounds? I expect it to make much more, of course."

"All right," he repeated. He took the form that she had now signed. She put the pen back in the case, locked it, and stood up, holding out her hand. "Thank you so much for calling us," she said. "The rates of commission are on the notes on the reverse of your contract . . ."

"I'm sorry if I said something out of place," he said again.

"Not at all," she replied.

She looked him in the face, but he saw her feeling written there. He knew it too well himself to mistake it.

"The sale is next month," she said. "If you want someone to transport the dresser . . ."

She talked her way out of the door, rapidly walking up the hallway. Sunlight was pouring in through the porch. All down the stairs, green reflections shone through the window.

But she still didn't notice it. She turned and shook his hand again on the threshold.

He watched her walk to her car, head down, face averted.

He locked the outer door and went back into the house, pausing outside the drawing room. Disabling the alarm, he went in, the heavy oak door swinging back under the pressure of his hand. Once inside, he locked it again manually behind him.

The room was not flooded with the same sunlight. He kept the blinds permanently drawn. They had been the first things to be fitted, long before his possessions arrived.

He walked into the center of the room and closed his eyes, taking the miniature from his pocket and holding it gently in one palm, covering it with the other. The painter whispered from the enamel disc.

He couldn't believe that he had left it there in full view of Catherine Sergeant. He couldn't believe that he had forgotten it. The miniature had been resting on the dresser all the time that he had been working down at the weir with Peter Luckham.

He walked slowly through the crowded space, opened the drawer on the cabinet, and put the miniature where it belonged, among its dozens of brothers and sisters.

6

Mark Pearson was in the garden when his wife got home, digging the broad herbaceous borders of the garden. He watched the car pull in the drive, and then Amanda sat for a few moments, gesturing to him through the window that she was on her cell phone. Eventually, she clicked it closed and got out.

"Is Catherine at work?" she asked, meaning the offices. "I'm trying to ring her."

"On a Saturday?"

"OK, I'll try her cell." She considered the garden steadfastly for a moment. "Where's that tree going?" she asked, nodding at the cherry tree he had bought that morning.

"By the hedge."

She frowned. He dug the fork into the garden soil and dusted off his hands. "Did you know there's mare's tail in here?" he asked.

"No," she said. "How long has Robert been gone?"

"It'll never come out," he said. "The bugger's been found in coal mines, you know. That's how deep the roots are."

"Mark," Amanda said, "I saw Robert at the airport. Catherine's Robert."

"So?"

"Well, did she say that he was out of the country? She never said so to me."

"No. What was he doing, coming or going?"

"He'd been to Rome on business."

Mark smiled at his wife. "Isn't that allowed? Going away on business?"

Amanda gave him a withering expression. "I'm just surprised she didn't say anything to either of us."

Mark shrugged. "I could do with some tea," he said. "I'm dying of thirst here."

Amanda didn't move. "He looked peculiar," she said. "I've been thinking about it all the way home."

"How peculiar?" Mark asked. "Hand me the shears, darling."

She did so, absentmindedly. "I don't know," she murmured. "Has Catherine said anything to you?"

"About what?"

"Oh, for God's sake. About Robert. About them."

"Why would she?"

"Well, you work together every day."

"You work with her, too."

"I'm stuck in the office," she pointed out. "It's you two organizing the sales, seeing people."

He was gazing at her in confusion. "Is there something the matter?" he asked.

She shook her head, turning away. "Men," she muttered to herself. "Absolutely bloody useless."

Amanda had first met Catherine when Mark engaged her as his partner. Charles Wellesley, his senior partner, had just retired. Catherine had come down from London.

Amanda recalled the day, Catherine coming into this very garden, with Robert following her. Amanda's first thought had been that she was not as she had expected. With Catherine coming from Bergens,

Amanda had a mental image of someone much more forthright. Louder, if you like. Briskly confident, even overpowering. But as Catherine began to speak over lunch—they had brought the food out to the garden, looking so much prettier in the summer—Amanda had begun to approve of her. She liked this quietness. She could see that the woman was no fool, she had a sharpness in her gaze, especially when listening to others talk. Which had been something of a relief, seeing as her husband was about to sink his money in his opinion of this stranger.

They had walked down to the orchard together.

"Mark's been trying to get these trees to produce properly for years," Amanda had said as they paused under the apple trees and looked up through the sparsely laden branches. "He's begun to take it personally."

Catherine had looked around her. "My parents had a house in Sussex with a garden like this," she said. "There were fruit trees there, too . . ."

"It must have taken all their time."

"Actually, no," Catherine had replied. "They worked abroad. Someone came in to do it. They always said they would take it on when they retired."

"And did they?"

"No," Catherine told her. Amanda saw a shadow cross Catherine's face. "They died before they could."

"Oh—I'm sorry."

"Well . . . it was sudden. A road accident."

"A crash? My God." Amanda put a sympathetic hand on the other woman's arm.

"They were in Nigeria. It was where they were working."

"So they were relatively young?"

"Yes," said Catherine. "They were."

The day was hot. Robert came down to join them for a while. Mark was cooking lunch. If Amanda had taken to Catherine straightaway, the same couldn't be said for Catherine's husband. He was much too formal, Amanda thought at first. Then, later, she saw that it wasn't formality so much as an actual coolness. Robert was rigidly polite, asking all the right questions of the house and themselves. But it was Catherine, who, after her initial reserve, would engage in the most interesting conversation. Give a little of herself. Unbend. And Amanda soon realized that she had almost given her own life history away before she returned to the subject of Catherine herself.

They had been sitting back after lunch, gazing at the trees and the valley beyond.

"Mark tells me you've written a book," Amanda said.

"That's right," Catherine replied. "A Victorian painter, Richard Dadd." She smiled. "Minor fixation, I'm afraid."

On Mark's request, Catherine had brought the book with her, but took another prompting before she took it out of her bag and laid it on the table. Amanda lifted it up and weighed it in her hand. It was very slight, but rather beautifully done, with artwork on each title page, grasses and tiny figures.

"This is very nice," Amanda told her.

"Thank you." Catherine smiled. "A few years ago now. For an exhibition at the Royal Academy."

Mark gazed ruefully at them both. "I'm not sure we can live up to the heady glamour of the Academy, not in Pearsons." He grinned. "The most you'll see there is prints and pisspots."

"Oh, how very charming," Amanda said, and threw a crumpled napkin at him. "Just what we all wanted to know."

Catherine laughed. "It'll be nice to get in the real world," she said. "It'll be something different."

That night, as they got ready for bed, Mark had referred back to this conversation. Standing half-dressed at the foot of the bed, Amanda had asked him what he was thinking about.

"Catherine," he told her. "Wonder if she'll stay."

"She seems very straightforward."

"She is," he replied. "Straightforwardly too good for us." He had taken off his shirt and slung it into the laundry basket. "You know she's quite well known? An expert. And she's only come here because of Robert?"

"Has she?"

"He wanted to be near his grandmother, apparently."

She raised her eyebrows. "Must be very close."

"Bit of a comedown from Bergens. That's what I'm worrying about. Bit of a backwater."

Amanda walked over to him and put her hands on his shoulders. "Look," she said. "The woman's come down here to support her husband. She needs a job. And if she's an expert, all the more reason to snap her up. We could extend the paintings part of the business. Do more fine arts sales."

He had smiled at her. "You like her," he said.

"Yes," she told him. "I like her."

But, in all honesty, she really hadn't liked Robert.

The more they met him over the next few months, the more Amanda's misgivings grew. Robert did not make conversation; he didn't even try. He was the least sociable man she had ever met.

"What Catherine sees in him, I'll never know," she told Mark one day after Robert had come into the offices at lunchtime.

"What's the matter with him?" Mark had asked. "Perfectly decent bloke."

"Yes," she'd murmured half to herself as she fed more paper into the printer and at the same time watched Robert through the window as he walked out to his car. "A perfectly decent bloody cold fish."

And now today. Today, at the airport.

Amanda stood, watching Mark plant the tree, her mind entirely elsewhere.

She had seen something in Robert's gaze; a look in the eye—a stubbornness so deep it was almost aggressive. A stubbornness in the set of his mouth, and the straightness of his stance. It was as if she were about to challenge him and he was ready—ready to rebuff a threat, ready to field an answer.

And with a sudden dropping of her heart and a lurch of anxiety, Amanda wondered what it was that Robert had expected to be asked.

7

John Brigham had met his wife, Claire, when she was working in the West End.

She had only been in London for two weeks after a year in the provinces, touring. She was a designer for a theater company. She always joked that John had snatched her straight off the train. She had a beautiful voice, so beautiful with its soft Dumfriesshire burr.

For those first few dates, John would meet her when the theaters came out, in the crush on the corner of Wardour Street. For a while, they met only then, late at night, going to a restaurant in Chinatown. The first few times with her, he would get home at one or two in the morning and spend the next hour or so too wired to sleep, looking out of the window at the castellated gable end of the house that faced his, absorbing every last detail of its white-on-gray pattern until the very texture of the bricks came to mean Claire, and the way that the lights from the street crept only into one corner, and all the rest was hazily dark.

And then one night she came home with him.

He didn't even go into the office the next day. He sat with her, watching her face with its sunny smile; her neat and practical hands fastened around a coffee cup; listening to the swing of her skirt against the stairs as she ran down them, late, to go to the theater.

One night he went to the Apollo and saw the play.

He was on the end of a row. Directly behind him sat two women in their fifties, equally discussing the clothes and the amount of the surgery that the leading actress was reputed to have undergone. His attention on the morose one-woman play had wandered; he tilted his head upward and looked at the ornamentation of the boxes, the doorways, the roof. He looked at the stage and imagined Claire in the wings, hardly fifty feet from where he was sitting, and had a barely controllable urge to rush the stage, go into the wings, and find her.

When they got home that night, she told him that she was going away.

"She's taking the play to Broadway," she said.

"Who?"

She named the actress.

"And you go with her?"

"That's what she's asked."

He tried to absorb the information, what it meant to him. "When?" he asked, eventually.

"In the summer. It's a big deal." She didn't meet his eye.

He felt as if the blood were draining right out of his body. He had known her precisely three weeks.

"I have to go. It's my work," she said. "It's a dream chance."

"Couldn't you work with someone else, here?" he asked. She had said nothing, her eyes lowered. He wondered if he ought to dash the dream. He wondered if he could.

"Do you want to go?" he asked.

"I would like to see America," she said.

Moments passed. He had lived a bachelor life until then; he had told everyone that he would never marry. He couldn't imagine ever being in the frame of mind to commit his life to another person.

"I'll take you to see America," he said.

She had given him a quizzical smile. "Oh, yes?" she asked. "When, exactly?"

"This summer," he'd replied. "On our honeymoon."

They bought a house in Rotherhithe, near the Tube, on a road that thundered all day long with lorries ferrying backward and forward from the new Docklands houses half a mile away. Their own was not new. It wasn't appealing, either. Not at first. Not until he set to work on it. It had once been a pub, and had been boarded up for over a year. The windows and the roof were rotted through. He drew up plans that kept the anonymous face it turned to the road, and extended it back, behind the nine-foot walls of the old delivery yard.

When they took the windows out, they found farthings that had been brand new in 1840, with a young queen's head on them. In the narrow chimney, among two centuries of rubbish that came raining down, were pewter buttons, a tattered shoe, the door of an iron birdcage. Under the floorboards were more superstitious gifts to the house: horseshoes, plaited twigs, a comb, a cup and saucer wrapped in cotton, and, a kind of miracle, a wineglass, without a crack or a mark.

He sold his flat and he and Claire lived there, among piles of bricks and piping. The first night they had a mattress on the floor, no bed. He had never slept so well, and woke up to the sound of rain pouring, hammering on their newly secure roof and blowing through the windows they had left open in the warmth of the evening. Claire had walked out to the bathroom, laughing at herself, shaking rain from her hands. He looked at the trail of wet footprints on the dusty floorboards, saw the arch of her foot in the print, the long area that barely touched the floor. It was as if she walked without touching her heels to the ground. He saw that imprint over and over again. He saw it in Spain and he had seen it once here, in the Dorset house.

Closed his eyes every time, waiting for it to vanish.

The following year, the year after they married, Claire changed her job. She started to work at the Victoria and Albert Museum. Costume. She told him that she wished she'd done it long before. To be no longer at the mercy of a production, of whatever flavor, was like being released from prison, she said. He knew that she was happy; she would go out of the house at more of a run than usual. Occasionally she would accept a lift from him, fretting at his later start, or his ability to be distracted by something he wanted done in the house during the day.

His love for her never altered, not in a single direction. It felt fresh, newly minted, interesting, as if he were looking daily at something he had never seen before, and was surprised by it all over again.

That particular morning—that unforgettable morning—was cold. It was March. Not a particularly noteworthy day. Not bright. Not cold. A mild, gray day. As he turned the car around in the yard, he saw her talking to the builders. She was wearing a reddish-colored coat. A long coat. They said something to her and she laughed. She looked at the car and nodded in John's direction, paused, and then turned and added something. As she walked away, he saw the three men look at him, their faces betraying a mixture of reactions: envy, affection, surprise.

The traffic was bad. They got out of Rotherhithe, having crawled all the way down Salter Road toward the tunnel. Claire was putting on her makeup in the vanity mirror over the passenger seat. They'd argued about the route. She had a lecture to prepare, she said. She had an appointment that morning at nine. She wanted to be early.

"I'm getting out at Bermondsey tube," she'd told him, hand on door. "I can change at Westminster and be at South Kensington before you've got past this next set of lights."

She was always impatient. Pointless to try and dissuade her. With one eye on the road, he turned to kiss her.

Her hand was still on the door. But her face had a strange, abstracted expression.

"What is it?" he asked.

"Something's happened," she said.

When he looked back at that day, he always wondered in what freakish split second she had managed to say those words. At the end of the sentence, her mouth stayed dropped slightly open. Then she

leaned to one side. Not slumped. Leaned, almost a conscious movement, as if she were trying to avoid something that was coming toward her.

"Claire," he said. "Claire?"

He pulled the car to the side of the road. It was a bus stop. The
queue all stared at him as he leapt out and came round to her side of
the car. He opened the door. In those few seconds, she had closed her
eyes. She was perfectly limp, like a toy, like a doll. He tried to prop
her head up a little. A bus came. The driver blew his horn to get him
to move the car.

A woman came out of the queue and touched his arm.

"Is something wrong?" she asked.

He looked at her.

"I'm a nurse at St. Thomas's," she said.

They both leaned down to Claire. A line of saliva was running out
of his wife's mouth.

"Have you got a phone?" the woman asked.

"What?"

"A cell phone."

He was looking about to find something to wipe Claire's face. In
peculiar exasperation, he pulled on his wife's elbow. "Wake up," he
said.

The woman reached behind him and took his cell from the dash-
board. She took his hand from Claire's arm and put the phone into
his hands. "Dial 999," she told him.

He drove behind the ambulance, his eyes fixed on the rear doors.
Nothing else. When the journey finished, he couldn't have told anyone how many sets of lights they had passed through, anything at all,
in fact, about the journey. But he remembered the doors.

They took Claire inside and straight into a cubicle, and they asked
him to wait in reception. He had to stand next to a ridiculously small

glass window and give them Claire's details through the tiny pane of glass. He couldn't catch what the receptionist was saying.

Then he stood in the center of the corridor and waited.

After a minute, a nurse came along. "Would you like to sit down?" she asked.

"No," he said.

"Would you like a cup of tea?"

"No," he repeated.

He watched as they took Claire away again, along the long and brightly lit corridor. He watched them go into the lift, watched the lift doors close.

"Where is she going?" he asked, more frightened than he could say by the obvious urgency with which they had brought her out of the room.

"She's going for a scan," the nurse said. "Sit down." She guided him to a seat.

They were gone for a long time. Forty minutes. In that time, a little boy was taken into the opposite cubicle; John could hear his mother saying that the child had fallen down during a game of football. Then the doctor's careful explanation that the cut needed stitches.

"It'll be all right," the mother kept saying to her son. And later, when the tears subsided, "We'll go for an ice cream," she was murmuring. "You can tell Daddy you had a whole ice cream, the big kind."

John started to plan what he and Claire would do when this was over, when they got out of here. What he would say to her. He would take her on holiday. They would go where they had been saving to go. Not save any more. Just go. They had been planning a holiday in Mauritius next year. They had the brochure. He would go straight from this hospital, he told himself, and book the flight. He would book the hotel she liked, the one with the little villas facing the sea.

And he kept repeating the other woman's words to himself.

It'll be all right. It'll be all right.

His fingers flexed and unflexed. He saw himself turning the brochure pages in the shop. Giving them his credit card. He rehearsed it in minute detail, watching the clock above his head.

The mother and the boy passed him.

Someone else came along, an elderly man on a paramedics stretcher. He was put in the same cubicle, and the paramedics came out and walked up to the nearest nurse.

He looked at them, two burly men in their fluorescent lime yellow jackets. He tried to make sense of what they were saying. Something about a stroke. Something about what they were doing after work. John tried to connect the two, the information about the patient, the plans for that evening.

The lift doors opened. The doctor who had been with Claire came out, looked up and down the corridor, and then walked toward him.

And he knew before the man uttered a single word.

He walked a long way. He crossed the river. By then, it was lunchtime.

When he first came out of the hospital he had turned right and found himself in the curious labyrinth made for cars, not people, that led to Waterloo Station. He had stopped, puzzled, trying to remember where he was headed; then he went back and walked over Westminster Bridge.

When he had first come to London, a newly qualified graduate, this view had thrilled him. All this area. The Houses of Parliament, the Cenotaph, St. James's Park, Horse Guards. He had come down here maybe a hundred times, just to walk it. Westminster Abbey with the oldest garden in England; the Tate at Millbank, where the awesome New Penitentiary had once stood, packed with industrial workshops and stables. He had walked the route of the eighteenth-century builders, the Cubitts and Johnsons, Gibbs and Flew. He had walked right through Kensington, where the Rutlands and Chamberlains had once occupied the new Italianate villas, and down through

Hammersmith, where speculators had thrown up five-storied terraces over the market gardens. Up again through Holland Park, where the walls of Debenhams peacock house had once been covered in blue and green tiles, and a draw to endless crowds; back through what had once been piggeries and potteries. Fulham and Hammersmith, that had been once famous for spinach and strawberries, destroyed by builders of the railways. Ealing, with two hundred market gardens, disappearing under tram lines and pavements.

He loved the city. He knew it. He could feel its organic growth beneath his feet. And yet that day, walking across Westminster, he felt that he had been put down in a foreign country. He couldn't recognize anywhere; even the street signs didn't make sense. He almost stepped out in front of a bus on the other side, on the corner of Parliament Square. He looked up at the Abbey and felt nothing at all, except perhaps a dreamlike fluidity like the motion of waves.

He walked until he felt tired, and found himself in a square, with trees in the center. He had stared at it. It could have been anywhere in London. He glanced up to his left and saw the long shallow steps of a house and a sign on the door. It was familiar. He knew that he'd been here before and that it held some significance for him. He had the oddest conviction that if he could get inside he could rewind, replay the day, start it again. He would be safe. His eyes ran over the lettering of the black-and-white sign without making any sense of it. It might as well have been in another language. He knocked on the green paint of the door and a woman opened it.

"We close in fifteen minutes," she said.

"That's OK," he told her.

She opened it and he stepped inside.

"It isn't really enough time to see everything," she warned him, taking his money in the dim hallway.

He wandered forward. Every inch of wall was crammed with objects. He walked into a dining room painted red and full of mirrors. Above the fireplace was the portrait of a man. He went on, into a narrow space with an ancient writing desk that looked out past pale green panels into a courtyard. He passed a hand over his face. His skin was covered in a cold sweat. He felt dazed. There were architectural fragments everywhere, casts of cornices and capitals, statues, plaques, tiles, medallions. Fragments of a life. Fragments of his. The pieces reached right to the tops of the walls and spilled over across the ceiling: hundreds. Perhaps thousands.

Beyond the room he could see many more, all colored by the light that came filtering down through a far-off rooflight. He stepped into a three-story shell of more stone, more statues, more paintings. There was a marble sarcophagus below him. Paintings crammed frame to frame. He looked up and saw implacable stone faces, carved leaves and vines, animal heads. And funeral urns.

"It's Seti the First," said a voice beside him.

He turned. There was an attendant in a green uniform. "Thirteen hundred years before Christ," the man said. "It's carved out of a single piece of alabaster. When Soane brought it here, he invited a thousand people to look at it, and he lit the rooms with three hundred oil lamps."

John stared at the man. Then, at last he realized where he was. "It's Soane's house," he said. "Soane, the architect."

The attendant looked back at him, frowning.

"It's Soane's house," John heard himself repeat.

"Yes," the man said.

"I saw his drawings," John whispered. "I did a paper on them." He shook his head slightly. "Six years ago. Seven."

The man touched John's shoulder. "Are you all right?" he asked.

John turned away. He was stifled and breathless. He wanted to get out, but he couldn't find the way. He tried to get back to the first red room and found himself in another gallery, where the paintings were hung in movable racks as well as on the walls. It was a dead end.

Another attendant glanced up at him.

"The way out," John said.

He followed where the man pointed, brushing past the model of a tomb.

Made for his wife after her death, said the printed label.

He gasped at it in the shadows.

Made for his wife after her death. St. Pancras Gardens. 1815.

He got out somehow, out into the dusty end of light in Lincoln's Inn Fields.

He walked over to a bench and sat down on it heavily, trying to stop the pavement under him lurching; trying to stop the stone spinning drunkenly wherever he looked.

Getting out his phone, he dialed his sister's number, hoping it was still the same. He hadn't spoken to her in a long time. All he could think of was that he needed someone who had never met Claire. Even if that someone was Helen.

"Hello," said a voice, inflected with a questioning note.

"It's me," he murmured. "Helen, can you help me?"

Columbine

1854

There were no women in Bedlam, at least none that Richard Dadd could see.

Sometimes at night he thought that he heard their voices: he thought that he heard screams, a sound so frightening to him that he would crawl into the corner of his cell and sit with his knees drawn to his chest, his head buried in his knees.

When he was a young man, he had painted a girl in a white dress, holding a rose. It had been in 1840. Late spring. The magnolias had finished flowering and the roses were in first bloom. He was twenty-three. Looking back on that part of his life was like putting a telescope to his eye and seeing the years made inconsequentially tiny. He had been admired then; he had been out in the roaring and peopled world; he had been adored and feted. Admitted to the Schools of the Royal Academy at fifteen, he was thought to be a genius. His work was commissioned; his work was bought. It was rumored that he would not fail, nor starve in a garret. He would rise to prominence; he would be famous. He would be courted. He would be loved.

He had friends then. Other artists who had not been ashamed of his reputation or company. Other men who understood him and came to see him. They had a company, a group, to which others yearned to be admitted. They called themselves the Clique. Frith was one, Egg and Phillip and Ward were others. There was no animosity between them, no jealousy. They formed a committee to outdo the old academicians, to bring the light of new painters out into the open and not have them suffocated by age.

Someone had once told him, in that time, that he was the brightest of them all. He had kept the letter and wondered where it could be now. "Sportive humor, innocent mirth . . . of the kindest and the best, as well as the most gifted . . ."

She had written it to him, the girl in the white dress. She was Catherine, the wife of his oldest brother. He had persuaded her to sit for him one afternoon, the afternoon when the roses first came into color. He had picked the rose; it had been yellow. The name of it escaped him now, but his memory of her did not. She sat on the bench outside the house, self-consciously holding the rose that he had given her, the dark hair falling to her shoulders. Catherine and Robert had been married the year before his imprisonment: the year before his possession by demons, the year before the voices. He wondered if she had once come to see him on the arm of his brother, or whether he had simply imagined her presence.

It was ten years now. A little more than ten years.

He had been sketching a great deal lately. In January, he had painted The Packet Delayed, a child's game on a riverbank. He had been thinking of Robert then. Two boys hold on to a branch while trying to retrieve a toy schooner from the water of the stream. He painted the masts of the schooner so clearly, so defined, that it was almost an engraving rather than a painting.

As winter progressed to spring, he painted David sparing Saul's life; and sketches of the passions of brutality and pride; ambition; agony; raving madness. Drunkenness. Avarice, melancholy. In the same week of June he painted two groups: all men conversing, settling disputes. One of them stood over a painting, inspecting it with a glass. Somewhere in the paintings, somewhere in the paintings he painted within paintings, was the answer. Paint within paint within paint. Detail under detail. He sketched hands and mouths; hands extended, pointing, and holding.

Mouths open in conversation. Faces turned to other faces, rapt in concentration.

When he sat back from A Curiosity Shop—*done in such a hurry, done from ten in the morning until three in the afternoon, missing luncheon, deaf to the instructions to come to the table*—a sadness swept over him.

He had no society of equals. He had no conversations. He could not make out liveliness or appreciation of intellect when others looked at him. He had lost it somewhere, by some action he could not fathom. He painted friendship, but he had none. He had been alone for over ten years, and never touched another human hand in admiration.

He took up the brush again and painted Columbine. *Looking toward him over her right shoulder, the smile playing on her mouth. He completed it in a matter of minutes: it was not difficult. She inhabited his soul.*

When it was over, he sat at the easel in the dying light of the afternoon and wept for company. He was dying here, alone, forgotten, alive only in paint, in the fantasies he created. And paintings were fragile. They did not last. He could destroy Columbine *in a second, if he wished it. Even if she survived, she might be lost, torn, put away in the dark. She was not real. She was only a memory. In a flash of clarity, he wished violently for someone to talk to. Someone alive and substantial to love.*

For Frith, and Edward Ward, and John Phillip. For his own brother.

And for a girl in a white dress, holding a rose.

8

Two days after meeting Catherine at Bridle Lodge, John came out of the hospital at eleven and turned toward the town center.

It wasn't far to walk, and the day was lovely. He noticed as he came down East Walks—down the hill, and in the distance the water meadows and woods and fields—that there was color in the chestnut trees. Another few weeks and these same trees would be green towers, banked with white candles, he thought. Unexpectedly—or, perhaps it was to be expected, today—a lump came to his throat. He had the sudden conviction that he wouldn't see them flower, and he fought it all the way down the hill, an unseeing gaze fixed ahead of him. He told himself as he walked, *Don't be stupid*, over and over, a mantra keeping pace with his footsteps.

Almost as soon as he came into the main street by the church, he saw Catherine Sergeant.

"Hello," he said, as he caught up with her. She was walking slowly along the line of little shops.

She looked up. Color rose in her face. "Oh, hello."

"Window shopping?"

She looked into his eyes only briefly. "Yes," she said.

He glanced around them. "Not exactly busy in town today," he observed.

"No one's here," she agreed.

Just the very act of saying this seemed to affect her. She began to frown, and put a hand to her face.

"Are you all right?" he asked.

She took a deep breath, a gasping breath. In the same second, he remembered himself on the seat in Lincolns Inn, and Helen on the other end of the line, repeating his name. *"John? . . . John?"* while he tried to get air into his lungs.

He took Catherine's arm. "Come with me," he said.

"I'm all right," she protested.

"I don't think so," he said. "Come and sit down for a minute."

He walked her along the street. She made absolutely no resistance. They turned up Colne Lane, a small cobbled alley that connected the two streets of the little town. She followed him, past clothes shops—frames of color in plate-glass windows; past the cosmetics chain store with its familiar scent of fruit and incense washing out of the door. There was a florist, and she paused for a fraction by its display. He eventually linked her arm, guiding her to the café on the corner at the top of the lane. He pushed open the door and she walked to a table and sat down. Sitting opposite her, he was touched by the bewilderment in her expression.

The waitress came to the table and he gave her the order. When he looked back at Catherine she was leaning forward, a hand raked through her hair and her body weight leaning on the hand.

"You look very tired," he said.

She said nothing for some time. She seemed baffled. Then, abruptly, she asked, "Where is your wife?"

He had been thinking of Claire so much lately, remembering her in the car, remembering her turning away from the builders and their expressions as they followed her, remembering the wet imprint of feet, that he was actually shocked for a moment. It was as if Catherine had looked into him and asked the one question he never stopped asking himself.

"She died," he told her. "Almost eleven years ago, of a brain hemorrhage."

Catherine suddenly sat up. "Oh, God," she said. "I didn't realize."

"It's all right."

"No," she told him. "It isn't. I don't know why it should have occurred to me. I shouldn't have asked. I'm sorry."

The drinks came. She stared down at her cup after the waitress had left. He watched her, not touching his own coffee, waiting.

"I thought perhaps you had parted," she said. "You seemed quite calm. I thought perhaps that you had left her."

"Left Claire?" he echoed. "No."

"No," she repeated in agreement. "No, of course." A kind of dull, bruised color had come to her face. "My husband left me two weeks ago," she explained, finally. She raised her eyes to him.

"I see," John said. He paused. "Now it's my turn to say I'm sorry."

"I only want to know where he is," she told him. "I only want an explanation."

"And he didn't tell you where he was going?"

"I found a letter."

"That was all?"

"Yes."

"There was no discussion beforehand?"

"No."

He paused. "And the letter didn't explain or give a reason?"

"No," she said. "Just that he was leaving. Had already left."

They sat perfectly still. Someone else came in the door. There was a rattle of the bell, the clatter of another couple sitting down.

"And the stupid thing is . . . this is such a stupid thing, I mean, it doesn't really have any significance, I suppose . . ." She paused, then carried on. "I found a catalogue, and this piece of jewelry, a necklace . . ."

"You mean some kind of sales catalogue?"

"For an auction."

"He bid for this at an auction?"

"I don't know," she said. Then she put her hand over her eyes, smiled crookedly, and dropped her hand. "As I say, it's just stupid. It's meaningless."

"Not if it's upset you," he said.

"I've been wondering today if he's having an affair. If that's why he's gone."

"Would that be possible?"

"Anything's possible," she said.

"But did you see any signs of it?"

"No," she admitted. "Well . . . maybe. With Robert, it's hard to tell." She glanced at him and caught his puzzled expression. "He's quiet," she said, lamely. "Very quiet." Then a breath escaped her, hardly a smile. "Silent, in fact."

He waited a moment. "Where could he be?" he asked. "Do you have any theories?"

She looked up at him. Again, there was no direct answer. She only said, "I'm so angry, I can't sleep."

"I would think that was normal."

"I don't cry," she murmured. "I just rage." She shook her head. "I'm so angry at wasting everything," she said. "The time."

"You feel that time's been wasted?"

She picked up the coffee cup, looked at it, but didn't drink, returning the cup to the saucer. "Wouldn't you?" she asked. "He's gone off somewhere, with someone, for all I know. I feel ridiculous. As if I didn't get the punch line to some cruel joke. As if I've been too dim, too slow, to pick it up. Does that make sense?"

"Yes," he told her.

"I'm just so angry."

He hesitated to speak. She seemed frozen in place.

"Catherine?" he prompted, at last.

She closed her eyes briefly. "I came down here five years ago to be with him," she said. "To be where he wanted. His grandmother lived in Milborne Port. It's about ten miles away. She was ill. He wanted to be near her." She sighed. "His own parents were unconcerned," she said. "They tended to be unconcerned generally. About everything. Anything. Especially their own family."

"And you came down here with him," John said. "To live."

She leaned back in the chair.

"You supported him," he said. "That was the right thing to do."

She appeared not to hear him. "His grandmother died within the year," she said.

He looked closely at her, but she was far away, standing at another hospital gate next to her husband, who had been so affected by his grief, the first and last time that she had seen him so distressed. She had tried to gently pull him forward, and Robert had pulled away. His fingernails had caught against her wrist, scratching her, raising a red weal. She didn't even notice that until later. All she had wanted was to get him in the car, to protect him from the gaze of passersby.

"There was the house to clear," she said quietly. "She had all these objects . . . Doulton figures . . . and red Carlton. Rouge Royale."

They had done the house together, the brutal task of going through all his grandmother's possessions. All the drawers and cupboards. Sorting through clothes. All the poignant paraphernalia of the elderly: the tablets lined up by the kettle, each bottle marked with different colored dots by a wavering hand. The half bottle of brandy in the cupboard. The wooden tray of ironed silk scarves. The old monogrammed towels, unused for decades. The camphor of mothballs between two ancient furs hanging in the satinwood wardrobe. The little travel clock, in a leather case on the bedside table, and the parish magazine from the church, and a small Bible with tiny print and gold-leaf-edged pages, which smelled astoundingly and powerfully of lavender, as if it had been absolutely doused with scent.

The Rouge Royale was in the sitting room, in a glass-fronted cabinet.

There were about a dozen pieces: some little ornaments, small jugs and plates, and then several large bowls. The color, by which these were catalogued, was a deep scarlet, with a wonderful glaze that had a touch of opalescent blue, like oil glimpsed in water in sunlight.

They took them down to Pearsons. It was Robert's decision.

Catherine had taken them from the wrappings herself and displayed them on an oak chest, far away from the door, close to the auctioneer's desk.

Robert had come in that same morning—there were a lot of his grandmother's things in the sale, chosen after agonizing hours of discussion as to what he wanted to keep and what he wanted to sell—and, walking up the aisle, he had suddenly noticed the Carlton on the chest, blazing away in the daylight.

Even she had experienced a moment of anxiety when she had unpacked them. They had been so precious and so personal, she knew that. Collected over years. And they looked so forlorn here in public, as if Robert's grandmother herself were laid out for inspection. Even Catherine had thought it heartrending, and so the expression on Robert's face when he turned to look at her as he stood by them had not really shocked her. She had expected it, for him to feel desperately sad.

But not what actually came.

"You're selling her," he had said.

"What?" she said. She had tried to hold his hand.

He had stepped back. "You're selling her," he had repeated. "And taking a bloody profit."

Catherine looked back up at John.

He was waiting, his hands crossed in his lap.

"There was so much that went wrong after that," she said. "And as time went on . . ."

Time. John wondered if she felt time as acutely as he did, the very essence of time slipping through her fingers, the impossibility of grasping it and making it stand still.

If only he could make it stand still. For a week. Or a month.

She abruptly dropped her hands to the table and looked horrified.

"What am I doing?" she asked herself loudly. "Why am I wasting *your* time like this?"

He smiled. "You're not."

She glanced around herself. "I am," she said. "I can't believe I've made you sit here . . ."

"It's no time at all," he said.

She looked at him acutely.

"It will pass," he said. "I know it doesn't seem that way."

She shook her head.

"You'll get an explanation, or you won't get an explanation," he told her. "And it will pass."

She suddenly slumped back in the seat, gazing at him, as if really seeing him in depth for the first time. "You're very patient," she said.

He almost laughed. "Actually, if there's one thing I'm not, it's patient," he told her. "Especially just now."

"Just now?" she echoed.

He shook his head, not wanting to go into details that even he couldn't face. He met her look; they exchanged smiles.

"Would you come out to dinner with me?" he asked. The question, which he had not even had in his mind, came rushing out of his mouth unbidden. It astonished him; it had sprung from looking at her, from the tremor he had felt in her hand the other day, from her profile while she looked at the Wedgwood trials—something, perhaps not even any of those things, perhaps all of them—and, now that he had asked the question, he felt himself to be suddenly hugely inept and unfeeling of her situation.

She had not responded.

"I'm really sorry," he said. "I just meant a dinner." And he found himself laughing out loud in exasperation. "Christ, that sounded crass. I just . . ." And he waved the subject away.

She began to smile, and then, to his surprise, to color. She looked away from him. She didn't answer his question at all. Instead, she crossed her arms over her chest, almost defensively. "Time," she murmured, regressing to the previous subject. "It feels strange. Not normal, not as usual. It's all stretched out and distorted. Hours and hours."

He took a breath, trying to follow the route of her conversation, the pattern of her thoughts. But it wasn't difficult. He knew this curious, rootless sense of bafflement and abandonment so well. "Circular hours," he murmured. "Where nothing progresses, and you come back to the beginning."

"That's right," she said. She looked back at him.

"It's all relative."

"Is it?" He could see that she doubted it.

"Of course," he told her. "Think about the endless days in a classroom, or behind a work desk in a job you hated. Or the afternoon when you were a child, and playing, and the sun stopped in the sky, and the trees never moved a leaf." He smiled at her. "You see?" he said. "All time is relative."

She considered him closely.

He leaned back and looked out the window at the traffic.

"If you think about it," he murmured, "there's really no time at all."

She began to gather her things together. "Well," she said, "whether it exists or not, I've taken too much of yours."

He stood up with her.

She put her handbag strap over her shoulder and put on her gloves. He stepped past the table and opened the door for her, looking back to the counter, ready to go back and pay the bill and let her walk away on her own.

Then she stopped on the threshold. "Thursday," she said. "Perhaps Thursday?"

And she glanced back, just once, as she walked down the street.

9

As Catherine arrived home, pulling her car up at the curb, she saw that a man was standing on the doorstep. His hand was just dropping from the action of knocking on the door; turning, he looked at her as she got out of the car.

"Mrs. Sergeant?" he asked.

"Yes," she told him. She had never seen him before.

He held out his hand to her. She noticed that he was carrying a briefcase.

"If you're selling something," she said, "I'm afraid the answer's no."

He smiled. "I'm not selling anything," he said. "I've been asked to call on you. My name is Styles." She considered him. He was about fifty. Brown haired, florid faced, in a suit too small for him by at least one size. He looked hot, despite the temperature of the day. He handed her a card. *Wade and Charleton*, it read. *Solicitors.*

"Do I know you?" she asked.

"I'm working for your husband," he told her.

Sitting in her kitchen, Michael Styles looked even larger. Catherine made him wait while she made tea, almost holding her own breath all the while, knowing that there was no way that this was going to be good news. She opened the window onto the small courtyard garden that she had planned so meticulously last year. The star magnolias were just coming out, white flowers on bare branches. They were only shrubs. She had discussed with Robert—only recently, was it only recently, was it only in October or November?—that they might have to move them when the shrubs got a little larger. They had stood at this very window and discussed the magnolias, discussed something they would do together in four or five years' time.

The kettle boiled. She laid a tray. She fought down another image, of Robert long ago, in some other tiny garden in London, before they had ever come here. Robert moving behind her, passing his arms round her waist. And, despite herself, despite Robert, she thought of John and the feeling of excitement that she had been holding until she had seen Michael Styles on her doorstep.

She closed off the memory, turned with the laden tray, and put it on the table.

"That's nice," Styles said.

"I'm sorry?"

"A teapot," he said, indicating it with a nod. "People don't bother, do they? It's nice to see a proper pot of tea." He blushed as he spooned sugar into his cup.

She sat down opposite him, pitying his obvious discomfort.

"Where is he?" she asked.

"I'm afraid that I can't tell you that," he said.

She put her hands in her lap, hiding them under the table so that he wouldn't see her balled fists. "What does he think I'm going to do?" she asked. "Run after him with an axe?"

Styles looked at her.

"It was a joke," she told him.

He opened his briefcase. "I've been instructed to bring these to you." And he pushed three or four sheets of paper across the table toward her.

She looked at the upside-down documents.

In the County Court, she read. There was a circular red stamp at the top of the page. Robert's handwriting filled the sheet.

She turned the papers around.

There was a date, the date of their marriage. And the place.

The petitioner and respondent last lived together as husband and wife . . . And then the address. This address. Their home address.

She looked up at Michael Styles. "Robert filled these in?"

"Yes."

"And left them with you . . . when?"

"A month ago."

She shook her head, trying to work out the exact details. "He filled this in, delivered it to you, and told you . . . what? To bring it to me?"

"Yes."

"Today? Specifically today?"

Styles spread one hand in a faint semblance of apology. Or perhaps embarrassment. "We had an instruction to bring this to you at a time to be notified."

"And he's now notified you."

"That's correct."

"You mean he's been in touch with you?"

"Yes."

"He phoned you, wrote to you . . . this week?"

Styles didn't reply.

She paused, looking down at the rest of the sheet in front of her. *There are no children of the family living . . . no child has been born to the respondent during the marriage . . .* Robert had put a black line through both clauses. She turned the page. *The said marriage has broken down irretrievably . . .*

She looked closely at the page, at the reasons given for the divorce. She read the two sentences twice. When she saw what he had written, something rushed through her: not anger, not any specific emotion, but more a physical reaction, a kind of roaring increase, as if her body had suddenly gone into overdrive. Blood raced round her heart while she leaned, head down, over the pages. Eventually, she managed to stare back at Styles. "You've read what it says?" she asked. "About the grounds, the cause?"

"I have."

"You accept what it says?"

He met her gaze. "It isn't my business to accept it," he told her.

"Only to deliver it," she said. "And is it true, what it says here?" She prodded the clause with her fingertip, making the paper slide across the polished tabletop.

"I couldn't say."

"You mean you won't say."

"I mean that I don't know the actual facts, but I accept them as my client's word," he replied. He was measured, she would give him that. But then, it was easy for him to be calm.

She pushed back her chair and got up. "Do you do this all the time?" she asked. "Do you come to someone's home and bring them stuff like this?"

"No," Styles said. "It's very unusual."

She glared at him. It wasn't his fault—she was well aware of that—but she felt in that moment that she could have struck him, hurt him, for sitting there, for opening his briefcase and putting this cold and outrageous insult on the table.

"I don't suppose he told you what he was doing," she said.

"The divorce?" Styles asked, perplexed.

"I don't mean the fucking divorce," she retorted. "Did he tell you that he was leaving, that he was going away, that he wasn't telling me beforehand? That he was going to walk out in the dark one morning before I was awake, without discussing any of this with me?"

Styles remained silent, looking increasingly awkward.

"I mean," Catherine said, aware now that her voice was rising, that it was running away from her with a hysterical pitch, sounding unlike herself, sounding like the typical hysterical woman, and that Styles would be thinking, *So this is what he was running away from* . . . She couldn't help it. "I mean, is it reasonable?" she demanded. "Is that what a reasonable man does? What did I do, that he couldn't speak to me? Not say a word, a word . . ."

The doorbell rang.

Styles got to his feet.

"I haven't finished," Catherine said.

He looked to the door.

"I haven't finished talking to you," she repeated.

It rang again.

"Oh, shit," she muttered. She went out of the room, up the hall-way, and wrenched open the door.

Amanda was standing on the step.

The other woman saw her expression. "What is it?" Amanda said. "What's the matter?"

Catherine held the door wide for her. "You might as well come in and join the party," she said. "The more the merrier."

Styles had come out of the kitchen and was hovering in the door-way. He looked at the two women, his briefcase in his hand.

"This is Mr. Styles," Catherine said. "Robert sent him."

Amanda looked from one to the other. "Robert?" she echoed.

"Mr. Styles is a solicitor," Catherine added. "Did you know that they did house calls?"

"No," Amanda said. And she gave Styles a hesitantly sympathetic look.

"Neither did I," said Catherine. "Wonderfully good of him, isn't it? Apparently Robert asked him to come here. You know, just to dot the i's and cross the t's . . . like, like, it's something Robert just thought of at the last minute," she floundered. "You know, as you're going out the door on holiday or something, and you suddenly realize you've forgotten to tell the paperboy to stop the paper? And you grab some-thing—you grab a scrap envelope and you scribble your instructions down, and you leave it on the side and ask a friend to drop it in for you. Just drop in this bloody note to say you're going away, and—oh! by the way!—you won't be coming back."

Amanda and Styles stood stock-still.

Amanda then gently put a hand on Catherine's arm. "Where is he?" she asked. "What's he done?"

Catherine merely nodded grimly, staring at the man in front of them. Styles took a step forward. "I've left the papers on the table," he said in a low voice, half to Catherine and half to Amanda, who was now holding her friend's shoulders in a protective gesture. He edged past Catherine, got to the door, and said, "Thank you very much for the tea," before he opened the door to the street.

"Shit," Catherine muttered. "Shit."

Amanda waited. "Any way you want to start me at the beginning?"

Catherine stared at her a moment. She let out a long breath. Together they went back to the kitchen. Catherine slumped in the nearest chair. Amanda picked up the papers and read them slowly, carefully. She put them down on the table again, went to the cupboard, took out an extra mug, replenished the pot with hot water, and sat down opposite her.

"I knew," she said.

Catherine looked up. "What?"

"I saw Robert in the airport on Saturday," she said. "I meant to tell you, but . . ."

"You knew?" Catherine echoed. "You knew about this all along?" And she waved at the divorce paper.

"No, no," Amanda replied. "I didn't know that. But I saw him, I spoke to him, and he had this strange look on his face . . ."

"You spoke to him?"

"Yes."

"What did he say?"

"Nothing," Amanda replied. "At least, nothing of any consequence. He said he had been to Rome on business."

"Rome!"

Amanda looked at Catherine acutely. "I take it that was a lie, then," she said.

Catherine was breathing heavily. "I don't know what's a lie and what isn't," she murmured. "Rome . . ."

"Have you spoken to his office?"

"They said he's on vacation."

"And how long has he been gone?"

"Two weeks . . . nearly three."

Amanda stared at her, then a slight color heightened in her face. "He left you three weeks ago and you've been on your own here, and you never said a word to us?"

Catherine shook her head, then leaned forward on the table and rested her forehead on both palms.

"I can't believe it," Amanda said. "That you wouldn't say a thing to us."

"It's just been surreal," Catherine murmured eventually. "I kept telling myself that he would come back." She took her hands down from her eyes and laid a fingertip on the divorce papers. "Now this," she said. "How could he do it? Why would he do it?"

Slowly, Amanda picked up the papers and read through them again. When she came to the reason quoted for the divorce, she put a hand to her mouth, then looked up at Catherine. "Is this really true?" she asked. "There's someone else?"

"I don't know."

"He didn't tell you?"

"He didn't tell me a thing. Not even that he was going. He disappeared one morning and left me a letter."

"Jesus Christ!"

"It didn't say anything about another woman."

Amanda took a moment to digest this information.

Catherine let out a gasping laugh. "You see what he did? He filled in the whole bloody sheet for me to sign. Divorce on the grounds of his adultery. Good of him, don't you think?"

The two women regarded each other levelly. Amanda drank a sip of tea. Then, replacing her cup, she said, "Look, I'm not defending him. God knows there isn't any bloody defense in the world for acting this way. But this is so out of character." She shook her head. "Someone like Robert doesn't do this. Is he all right?"

"What do you mean, 'all right'?"

"Well, has he been stressed about anything?"

"You think he's had a breakdown?"

"I don't know what to think, Cath. It's all so incredible."

There was a long moment of silence. "Christmas," Catherine murmured. "There was something just before Christmas."

Three months. In the week before they broke for the holidays. She tried to recall it exactly. In the normal course of things, it might not have any significance at all. But, at the time, it had briefly bothered her. Not enough to mention. Not enough to argue about. But enough to puzzle her. Robert coming home late, but not tired. Wired-up somehow, a tremor in his look, a vibration, as if he were coming down from a high. In any other man than Robert she might have guessed he were drunk; but he was not drunk. He was fired by some inner victory or revelation. She remembered wondering if he was going to be ill, feverish. He had gone to bed early, and when she had come upstairs he was asleep. Soundly asleep, unwakeable, the sleep of the dead or the just.

Or the adulterer, she thought now, stringing Robert's sleeping look, the heavily weighted look of an exhausted child, with the colors of Christmas that year—and the sale that Pearsons had had that same week, the paintings and jewelry sold, the unusually good-natured talk of the dealers.

She looked up at Amanda. "The necklace," she said.

Amanda frowned. "What necklace?"

Catherine got up and went upstairs, found the catalogue. When she came back down, she threw it on the table. "Lot 543," she said.

Amanda looked at it.

"It was in the drawer," she said. "The page folded back." She, too, looked down again at the illustration of the piece.

"Pretty," Amanda commented.

Catherine sat down again on her chair. "We had a telephone bidder," she said. "The only telephone bid in that section."

"And you think this was something to do with Robert?"

"Well, why is it in his drawer?" Seeing Amanda's doubt, she snatched the catalogue away. "It doesn't matter," she said.

"Not in the greater scale of things right now," Amanda said.

Catherine stared at the tabletop for a second, then looked up. "Who is she?" she murmured. "Are you sure he wasn't with anyone at the airport?"

"No one I saw."

"You're sure."

"I can't be sure. But certainly there was no one standing with him or even near him." She paused. "But . . ."

"But what?"

"I said to Mark when I came home, Robert looked peculiar. I couldn't place the expression on the day. But perhaps he was nervous. Frightened that I had seen him."

"Guilty?"

Amanda considered. "No," she decided. "Just wary."

"And this was last Saturday."

"That's right." Amanda leaned forward, elbows on the table. "Couldn't you have told us?" she asked. "Didn't you trust us?"

"It wasn't a case of trusting you," Catherine replied. "I just . . . hoped it would solve itself somehow."

There was a long pause. Catherine pushed her chair back, but made no move to get up. The two sat facing each other, the divorce papers still between them. As Amanda looked at Catherine, she could see absolutely nothing in her friend's expression.

And she was right. Catherine was feeling nothing at all. She felt blank, empty. She closed her eyes, and the afternoon that she had spent etched itself on her mind. She had been to see Mr. Williams, the man who had owned the painting of the girl that had been in the most recent Pearsons sale. Mr. Williams, who had so loved the painting that looked like his wife. He lived alone in a great stone house at the end of a drive of overgrown laurels, two villages away. It was next to the church on the hillside, and was decaying slowly behind its huge walls, weeds growing in the gravel paths and in the old tennis court.

"I went to see a man today," Catherine murmured.

"About this?" Amanda asked. "About Robert?"

"No," Catherine said. "About a painting he sold. I went to see why he had brought it in, when for months he's held on to it. Selling other things in preference to the painting. It hung on his landing. You saw it when you came into the house, and as you climbed the stairs. And he sold it."

"Perhaps he needed the money," Amanda said.

"He did," Catherine agreed. "He lives in Sandalwood."

"That old monster of a house?"

"Yes, the same one."

Amanda watched her. "What made you think of him?" she asked.

The first time that Catherine had visited Mr. Williams, he had told her that he and his wife had lived all over the world. Been posted to Burma when it was still Burma before the war. Traveled in Malaysia. When war had broken out, he had enlisted in the navy. He had been on the Arctic convoys. He had described Riga to her, a black outpost in a white-gray world. He had traded American dollars for czarist porcelain there, cigarettes for Fabergé. He and his wife had settled in France after the war.

He had taken his life to auction to pay for repairs on the house: the porcelain, and the surrealist sketch by Delvaux, and the Balinese figures, and the dancer's bracelets hung with Sri Lankan silver dollars, and silkwork from Paris, and two bronzes he had brought out of Berlin.

Catherine had known him for the five years she had been here. A lonely old man living in what had once been a house full of the past, a house he had consistently stripped of his memories.

"What did you sell your painting for?" she had asked him that afternoon, over tea that he had made for her. A gentle old man moving slowly about his kitchen, laying a proper tray for her, carefully arranging it on the table. He always had a sweet, polite smile and was the soul of old-fashioned civility.

"It was only a painting," he had told her, and he had closed his eyes as he had stood on the doorstep. "Things are no good to me now."

She had thought that he was crying, but she had been wrong. He had opened his eyes and shaken her hand as she had given him the check for the painting. A dry businesslike shake of the hand, an unsettling touch of veined skin and bone. The same sweet, sad smile as he waved to her when she drove away.

And then she thought of John Brigham's hand. To her surprise, her heart turned over. One soft turn of desire. She paused, listening almost objectively to the increased beat. John Brigham's hand; practical, long-fingered, sensitive. The warmth of his palm and fingers. She closed her eyes for a second, catching her breath. He had looked at her today with candid directness, with humor. And yet she had had the strongest feeling that he was not just giving away what he had loved, like Alec Williams, but readying himself for some moment. Readying himself at the edge of a precipitous leap. There was also something else: something that had happened in his house that had struck a strong chord of familiarity in her. The same something that had nagged at her over the last few days.

He had turned and taken it from the dresser.

That was it. That was the thing that she had been trying to remember about that day.

He had taken . . . she tried to remember what. She had seen the movement. The way that the same hand that had touched hers today, and lingered on hers, had moved to snatch something from the dresser shelf. At the time, she had been distracted, nearly transfixed, by John's gentle, briefly caressing, touch. The item had been small enough to be put in John Brigham's pocket. She frowned now, irritated at the memory and its intrusion. She had not been concentrating then; she had been sunk in apathy. She had seen it; seen it lying there. Yet her gaze had drifted over it.

She took herself through the house again. Followed him along the hall. There were William Morris panels on the stairs . . .

There was the dresser, and the glass-framed trials . . .

And then, exactly then, she remembered.

She stared past Amanda, seeing the enameled disc in her imagination. The disc that John had put into his pocket with such haste. The disc that she had glanced at for a second or two.

She recalled it now, where her mind had submerged it before. It was a tiny, infinitely delicate portrait of a child. There was a perfectly rendered chessboard spread on a table in front of him, and by his outstretched hand, a walnut shell halved and turned into a sailboat. There was an unmistakable, unforgettable expression on the child's face.

Once seen, never forgotten.

She sat back suddenly in her chair, straightened, and stared at Amanda.

"What is it?" Amanda asked.

But Catherine couldn't tell her. Robert had vanished momentarily from her mind. All she could think of, all she could see in her mind's eye, was the fantastic, the impossible. The child in the locket.

And the painter of the child, the engraver whose world had been reduced to these few lines. Lines on paper. Like the configuration of lines on the papers in front of her on the table. Just a few lines. So much significance.

"Oh, my God," she whispered to herself in amazement. "Richard Dadd."

10

As he climbed the stairs, Robert's fingers closed around the key in his pocket. He suppressed an almost childlike need to run up the steps two at a time, and only the fact that the stairway was narrow, and the landings and turning so ill lit, stopped him.

He got to his door and opened it.

There were only three rooms: a bed-sitting room, a bathroom, and a kitchen. He walked across the carpet and stood with his hands on the windowsill, looking out at the view of London.

In fact, there wasn't much to see: part of a wall and some heavily netted windows to an office, part of a higher building that backed onto the apartment block. When he had been shown around before, it had been getting dark and he had seen people moving about across this narrow gulf: a gray-haired woman, a man at a desk. Fluorescent lighting behind them, and banks of VDU monitors. Passing the door in the street below, he knew it was some sort of broker. Some anonymous business. Anonymous, like him.

He turned his back, still relishing his namelessness. This is what he had wanted: to be left alone, to relinquish an identity, even if it were only for the relatively short times between work and sleep. The rooms belonged to the company he now worked for, the job that he was about to start in a week's time. It was a courtesy flat until he found a house or an apartment of his own. Not that he would be in a position to buy anywhere until the divorce settlement came through.

At the thought of Catherine, his face clouded over. She would have got the papers today. It was done, then. She would realize his intentions. And perhaps she would be angry enough not to oppose him. That was what he wanted. Not to be opposed. Not to be questioned. Just to be released.

He walked over to the two suitcases, still on the floor of the sitting room. He had only had time to take out a few clothes so far. Now he began in earnest. It was only when he got to the bottom of the case, some five or ten minutes later, that he thought of Catherine in any real depth, in any way other than a convenient caricature of anger.

For some reason, he had brought her book.

Why he should have seized on this as a memento was still beyond him. It was the book that most irritated him, the symbol of her success. He looked at the cover now for some time, a glossy representation of a fairy scene; Richard Dadd's painting of the meeting between Oberon and Titania.

He found nothing attractive in it; he never had. He had never, for a single second, understood her obsession with the painter. And this was one of the least appealing female figures you could ever imagine, this matronly profile, this expression of bland indifference.

He went over to the only chair, book in hand, and sat down, resting the picture in his lap.

The strange thing was, the woman in the painting looked almost the same as the woman he had met before Christmas. Not anything he willingly wanted to recall.

He had met her at a sales conference. He had only been involved peripherally; only attended because one of their firm's clients had asked him. As their auditor, he had overheard the plans for the party and been invited. It had been the last day of the conference, in some dirty-looking hotel in Bloomsbury that turned out to be marginally better inside than out.

It was well into the evening; he had probably had a drink too many. He had found himself sitting next to her in a booth of the hotel restaurant. He didn't know who she was; he had never seen her before. She wore a gray dress, a rather sacklike dress that showed brown shoulders. He would have passed her by in the street without noticing her. He supposed she was older than the usual office girls, maybe thirty-five. Perhaps even older than him. Perhaps forty.

"You've got a tan," he had said.

"I've been on holiday," she told him. "Morocco."

They talked about that for a while. And, if he remembered rightly, about Italy, and about the fact that she was learning Italian.

"You never know when you'll go somewhere," she'd said. He had heard the first slurring of her words.

"You're planning to vanish, to go?" he'd asked.

"Maybe," she'd said.

Only later, much later, they were left alone in the booth.

"Robert," she had said, "what do you want out of life?"

He had tried to look past her; he had thought someone was ordering a taxi. He had wanted to leave, having some vague idea that he could still catch the last train. "Ordinary things," he had told her, partially distracted. "What does anyone want? Security, health."

"Security," she had repeated to herself, and started to laugh. "Is that all you want? Just that?"

"Is it such a bad thing?"

She'd put her hand on his thigh. Outside, in the rain, he hailed a taxi, intending to try and leave her on the pavement. Yet when it came she stepped straight into it, and he found himself saying the name of his hotel.

It had probably been one of the worst events of his life. And yet it had had such consequences.

When they got to the hotel, he already knew that he didn't want her. He particularly didn't want her in his room all night. So as the cab drove away, he took her by the elbow and led her to the side of the building. There was an alley here, a walkway through to a rusty little garden beyond. The wine bar down here was closed. They stood in the unlit doorway.

"I'm sorry," he told her. "Very sorry."

It was then that she abruptly stood with her back to the locked door and told him exactly what they were going to do. He found himself to be both hungry for and numb to her touch.

"Not here," he had said. "Not here in the street."

But it was exactly there. The pleasure of it was overwhelming, the sense of thieved satisfaction. She was not even pretty, and yet his desire had been fierce, a kind of desire to be robbed of himself, to be obliterated, out there in the dark, to the rattle of the door frame and the sound of the rain.

Insanity.

And then, just at the last moment, he found that he couldn't do what she wanted. She had pushed him away impatiently, standing looking at him in frustrated astonishment. He had been humiliated by her silence more than if she had laughed at him.

Thank God, he never saw her again. No one remarked on their leaving together; probably no one knew.

He began to think about her and what she had said in the booth. "Is that all you want?" she had asked him. "Just that?"

He realized that this was exactly what he did want: the security of being alone. He wanted to be freed of the claustrophobia of need, both his and Catherine's. In fact, he would prefer to have no needs at all.

He had gone to see his mother that afternoon.

That was another need, another duty. He didn't know why he had bothered.

She lived in the old house in Bedford Square, the very last one to be undeveloped and smartened up. It was a yawning great warren of a house and his mother had largely abandoned it, preferring to live in the basement kitchen for most of her time. He had rung the bell and she came eventually, greeting him with a cigarette in hand.

"Ah," she had said, smiling. "The wanderer returns."

She stepped back and motioned him in. He kissed her cheek, which she had pointedly offered him. He followed her down the hallway and went into the sitting room, in a corner of which she had been sitting in a vast wing chair, watching the television.

"I've come to live in London," he told her.

She sat down with a sigh. "With Catherine?"

"No."

"I thought as much. She's been on the phone to me."

"Has she?"

"Asking where you were."

He remained standing. His gaze edged round the room at the sofas covered with plastic and the oriental pieces dulled under a layer of dust.

His parents had worked for a tobacco company in the Far East for years. The good old days, his mother called them. Gin and orange at four, cocktails at six, dinner at eight. Endless rounds of entertaining and being entertained. Upstairs, in her bedroom, the wardrobes were still stuffed with fifties frocks, all flowered crepe-de-chine in tissue paper. And she still had all the Hong Kong twenty-four-hour tailored dinner suits made for his father; vintage suits with ribbed silk lapels and black satin covered buttons and cream satin linings.

And on the floor above that was his old room: a stripped bedframe and ticking pillows, and his old bookcase with his copies of the *Royale Encyclopaedia for Boys*. Once, when he was just out of college, before he had met Catherine, he had made the mistake of bringing a girl-friend home, and his mother had mortified him by giving the girl the grand tour of the house, from the cobwebbed rafters to the base-ment. The girl had picked on his encyclopedias, reading out from the first paragraph she turned to.

He could still hear her. "E is for the Eastern Question," she had laughed. "How very colonial! And East Lynne, and Eddystone Light-houses, and Edward the Confessor."

"He always was a bookworm," his mother had said. "I never saw such a stultifyingly silent child."

"You never saw any children at all," Robert had commented, caus-ing his girlfriend to laugh all the more, even though it was the truth. His mother had never wanted any friends in the house, a fact of which he had been secretly glad, since she and the house smelled of smoke and damp, and she had taken to stacking newspapers in the halls and on the stairs and leaving clothes where they dropped, and the sight of her had simply revolted him.

"Where are you living?" she asked him now.

"Hotels," he lied. "I'm not in any place very long. Auditing abroad, mostly." He didn't want to be expected to live here.

"What about your house back there?"

"We'll sell it."

She began to laugh. "Better tell your wife," she said.

And, even though he had left Catherine, he hated that. She wasn't to be laughed at. She was, he supposed, to be pitied.

He got into bed early that night.

He felt that he needed to sleep for a very long time. He was not tired. He was just irritated with a world of emotional desire and ab-sorption pressing in on him. He lay on his back and looked at the rec-tangle of reflected light that lay across his bed through the window.

All he wanted was to lie in the dark, with the skewed square of light coming in at the window, the residue of reflected light from the street below.

11

Since John had come back, if he dreamed about anything, it was the house near Alora.

He was walking now, while he slept, while he dreamed, along the dusty road toward it; a finca of olive trees on a hillside. The grit got into his shoes; he stooped and took them off, and carried on walking with the sandals in his hand. Sun was beating on his back, and the house was exactly as he had first seen it after Claire's death.

It sat just below the brow of the hill, a bare block on a cement stand. No roof, no glass at the windows, just a half-finished project that someone else had abandoned. There was no driveway, just a rutted track turning off the lane that led to the farm on the other side of the hill.

He turned and looked back down the hill.

He wasn't a visionary. He had never considered himself to be one, even when he had the art of concept. He could tell a client about his plans for their own house and see it in technical shape. But he had no visions, no emotion. Except, of course, with Claire. From time to time in Rotherhithe, he had experienced a flash into the future that had all the detail and warmth of actual life. But that had been very rare.

Yet now, as he stood in front of the abandoned house, the roofless block, he did have a vision, a sensation of himself as the man who could live here. He saw himself sitting here at night. He saw the pool he would build in the back; not a clean architectural device but a deep, green-walled bath, not pretty, not tiled, not terraced, and with no steps, but a shaded dark-watered tank under a ceiling of bougainvillea, with no formal garden, but the tamarisk trees growing wild around him.

And he saw the rooms. Cool plain rooms. A kitchen, a bedroom, a studio at the back where the sun only came late in the day. A wood-burning stove. A desk.

A year later, when the restoration in Alora was half completed, he left everything else to the tenants in Rotherhithe. It was so much easier to leave behind the house that he and Claire had shared in London. It had been four years, and he thought that he had her death in proportion.

He made the mistake of taking the china they had bought together. Unpacking it in the new Alora house in Spain a fortnight later, he had wept like a baby over the pattern, a stupid pattern of ribbons and oranges, a sentimental pattern that he found he couldn't bear. He had gone down to the local market in Alora on the second weekend and bought brown plates and cups; red clay undersides and glazed brown tops. He found it hard to eat when he was first there—the loneliness was almost tactile, alive, like a snake coiled behind every door. But there was time, empty time he had never allowed himself before. And so he forced himself to stare it down, and then fill it, even though the ache of loss was more acute in a strange place.

He would stare for minutes at a time at combinations of colors. And it was not getting himself used to the broader, blanker silences on the hillside that eventually saved him, nor the technical work, building work on the farmhouse. It was the colors. Different shades of green as the light came across the valley in the morning. Food on his plate in primaries of pepper and tomato and lemon. The skin of aubergines and plums. The olives, when they came in season. Deep lilac shade that crossed his bedroom at night in summer.

And he saw himself there now, dreamed himself there now. He

saw himself alone in the dark pool behind the house, the temperature over a hundred degrees, the country asleep in the dry heat that drugged the air, a sky of violent blue blazing above him through the trees. He had hauled himself out onto the side and lain on the baking stone, and he had seen Claire's footprints, wet footprints, as if she had climbed out of the pool alongside him.

And he saw what he had not seen then. A body materialized next to him. He saw the shape of the naked woman's shoulder in his dream, her skin reddened slightly by the sun, and drops of water running down her back. He pressed his mouth to the drops of water and felt the heat under the slippery surface.

In his dream, he ran his hands down her back. She turned to him, laughing, lying back, her hands touching his face, saying something, whispering something, as she pulled his face to hers and took his hand and guided him to her. Now wriggling upright, her hair falling over her face, wriggling upright to sit astride him, the sunlight flickering across her, the stone under him hot to the touch, the body warm and silky in his grasp. He put his hands on her waist and she threw back her head. In the arch of her neck he saw the artery pulse; he closed his eyes in the dream and he felt her enclosing him, burning in his breath.

He took her greedily, urgently, altering both his body and hers so that eventually she was on her back and he was above her on the edge of the pool. She kept his gaze; her arms were spread out at her sides, she wrapped her legs around him. Nothing had ever felt so good, so right, to be lost with her.

He looked in her eyes and closed his mouth on hers.

And in the very same second he knew that the woman wasn't Claire at all, but Catherine Sergeant.

He woke with a jolt of shock to the cold darkness of his own bed.

12

The van from Pearsons arrived at Bridle Lodge at nine the next morning.

John had watched it from the kitchen window coming up the drive, and seen Catherine's car directly behind it. He walked out now onto the doorstep just as she got out. She walked across the gravel, smiling at Frith, who ran in circles around her.

"I didn't expect you," John said.

"I didn't plan to come, until last night," she told him. She paused, another flush heightening her color. He watched her blush with surprise. She put a hand to her face, smoothed her hair, turned away, as if she were embarrassedly aware of it. She stepped ahead of him, following the gesture of his hand into the house.

He showed the porters through to the kitchen, where everything that had been in the dresser was now laid haphazardly on the table. Without a word, they began releasing the backboard. John switched on the kettle for tea.

"Do you want the doors removed or taped?" Catherine asked.

"Taped," he said.

She looked around at the table.

There was plenty of mundane stuff from the drawers: receipts, maps, the usual stack of bills. She picked up a paperback, read the back cover, replaced it. He tried not to look directly at her. Every time he did so, he saw drops of water on skin and felt her fingers urgently laced over his.

They exchanged small talk, watching the dresser being loaded onto the van. After ten minutes or so, Catherine let the men go without making any effort to follow them. Instead, she came back to the kitchen with John and sat down, looking speculatively at him.

"Do you have any paintings?" she asked.

The question, out of the blue, shocked him. Automatically he glanced at the door to the hall, to the alarm outside the drawing room.

"Yes," he told her. "I have some."

"Any particular period?" she asked.

He paused. "Victorian," he said.

"Figurative?"

He sat down alongside her, putting the items from the dresser into piles, not replying for a moment.

"You saw the miniature," he said.

She took a deep breath. "Yes, I did," she said. "*The Child's Problem*. Is it a copy?"

"No."

She put a hand to her throat. "Original? Genuine?"

"Yes."

She looked up at the ceiling, closed her eyes, opened them again with a smile. "Oh, my God," she said. "My God."

He got up and went out of the room. When he returned, she was still sitting in the same position at the table. He put a small box in front of her, took off the lid, and folded back the tissue paper.

She looked at him and then leaned forward. She took out the disc slowly, resting it in the palm of her hand. She said nothing for a long time.

Her utter immobility was fascinating to see.

For her own part, shock was the first emotion; it felt almost like walking through a brick wall, something she had previously felt to be impervious, immovable. But it was not only the accepted logic of

Dadd's history that was fragmenting here—the knowledge that he had painted more than she knew, and might have painted far more, if he were as industrious as this—but it was herself, her own image of what she was. It was that which was changing, and more rapidly.

She was not in control; she was out of her own carefully constructed picture. She felt so drawn to John that she could hardly look in his face. All the rules of reason were seemingly obsolete. She held an unknown Dadd in her hand, but more curiously still, she knew the stranger who had put it there, knew John intimately, recognized him, as if he had always been at her side.

She put a hand to her face briefly, as if to hide the pleasure that might be painted there.

John was still watching her acutely.

"You know this picture," John said.

"Yes," she said. "I've seen it in the Tate."

"It's not on public display."

"That's right," she replied. She turned the miniature this way and that in the light. "It's extraordinary," she said. "It's exactly the same. Exactly the same as the watercolor in the Tate. The scale is perfect."

He watched her face, seeing her appreciation. "Claire always thought it was disturbing," he said.

"It is," Catherine agreed. "It really is. It's the most peculiar and frightening painting I think I've ever seen. I've always thought so."

He drew his chair closer to her, and she tilted the picture toward him. "It's the child's face, the expression on the face," she said. "You think at first that he must have seen something terrible on the chessboard. You see the way he's reaching out his hand, as if he's going to move a piece, the castle?"

"Yes," John said. "White to play, and mate in two."

"Except for the contortion, the way the wrist goes . . ." She shook her head. "He isn't even looking at the castle. In fact, he's not looking at the board. He's looking beyond it, to something outside the picture. Recoiling from something horrible, terrifying." She sat back in her chair. "I always wondered what the problem was, the problem in the title. *The Child's Problem*. What was Dadd thinking of?" she said. "The problem isn't the chess move. I don't think it's even the knife beyond the chessboard, or the grotesque old man asleep in the chair alongside him. It's something else, beyond the board."

"Something that only Dadd could see," John said.

She shook her head. "There's another painting of his," she said. "Of a woman and two satyrs. The same eyes as these look out at you through leaves. The faces are pulled upward, as if something has hold of the hair. The brows go upward and the eyes slant. All Dadd's eyes began to look like that, eventually. Wide open eyes, showing the whites. Mothers, children. Even the babies."

John seemed to be about to say something, but had stopped himself.

Catherine glanced up again from the miniature. "Where on earth did you get it?" she asked.

"I found it," he said.

"Found it?" she echoed. "Where?"

He glanced downward. "In a flea market."

"No!"

She was gazing at him, a broad, delighted smile on her face.

He felt so guilty for the lie.

"You found a Dadd original?" she repeated, and started to laugh in astonishment. "But it must be worth a fortune!"

"It is," he said.

"How did you know it was real?"

"There's a signature."

She had put the miniature on the table between them, but now picked it up again.

"Turn it over," he said. "Look inside."

"I can't," she said. "I may damage it."

He smiled at her. "You mean you can resist looking at Dadd's signature?"

She gave him a quirky grimace of a smile. "Oh, Jesus," she breathed. With a slow, gentle movement, she prized the fastening apart.

"You didn't take it to an expert?" she asked.

"No," he said.

She opened the back. Inside, the fabric was folded tight, with a tiny piece of canvas backing held in place with a brass pin. She looked up at John, hesitating. "I can't do it," she said finally. "This is a job for a restorer, a specialist. I shouldn't touch it." She stared down at the canvas and the pin with a kind of longing, running the edge of her thumb along the rim of the metal. He looked at her with deeper interest, recognizing that look, that longing.

"It's painted on a little piece of stiff cotton, quite dirty," he told her. "Like a corner of a handkerchief, perhaps even a corner of a bedsheet. And there's a scrap of paper in there about two inches square. There's Dadd's handwriting on it."

"Dadd's handwriting is under this canvas?"

"Yes."

She sat back in her chair, smiled with delight, and replaced the miniature on the table. Then she stared at him. "You know that he'd killed his father? That he was in lunatic asylums, Bedlam and Broadmoor, for most of his life?"

"Yes," John said. "And to think that he painted something like this in prison . . ." His gaze went back to Catherine.

"*The Child's Problem* in the Tate has his inscription on the front top left," Catherine said. "In tiny little script. You almost need a magnifying glass."

"That's right," John said. "Only the date and address are different on this."

Catherine's eyes were fixed on his. "December 1857," she said. "Bethlehem Hospital, London. St. George's in the Fields."

"And this one," John told her, pointing at the miniature, "says, November 14th, 1885."

"A month before he died?" Catherine murmured.

"Yes."

"The last thing he ever did."

He nodded. "Probably."

"Even to the eyes," she said.

"Even to the empty eyes," he said. "Looking at empty spaces."

She sat back in her chair, regarding him. There was a silence for a second or two. "What did Claire think of it?" she asked.

"She thought I should get it insured."

"You didn't? Why not?"

"I don't know," he said. "It would mean telling people that I had it."

She looked at him questioningly. "Art galleries would be very interested in it. There are so few Dadds anywhere. Most of his paintings have vanished."

"I know."

"And to find a new one . . ."

"I know," he said, cutting short the conversation. He got up, picked up the miniature, put it into the box, and replaced the lid. She watched him; he felt her gaze lingering on him, and not just the miniature.

"Which is your favorite?" she asked at last.

"My favorite Dadd painting?"

"No," she said. "I meant which is your favorite from the others. You said you had other paintings."

John paused, passing the miniature from hand to hand. "I've never had them valued," he said.

"I didn't mean value," she replied. "I meant which one has the most meaning for you. Which one you like best." She saw his mixed expression. "You don't think I'm asking you so that I can assess them?" she asked.

He didn't reply.

"You think I'm showing an interest because I've got half an eye on commission?" she said. "Just in case you ever want to sell? I wasn't asking for that reason," she said, standing up. "I was asking out of interest. That was all."

"Don't go," he said.

"I must," she replied. "I'm late already."

"I'm sorry," he said. "I'm defensive about them."

"It's your prerogative," she said.

He stepped in front of her as she turned for the door. "I've collected since Claire died," he said.

"They're personal," she said. "I understand."

"No," he told her. "You don't."

"But I do," she replied calmly. "I've lost count of the number of clients who don't want to show me. Or who show me by degrees. I understand very well. But I wasn't asking you as a potential client."

"Look," he said, "please . . ." And he took hold of her arm. She looked down at his grasp and he released it almost immediately.

"I worked in London after Claire died," he said. "I wanted nothing in my life. I didn't even want the furniture we had owned together. And then, after a while, when I'd gone to Spain, I bought a painting. It wasn't expensive. It wasn't a Dadd, or anything like him. It was a surrealist picture. Nobody famous. I hung it on the wall." He moved his eyes away from her face. "I built my house, and that's all I did. Work on the house. Walk Frith. I walked for miles that first summer. I walked at night. I'd moved out there for the landscape, the difference. But I never looked at the landscape. I couldn't."

She stood still, listening, her gaze fixed on his downturned face.

"And then, one day, I bought the picture," he said. His tone had dropped. "And I thought . . . I can't say what I thought, exactly . . . that there was something here . . ."

"To fill the empty spaces," Catherine said.

At last he raised his eyes.

"Tell me your favorite," she said softly.

He knew which one. But there was no way he could tell her. She would know right away. If he told her the title, she would realize what he was talking about. See the weight that his life had become.

He tried to think of something inconsequential.

All he could think of was drops of water. The water in the river below the house as it fell from the weir. The cool drops of his dream, cool on warm skin. And the way he was drowning now.

"There must be something," Catherine said.

"There's someone called Sorolla y Bastida," he said. "Spanish. There's a wonderful painting . . . it has two women . . . the blue behind the women, it's beautiful. The sea, beautiful . . ."

He couldn't continue. He took hold of her hand. This time, she didn't resist. She let it lie within his. He put the miniature down on the table.

"What do you think Richard Dadd saw beyond the picture?" he asked. "That was so terrible?"

She didn't hesitate.

"The past," she told him.

He walked out into the hallway, taking her with him. He stopped outside the drawing room and keyed the alarm. When it was released, he looked at her only briefly before opening the door and taking her inside.

It was a large room with a huge window that must have looked out onto the lawn, but the curtains were drawn. In the gloom, Catherine saw only shapes: frames on the wall, what seemed to be a sculpture by an opposite door. The paneling close by them was exactly the same as that which ran up the stairway.

"Have you been in here before?" John asked.

"Yes," she said. "Mrs. Aston used to see me in here whenever she wanted to sell something."

They used to drink tea in here, she remembered. The frail old lady had held that tradition, taking an age to bring a little trolley by the window.

John switched on the light and he walked forward into the center of the room, but she stayed where she was. Shock rolled over her.

Three vast sideboards occupied the back and side walls, each one matching, and eight or nine feet long. They were Jacobean. Old oak, very dark. On their broad tops were dozens of items: Bow and Chelsea porcelain, vases, dishes, salt cellars, scent flasks, figurines, plates, tea canisters. There was silver, although much more porcelain than silver.

The nearest chest was simply a flood of ornate gilded blue; toward the back was a line of plates echoing the same shade, but simpler.

She recognized the soft-paste porcelain of Bow from the mid-1700s. The two salt cellars before them were the most complicated design of crayfish and shell, modeled in detail so that it looked almost alive. At one end was a small service, again from Bow, transfer printed in brown and painted with enamels of some Chinese design. Here on one cabinet was perhaps a hundred thousand pounds of delicate, infinitely perishable craftsmanship.

She walked a step forward and looked at the other sideboards. This was much more of a mixture. There was an 1860s plaster bust of Marianne, of the kind that sometimes were found over town hall doors in rural France; it sat on a small gilded chest, much battered and wormed. There was an unbelievable nineteenth-century Baltic bedroom cabinet on top of its Jacobean brother—a thin confection of white paint and crown-topped columns. And a white marble figure, barely sixteen inches high.

"This is Henri Laurens," she said.

She reached out and ran her fingers slowly along the contorted lines of the female nude, roundly misshapen, rigid-backed, heavy-breasted, arms raised over a head twisted on an impossibly long neck.

John still had said nothing. Catherine was aware he was standing behind her. She turned to say something to him, and saw the Sargent portrait.

She was on the far wall, behind where John was standing. She was half sitting, half lying on a seat by a window, her head tilted back, her arm lying extended along the backrest. Summer light flooded the picture and the face of the woman with her dark coiled hair, the glitter of diamonds at her neck, the bare shoulder above the cream-colored gown. She had a face of removed, even bored calm. Beyond the open window was a bank of roses and a distant parkland, shimmering in the haze of an August day. Below her, her dress cascaded to the floor in deep folds of cream satin. As the fabric fell farther from the light from the window, the painter had picked up its drop in swiftly executed single lines of color, shining in the shadows. A shawl, patterned with red and gold, had dropped to the floor of the room.

Catherine walked forward.

John Singer Sargent's style was unmistakable. The greatest of the Victorian portrait artists shone out in the subdued light, spilling a summer day into the north-facing drawing room, that, even with curtains open, could be dark. Voluptuous light, fresh and lovely; the woman's flawless skin gleaming above the dress. One of Sargent's heiresses. One of the endless procession of American and French women who had sat for him in the 1880s and 1890s, and in the end, along with the English aristocracy, finally bored him beyond endurance.

John was watching Catherine's face.

"Her name is Amy Clanville-Wright," he said. "She was sixteen."

Catherine said nothing. She couldn't. She walked to his side.

"I was given her to pay for a debt," he said.

Catherine stared at him. "A debt?"

"I built a client a house in Guadalhorce, and he couldn't pay," he explained. "He gave me this." He smiled. "I think he was a crook," he said. "One of those East End boys living in Spain to escape the long arm of the law." And he started to laugh softly. "I never did dare ask where he made his cash. And I never dared ask where he got Amy Clanville-Wright. I dread to think."

She shook her head. "John," she said, "this is serious money. Are you crazy, keeping it here? My God! This isn't a joke." She turned on her heel. "And this . . ." she said, waving her hand at the porcelain.

"I've bought it over the last eight years."

"All this? Everything?"

"All of it," he said.

"The Laurens . . ."

"I had to have her," he said.

She met his eye. Then she looked about herself again, trying to take it in. "I don't know what to say to you," she said.

"It isn't about money," he said.

"Not about money!"

"No," he said. "You know that, of all people."

She looked around at the whole room. She did know what he meant. She knew the fixations and passions. She knew what came out of loneliness, above all. She glanced back at John, with a glance of sadness.

"Don't pity me," he said.

"I don't," she said.

"I didn't buy them to collect," he said. "Although I *did* collect. I bought them because they reminded me of what the world was like."

She waited.

He went to the Laurens. He rested his hand on the figure's neck, on the cool and perfectly smooth texture. "It was made for love," he said, "not money or status. But because it had to be made. A compulsion."

He looked across at the porcelain. "A compulsion to make something wonderful," he said. "To be alive in the world."

He turned back to her and saw that she had her hands to her face. She turned half away.

"What's the matter?" he asked.

"It's nothing."

But it was something. She had begun to cry. "Catherine," he said. "Catherine."

She tried not to look up at him. She was suddenly overcome with memories. Herself, alone, bent over books while she studied. Herself as a little girl, and alone in a house, sitting at a window, very like the window in Sargent's painting. Looking out onto an empty garden. Playing with the flaking paint of the sill, making it into patterns, drawing with a pencil around the patterns, while the day drifted away. Saw herself with Robert, making do with less than she needed, for an idea of what he was, instead of what he really was.

Saw herself in the empty spaces. And John Brigham, too, scribbling in time, filling it with colors and shapes. Living in paintings.

That's all they did, she thought. *They lived in paintings.*

She turned her gaze to him.

He held out his hand, that same hand that had sent a rush of longing through her, a telegraphed impression of longing, just yesterday.

"Catherine," John said. He made another hesitant step, and then quickly took her in his arms. "Catherine."

It was nothing more than a whisper, in a room crowded with desire.

Contradiction: Oberon and Titania

1854–58

There were new rooms.

He had been told that the better class of criminal patients would be moved from the ordinary wards, and that the new rooms were large and airy and had pictures and statues. He thought of the rooms while he was on the ward, keeping silence while others ranted along the dormitory cells. In his silence, that leafless forest, branches locked over his head, footfall soaked into the earth, smothered by sandy ground, he waited.

Seeing airy rooms, airy rooms.

On the day that he was moved, he was shown a book of his confinement. He had been quiet and amenable, lost in his inner landscape, head bowed under the imagined ceiling of branches, so that when they came to take him, he was calm.

He looked at the book, laid out on the great oak table. There was written the date of his admission, and the date of his trial, and his transfer from Maidstone jail.

He had leaned over the page, tracing the copperplate, fixated on the curvature of lettering and the neatness of the figures. He put his hand on the page to absorb its contours, its ridges and rises, its mountains and valleys. Inside the scroll of the downward strokes were rivers, their moisture coiling in warming drops on the fine tipping slant of the R, the expansive curve of the D.

These things were in his name: rivers and drops of oil and drops of paint and drops of blood. In his name and the dates of his life were continents and countries. Here he came on 22nd August 1844—he pressed his fingertips to the line—in strait-waistcoat and his blue cloak, and his hands shackled, and a dark beard and combed hair, a Christ in chains, driven by the Devil.

It was May. In the new rooms was a calendar. It was the first thing he saw. He didn't care to view the country from the windows: the lost city, the distant gray edge of the Thames. He cared only to walk up and down the wall of the door that had admitted him.

He took a place in the corner, with his back to the light.

Edward Brigham, his new attendant, brought him his easel. Dadd drew a line on the floor to keep the other patients away. Behind the line, the Devil himself whispered and writhed, subdued by the changes, muttering in sleep.

He had begun this painting three years before. He thought that perhaps it would take him still another year. He marked out the picture in a grid, and worked from the bottom right-hand corner upward. It would have been easier to work in the opposite direction, downward from the left; that way he would not have to hold his arm and hand at such an impossible angle. But as his elbow and shoulder took the strain of the painting, they carried it, and he could feel himself crawling upward, inch by inch, slowly toward completion, like the snails and insects that inhabited his pictures, and took week upon week, month upon month, to illustrate.

Last year, in addition to Contradiction, *he had painted the last of the* Passions. *Sketches for each torment: duplicity, and disappointment, and grief, and anger.*

In Hatred *he could not help himself. He painted* The Duke of Gloster—*"see how my sword weeps the poor King's death"—but he didn't paint Gloster's face above the body; he painted his own, staring at the long blade.*

Jealousy and Hatred were painted within days of each other. He couldn't separate them; they were woven, knotted in his head. Murder was easy; his brush flowed. Cain standing above Abel, a club in his hand, the bodies almost indistinguishable from each other. This was what he could never tell others, not even Mr. Hood, who had been so understanding of his work. That he and his father were conjoined in the same way as the biblical brothers, sealed forever in the same terrible moment. He had stood above his father, connected to him by ties of blood in more than one sense. He would think about this often; the hand to the weapon, the weapon to the throat. Such were family ties: the constriction, the conjunction, the dispatch.

After it, his hand was shuddering. Brigham, with a kindness in his touch, took away the paints.

In the bottom of Contradiction, *he had painted an archer. Grotesque, with his arm drawn back, he is aiming at the fairy queen herself. Fairy sprites struggle to save her life, though she remains obliviously unaware. So unaware, in fact, that she has crushed another tiny winged figure under the ball of her foot. She is cruel. Bulky, unappealing and cruel, dominating the painting while scenes of frantic defense unravel around her.*

He couldn't bring himself to love her. His Titania was rigid, static, swollen with greed, sated with bodily lust. She had changed since he last drew her twelve years earlier; grown huge, self-satisfied, bored, unflinching. She was the very embodiment of anger, the central core of the quarrel between fairy king and queen. He disliked her with an increasing passion, an increasing need to be free of her. And yet she grew there in the center of his mind, taking on a bright yellow gown and a robe that hung from her hand and trailed below her feet, representing all the distortions and details and objects that had come to possess him. He longed to be free of her. He longed to rush out into the daylight and breathe fresh air.

He longed for that air to blow through him, and make him clean.

He finished the painting at the end of the month.

When he stood up at last and looked out, the year had turned miraculously to summer.

13

Friday morning, in the early hours, he heard a bird singing loudly in the night.

John had no idea what kind it was, only that the song was extraordinary and seemed much louder because of the silence of the dark. It was in a tree somewhere close to the house, and the song was a true melody. Lying flat on his back, he had been awake for more than an hour. There was no way that he could sleep.

He had met Catherine the previous evening in a local pub, a small place in the next village. Over the meal, the conversation predictably turned to Richard Dadd.

"I wrote a book about him," Catherine said.

"Did you?" he replied. "I'm sorry, I should have known that."

She shrugged. "I don't see why," she told him. "It wasn't exactly a bestseller. It sold about three copies."

"You're being modest."

"I'm not," she retorted. "I produced it when there was a retrospective for him. OK, it sold a few while the exhibition was on, but after that not many."

"I'd like to read it."

"It's more about the paintings than Bedlam or Broadmoor."

"So much the better."

She smiled and shook her head. "I rarely meet anyone who's even heard of him."

"Do you have a copy I can borrow?"

"Yes, I . . ." She paused, frowning slightly.

"What is it?" he asked.

"I have several," she said. "But I think Robert took one."

"He did?"

"There's a gap in the bookshelf. I'm sure it was my book."

"Is it so surprising that he should take a copy?" John asked.

She laughed faintly. "Yes," she said. "He thought Dadd was grotesque."

"Well, so he could be."

"Yes, but . . ." She lifted a hand to her face. "Robert thought it was all pretty much a waste of time."

"Just Dadd?"

"Art generally."

John frowned. "That is a lot of your life not to have in common."

"He wasn't obstructive about it," Catherine said.

"Nevertheless."

She had finished her food and put her knife and fork down slowly. "I met Robert when I first moved to London, straight out of college," she said. "Waiting for a train, actually."

"You were working there?"

"Yes. For an auction house. A little bigger than Pearsons." She smiled, then glanced away. "Though it wasn't a very nice time overall."

"Any particular reason?" he asked.

She paused for quite a long time. "Well . . . my parents had died a year before," she said. "A car accident."

"Oh, I'm sorry," he said. He waited for some other detail, but none came. "In London?"

"No," she said. "They worked all over the place. They were in Africa at the time." He watched her hand describe slow circles on the tabletop, pursuing the grain of the oak in the surface. "There was another car following them, they were on a dirt track. The driver be-hind—they were in a convoy of three—said that the car flipped so slowly, and landed so gently, that he was sure they would both be OK. But they weren't. My father was killed instantly."

He waited, trying to read her face. "Are you an only child?"

"Yes," she said. "Are you?"

"No," he replied. "I have a sister, Helen. She's younger than I am and she lives in London."

"Do you see much of her?"

He shook his head. "Actually, I haven't seen her for some time," he said. "She . . . she's very busy. She works in television."

"Oh," Catherine said. "As an actress?"

"No. She's a designer. I think the last thing she worked on was *Byzantium*."

He had named a well-known historical series that had come high in the year's ratings. Catherine nodded, impressed. "And she would . . . do what on that?"

"Come up with the concept of how it looked, the locations, the overall tone. Working with the director."

"But that's an amazing job," Catherine said. "She must be a very in-teresting person."

"Yes," he said finally. He did not want to talk about Helen, or what she represented to him. "She is quite interesting." He hoped she could not hear the irony in his voice.

The waitress came; they looked at the menu and ordered coffee.

Catherine glanced around the bar and back at him; then she ran her hand briefly over her face before resting her head on the same hand.

He gazed at her. He had been drawn to her earlier in the day, felt overwhelmed by the sensation of her in his arms; but something far more powerful, far more basic, took hold of him now. He looked at her hand, at the shape of it, at the smooth texture of her skin, at the shape of the fingers and the angle of the wrist, and suddenly wanted her. It took the strength out of him. He wanted to feel her skin; he wanted his mouth on her. He crossed his arms over his chest as if to hold the feeling in.

She was not looking at him directly now; she had been gazing for a second at the people at another table. Then she turned back to him. "How long were you and Claire married?" she asked.

"Four years."

"And was there someone in Spain?"

"In Spain?" he asked. "No."

"That's a very long time to be on your own."

He didn't reply. He felt Claire somewhere at the back of his mind, where she had been for the last two or three years. She had finally retreated out of his daily consciousness, which at first made him feel guilty, and then, slowly, saddened and relieved. She lived there, halfway to forgetting, an icon of what it was to be loved now, rather than a woman of flesh and blood. He would concentrate on her from time to time with a kind of two-dimensional longing. She was no longer living in his mind but, rather, reproduced there.

He realized that Catherine was watching him with a curious expression on her face. "I saw them afterward," she said.

"I'm sorry," he replied. "Saw who?"

She blushed slightly, made a slight face to herself, as if she had said something embarrassing, out of place. "It doesn't matter."

"Saw who?" he repeated.

She bit her lip. "Did you ever see Claire?" she asked.

He looked hard at her. He thought of the dream and the footprints. "I saw where she had walked," he said, quietly. "The imprint."

There was a perfect silence for a moment. She did not say, as he had half expected her to say, some placatory thing, that it was perhaps some kind of hallucination, some false memory. She accepted it; she nodded.

"They were in my room," she explained, simply. "About a week after the funeral." She sat back in her chair, her hands folded in her lap. Her face was calm, thoughtful rather than unhappy. "I came upstairs," she continued. "It was early in the year and got dark early. I hadn't put on the light, and I walked into my bedroom and saw them. I saw them standing . . ." She stopped.

"In the room?"

She frowned. "It was very odd," she said. "I don't mean just the fact of seeing them at all. But they were standing on either side of my bed, very straight, very still. And at the time I didn't think, How peculiar that you're here. That was the strangest part. I didn't think that at all, or anything like it. I just wondered why they said nothing. They were like sentries on either side of the bed." She crossed her arms. "I put on the light," she said. "And they stayed. They stayed for three or four seconds. I saw the light on their clothes, the colors come up after the shadows. I saw the color of my mother's hair. I saw the ring she always had on her thumb, too large to wear on her finger, an African ring."

John listened, thinking of the distinctness of Claire's footsteps in his recurring dream in Alora, and how they had lived with him, how he sometimes thought that he saw them when he was awake, and how he accepted their presence unreservedly. "Did it frighten you?" he asked.

"No," she said. "But I kept seeing the amber in the ring. It was amber in a thick silver setting, with a kind of hatched pattern in the silver. Do you know a painting called *The Last Chapter*? By Martineau."

"No," he said.

"Oh, well," she smiled. "It doesn't really matter. But I had a print of that. It's a wonderful painting for the firelight; a girl is reading a book with only the light of the fire, and . . ." Her voice trailed off for a second. "But she's wearing a sash, with a hatched, a crisscross pattern . . . the two stuck together, the colors of their clothes, the painting, the patterns. And sometimes Dadd did that kind of shading. I would glimpse that design, a sort of echo, when I was doing other things. Working, or sitting on a bus, or . . ." She shrugged a little. "I was crazy, I suppose."

"No," he told her. "That kind of crazy is sane. A repeating pattern, running through everywhere you look." And he thought of particular designs he had done after Claire's death, ones where he inadvertently used drawings she had made for a costume, the cut or angle of a shape. How it came out in everything. How everything was linked. Paintings, shade, shape, memory, feelings: longing or desire or preoccupation. How satisfying it was to draw the line and find that it linked two disparate objects in your mind.

They lapsed into silence and he paid the bill. After another couple of minutes, they went out of the pub together. Crossing the parking lot, they paused by his car.

"Thank you for the meal," she said. She was holding her own car keys in her hand.

"You're very welcome."

"Have you finished the work on the river now?" she asked. "The stream?"

"For now," he said. He looked at the keys in her hand. "Would you like to walk down to the bridge?" he asked her.

"Yes," she said, and put the keys in her pocket.

The village street was very quiet. Only one car passed them as they walked downhill, the long gentle slope to the eighteenth-century bridge that John had seen almost swamped by the floodwaters earlier in the year. It was a narrow bridge with two small niches on both sides halfway across, so that pedestrians might avoid the road traffic.

They stood here now, looking at the water meadows on one side and the river on the other. Two or three hundred yards out in the meadows were blurred white shapes.

"Can you see them?" Catherine asked. "The swans."

And so they were. Three pairs, heads dipped into the short grass, so that they presented curious shallow figures, almost horizontal. Six white ghostlike boats moving across the dark canvas of the fields. They might have been invisible altogether if it hadn't been for the moon.

He took Catherine's hand and crossed the little road, then stepped down onto the riverside path, a very narrow chalk path under the trees.

Two tributaries joined here: there was a wide, rushy gap of water and a few feet of gravelly shore. On each bank, trees dipped down to the river. He knew that behind him, the land stretched away to the foot of Derry Woods, though nothing could be seen of the woods now.

In fact, he could see nothing at all but the shadows of the trees and the lazy movement of the river, a slow dance where the waters merged, breaking up the reflection of the moonlight.

He realized that Catherine had stopped and was staring at the water.

"What is it?" he asked.

She stayed where she was. "I've been waiting for them to come back," she said. "I've been waiting for my mother's hand." She shook her head.

He drew her arm so that it locked behind his back. She said nothing, but turned in toward him. If he could have heard her thoughts, he would have heard her longing for him, the rush of desire, the electricity she felt when he touched her. But he could barely see her face, though he saw the lightness of her skin, the fall of her hair on her shoulders.

"They won't need to," he whispered. "I'll stand with you now."

She remained still for a second, and then put her head in the crook of his shoulder. There was nothing but the whispering of the river, the black-and-white photographic print of water and trees, so distinct in its contrasts that it was almost abstract.

They were part of a pattern, a ribbon of light and dark. He felt the world fragment, move and alter. He felt a change, a rush, a disorientation. He shifted his balance to hold her closer, pressing his mouth to her neck, her face. She tilted her head, returned the pressure of his touch. He lifted her free hand and pressed it to his mouth, then turned the palm over and ran his lips from fingertip to wrist.

He heard her intake of breath. She put her arm around his neck, tightened the embrace in the small of his back. What he saw in his mind was the light on the water; the moonlight breaking and rejoining, breaking and rejoining, as the water rolled past them, under the wide span of the arches and beyond the bridge.

John turned on his side in the bed now and felt the faint trickle of cold air from the open window. The bird had stopped singing; the silence it left was almost tangible. He listened for a while, hoping for a long time that it would continue, then turned back.

Catherine was lying at his side, asleep, her head turned down into the pillow so that he could not see her face.

Tentatively, he reached out and touched her, felt her warmth.

And, for the first time in years, certainly for the first time without grief, and despite himself, he cried, quietly and steadily in the dark, with his hand in hers.

14

The knock on the dressing room door of the London theater came just as Nathan Fitzgerald was leaving.

"There's a woman to see you." It was one of the front-of-house girls, still in her black uniform, with a coat thrown over it.

"I've seen them all," he said.

She grinned at him. He shut his door after him, slinging the rucksack over his back. He was always the last of the cast to leave, and tonight had been no different. Nathan had been interviewed for *The Evening Standard* while he lay on his back with his feet propped on the dressing room wall, the only comfortable position for a back that ached fiercely after every performance. He winced now, and the girl walking alongside him glanced at him.

"Still a problem?"

"Bloody chiropractor's no good at all," he complained.

"You shouldn't throw yourself around the stage, maybe," she observed. "Or anywhere else." They came out onto the stairs. The girl started down them, but pointed to the entrance to the stalls as she did so. "She's in there and won't leave," she said. "You'd better hurry up, Webster's wanting to shut up shop."

Nathan sighed. "Who is it, anyway?" he asked. "Has she got a name?"

"Brigham," the girl said, over her shoulder. "Helen Brigham."

He tried to remember, as he walked toward her, how long it was since he had seen her.

Maybe three weeks. Maybe four.

She was sitting near the front, her knees drawn up onto the seat, her large black velvet coat wrapped around her. She looked fragile. A small, thin body and a childlike face. She had cut her hair; it was cropped and spiky, and only added to her air of edgy vulnerability.

He deliberately didn't sit alongside her. Instead, he walked along the row in front and took the seat slightly to one side, and turned his body around so that he was facing her.

"I'm here," she said. "You told me not to come, but I did anyway."

"It's OK," he said. "I didn't mean for you to keep away forever."

She looked at him. "Didn't you?" she asked.

He avoided the question. "How are you?"

"I'm fine," she said. It was her standard response. She was always fine, even when in the throes of one of her moods. He studied her now, trying to gauge what state of mind she was in.

"Did you see the show?" he asked.

"No," she said. "I think I've seen it enough."

When they had been together, she had come often, sometimes seeing the whole show, or part of it. Sometimes standing in the wings, which he had tried to discourage, as he could feel her gaze.

"We've got another Daniel," he said, naming a character.

"So I hear. Is he any good?"

"Yes."

"Be taking the shine from you," she said.

"Nothing can do that."

She smiled. "Oh," she said. "That's right. I forgot. You're an actor."

There was a silence.

"How are you really?" he asked.

She looked to the stage. "I got fired," she said.

"What? When?"

"Today."

"Oh, shit," he sympathized. "How did that happen?"

She pulled the coat tighter across her. "I'm not allowed to have any opinion at all," she said. "And this . . . this Price."

"Price is directing?"

"Yes."

He had seen her tears many times; he almost could grade them according to authenticity. But this seemed sudden and real; she put her hand over her mouth, then both over her face.

He reached out and touched her knee. "It's a misunderstanding, surely."

"No," she said, still from behind her hands. "No."

Out of the corner of his eye he saw the manager, Webster, come to the door and signal him that he was shutting down the lights.

"Listen," Nathan said. "Come outside with me a minute."

She carried on sobbing, childlike snuffles that now, he guessed, were probably deliberately prolonged. He patted her knee. "Up you get," he said. "Webster wants to go home to his cocoa, and so do I."

She appeared from behind the hands. "You don't like cocoa," she muttered with a comic sad smile.

"Then we'll go to the Metro," he said.

She stood up almost immediately, the smile widening. She followed him to the edge of the row and linked his arm. "I've missed you," she said.

His heart fell about a hundred feet into an abyss.

The Metro was crowded.

Several people smiled when they saw him, then their gaze went to Helen and back again to his face. They were given a table facing into the body of the restaurant. Helen shuffled along the bench seat and wriggled out of the coat, looking around her. She seemed very pleased to be noticed with him, he saw.

"I'm not going to eat," he said.

"Oh," she remarked. "Just something."

"I'm not hungry," he said. "If you must know, I'm very tired, Helen. I really do have to go home in a minute."

She looked at the menu, then dropped it to the table. "We've only just walked through the door and already you're telling me that you have to go," she said.

"OK," he admitted. "I'm sorry. But I'm not hungry. You have something."

She did. She ordered a glass of wine and the Italian plate. He hid his frown. He knew it was a code; he knew her. They had been to Italy at Christmas, to Florence. He had hated it. He didn't like galleries. He didn't like churches. But she insisted; she even had a little notebook and camera. Research. She had been there before, as a student. She kept talking about paintings and how much, how intimately, she understood them. It was in Florence that he had known for sure that he could not bear to be with her anymore, and it had been sad, very sad, to be with her, with all her enthusiasm, taking the notes and the photographs, and to know that he would soon tell her that he was leaving her.

It had been her idea that they live together. He had always resisted it. She had talked about it almost from the first moment they met, and she could be very persuasive. My God, persuasive wasn't in it. She could be exhausting, monopolizing him. Very sexy at first. Very wearing, very boring after the first two months. And the moods.

Then he had lost his shared apartment. He took advantage of her, he could see that. But the realization of having used her to avoid looking for anywhere else was not a very appealing character trait, so he had tried to ignore it. But in Florence, he knew. He knew that there was no way he could spend any more time with her.

She had made plans. She was good at that. Good at organizing. That was her job, she would point out to him, laughing.

And so she organized everything; the holidays they had together, and the weekends. She was alarmingly generous and he had thought that she must have some sort of private money. They went to Paris.

They went to Crete and Sardinia. She booked them a long weekend at a place in Cornwall and tried to teach him to sail. She had been adamant about it. "You'll sail and look like those thirties film stars," she had told him. "It's amazingly good for the image, Nathan. Think about it. Outdoor guy, blue sea."

But he wasn't a sailor. He wasn't anything, it seemed to him, that she wanted him to be. He was an actor, but he wasn't literary, and he didn't like art, and he wanted to be down at the pub and perhaps go running with the two mates he had shared the flat with.

"I'm an ordinary person," he would tell her.

She had just laughed. "You're an extraordinary person," she would correct him. And she would wave a newspaper at him. "It says so here in the reviews."

"I'm an extraordinary actor," he quoted. "But I'm just a bloke. Don't make me something I'm not."

"You won't make a name for yourself propping up the bar in the Mile End road."

"I don't want a name for myself," he had told her. "I'm not some superannuated grandee of the bloody West End. I'm twenty-six."

"You're lying," she had retorted. "All actors are egotists."

Perhaps she was right, and the man-of-the-people was a name tag he wore, but he didn't want to go to showbiz parties or stand around the Royal Academy at the Summer Show pretending that he knew his arse from his elbow.

"Look," he said one day as they lay in bed, "you've got to understand this. I'm a boy from Salford. That's what I am."

"And that's what you want to be all your life?" she had replied, tauntingly, smiling.

"Yes," he had told her as he got out of bed.

He looked at her now.

"What have you been doing with yourself these last few weeks?" he asked.

She shrugged. "Working."

"With Price."

"For him. Much good it's done me."

"There'll be another job."

To his horror, she began to cry again. "There won't be another job," she said. "No one will take me."

"You're exaggerating."

"I'm not."

"You're just depressed over—" he realized what he'd said as soon as it was out of his mouth, but it was too late.

"I've got a good reason to be depressed, haven't I?" she demanded. "You walk out on me . . ."

He couldn't deny it. He had told her the moment they got back from Florence. In fact, just to lessen the tension on himself—selfishness, selfishness—they had barely put their bags on the floor of her flat before he told her that he was going. He just couldn't see the logic in unpacking his case only to have to repack it in the same week.

"Going?" she had echoed. "Going where?"

Of course he was sorry. But it had never been a long-term relationship as far as he was concerned. He was stupid enough, cruel enough, to tell her so.

"Why?" she had said, sinking to a chair. "Why?"

Because she was so helplessly clinging. Because she never woke up in the same mood. Because he was forever guessing what he had done that day to upset her. Because she would sometimes sing all day, or cry all day. Because she wanted, planned, visualized a future with the full entourage—the children, the admiring friends, the fawning fans, the full celebrity couple status. Because other people, who had known her longer than he had, told him that she was crazy. And they were right. Because she wanted to suck out his bloody soul with her questions. Because he wanted to breathe again, and not be looking over his shoulder, afraid she was at his back, watching him.

But he didn't tell her that.

"I'm not ready," he had said, eventually, "for everything you want."

"I'll change," she had offered. "I'll change."

She had held his hand tightly as he tried to get out of the door.

"I'll ring you tonight," he lied.

"Meet me tomorrow." She was clutching at his arm, his hand.

"I will," he said.

But he didn't. For two weeks, he ignored all her calls and e-mail messages and texts. Then he saw her by accident at the Royal Festival Hall. He had gone in to meet someone, a woman. Helen was just coming out of the bookstore. She stared at him and then made a little waving motion with one hand. He had turned away.

The food was delivered to the table.

She didn't touch it, just sat looking at it.

"I'm leaving the show in three weeks," he told her.

She glanced up at him. "You are?"

"I've got an offer in New York."

There was a second's pause. "Doing . . ."

"Doing the same play."

"On Broadway?"

"Yes."

It was hard to hide his excitement. He didn't mean to hurt her. As she looked at him, he knew in that instant that she had come back to him to try again. And, in the same second, it came to her that they would never be together. He saw a flash of some complicated, strange emotion pass over her face.

"Perhaps I should come to New York, too," she said brightly. "A new start. Perhaps they would like me over there."

He waited a beat. "Helen," he said.

She stood up. Her eyes were full of tears; one hand was laid across her stomach. Then she leaned down, kissed him on the cheek, and snatched up her coat.

He had a sudden, horrible misgiving, a premonition. "Why did you come tonight?" he asked. "Specifically, tonight?"

"It doesn't matter," she replied.

"But where are you going?"

She started to put on her coat. A girl at the next table glanced at them both and smiled behind her hand, and Helen saw the smile. She froze for a second, and then continued, eyes downcast, movements fumbled. "I think I will have a holiday for a while," she said. "I think I will go and see my brother."

And she nodded to herself, turned away, and went out of the door without once looking back at him.

Sketch to Illustrate the Passions: Treachery

1853

There was a new physician given to Bedlam in 1853.

Dadd was taken by Brigham to see him: a walk along the galleries and down a staircase. Past the pump room, where a vast cast-iron boiler was rattling behind the doors. He would have liked to stop and listen to the sound, the choke of steam echoing along the steps and tiled walls. But he was not allowed to stop.

They carried on—small high square windows cast smaller squares of ocher on the red floor edged with blue tile, as if streams ran along the edges—until they reached Mr. Hood's room.

Dadd painted him soon after. The physician was sitting on a chair without a desk before him, sitting facing the door, very composed, hands laced in his lap. He had a very solid gaze; he wore a dress coat of black, a black waistcoat and trousers, a starched shirtfront and black stock.

Remembering him, Dadd painted him in a garden, for Hood's demeanor and his office were gardenlike, he thought; none of the airlessness and suspicion of other men. He painted him sitting on a blue bench with a back made of entwined branches and ivy curling between his feet, and a puzzle of a leaf lying on his shoulder.

Whenever he thought of it, Dadd would smile to himself. No one had noticed it, the fact that the leaf—a large thick sunflower leaf—looked as if it might be both behind and in front of Mr. Hood. The perspective was twisted. It looked as if it might be behind the man's figure if you studied the head and shoulder; but the leaf tip actually lay over the nearest branch that formed the backrest of the seat. Mr. Hood carried the up-surging plant on his shoulders; it hung over him like a green umbrella. Pure foolishness, worthy of a lunatic left to his own dreams and devices for ten years.

In the background, the mountains and cedars of Lebanon; in the fore-ground, the iron lawn roller of an English garden. On the seat beside Hood, a Turkish fez, and that all-obscuring piece of cloth that hung over the face of the man in The Child's Problem.

Cloth had properties, he told Hood that first day. Properties of substance and flexibility. It could ripple and fall. It could be starched into ruffs that enclosed necks. Over and over again, he painted great folds of shawls; pleats in skirts; sculptural drapes that almost—almost, but not quite—covered feet, or faces, or hands. Inside the folds, what was hidden? Merely the cloth itself, perhaps. Or perhaps the depths of other things— the cocoon and wrappings of sleeping vices.

He painted Cupid and Psyche this year. Cupid had fallen in love with the king's daughter, but leaves her when she steals a look at him. The two are caught in a kiss; but he had not taken that right. He could not get the woman's face. The finished portrait was strange; her hair would not fall past her throat. The breasts and the curve of the shoulder and stomach belonged to some other, larger woman. And under the folds of the mate-rial, above which her own feet are balanced, came another foot, the foot of the chair: a griffin's claw, scales and bone.

You never knew what was hidden in commonplace objects, or com-monplace minds.

"Mr. Dadd," Hood had said, standing up, and holding out his hand. "I'm very honored to meet you."

It was probably five years since anyone had formally shaken his hand.

Dadd received it with interest, this touch of another flesh. The hand was cool and sanguine, without much pressure. It was a disappointment to him. He resisted the urge to inspect it, as he often inspected his own *fingers that had been responsible for etching his commands on other skin, and on canvas and paper.*

"Tell me," Mr. Hood asked when they were both seated, "what have you been painting this year?"

It was difficult. Dadd recalled Dymphna Martyr, *but he didn't wish to tell Mr. Hood of that watercolor.* Dymphna had been the daughter of an Irish pagan king and a Christian mother. After her mother's death, her father had wanted to marry her, his own flesh and blood. She fled to Gheel, where the king caught up with her and beheaded her, spilling what had sprung from him on the ground.

No, not to tell that. And not to tell The Death of Richard II: *four figures wrestling on the edge of eternity. Not to tell of* Hatred.

"I have painted a watercolor," he said quietly. "It is called A Hermit. It is peaceful. There is an hourglass and a book."

Mr. Hood nodded. "Do you have anything to read?" he asked.

"Mr. Brigham brought me a Bible."

Hood nodded approvingly at the attendant. "Would you like something else?"

Dadd considered. "Shakespeare," he said. "Poetry."

In his case notes that year, Hood would write: "A very sensible and agreeable companion, a mind once well educated and thoroughly informed . . ."

The interview was soon over. Mr. Hood was very busy, Dadd was told.

He was busy, it transpired, with all kinds of improvements. Every single window in the hospital was enlarged that year, flooding Dadd's sleeping cell with an unexpected brightness late in the morning, when the sun came at a particular angle. Busy with other changes, too: unheard-of things. Every ward had an aviary of singing birds.

Men crowded to them. Some tried to take the birds, but were defeated by the height of the cages and the welded doors. Others, like Dadd, could not bear the new voices. The birds sang at twilight and at first light. It seemed to him unbearably mournful. They had been imprisoned for no crime, and all they could do was call, and call, and call.

He struggled with his rages. He swore rambling oaths at Brigham. He spat his food on the floor.

When Mr. Hood next visited, he found that Dadd had begun a great raft of sketches of the passions. Poverty, and Splendour and Wealth, and Idleness, and Gaming and Treachery.

Hood examined the last watercolor closely.

"It is three Chinese," he said.

Dadd hardly took his eyes from the paper. "We are at war with China," Dadd said. "That is why they are treacherous."

"We were at war with China until twelve years ago," Hood murmured.

Dadd did not pause. "All wars and trickery have the same root," he said.

Hood looked at the painting: a flight of steps, an open door. A man on the steps relays some secret to another, hiding below. The long curved blade in the man's right hand waits for the unsuspecting figure stepping out of the house.

"The Chinese dress is very well drawn," Hood told him.

"It is not correct," Dadd told him. "It hangs wrongly from the waist."

"I can see no fault," Hood told him truthfully.

And Dadd finished it in that moment, writing his name and the date along the bottom step in the picture.

"Not all faults are visible," he murmured. He thought of his father, retching in the evening darkness on a public path, unable, even then, to let go of his trust. Falling, one hand clutched to his collar, looking about him for the murderer who could not be his own son, and his eyes finally resting on Richard in disbelief. That had been his last expression: blank disbelief.

"Treachery in those who suppose to love us," Dadd said, wiping the paintbrush on the corner of the paper.

15

When Catherine woke, first light was showing.

It was two months later, the warmest May for years, and the copper beech on the lawn was coming into leaf. She could see the crown of the tree now, through the open curtains. It was a glorious tawny red, made more distinct by the oak and tulip trees behind it.

"What's the matter?" John asked.

She looked across at him. "Nothing," she said. "It's OK. Go back to sleep."

He held out his arms; she eased herself into them and lay with her head in the curve of his shoulder. She closed her eyes, savoring this moment, the warm length of his body, the way he immediately responded to her touch. He caught her hand in his, raised it to his lips, and then wordlessly held it against his chest.

"Do you want me to go to the house with you today?" John asked.

She considered. "No," she said finally.

Robert had sent her a letter asking her to meet him at their home, giving today's date. It was now three months, perhaps a little more, since she had seen him. When she had gone back yesterday to check the house over, she had found the letter among a pile of mail. It was postmarked London and dated the week before. When she had come back to Bridle Lodge, she had held it out wordlessly to John.

"It had to happen sooner or later," he said.

"He will want to sell," she said. "That's all it can be."

"You don't have to do anything you don't want to," John had commented.

They had been standing in the hallway. She had been living here now for just over six weeks; since that first night, she had never really had any inclination to go home. Sometimes, she wondered even what life had been like with Robert. It seemed pallid when she looked back at it. A world she had stepped out of, like Alice stepping through the looking glass. Or a character out of a canvas. Except she felt that she had stepped from a dream into actual life, and not the other way around.

John gave her back the letter. He stepped down from the tread he had been working on: he was restoring the panels under the balustrade, tracing out the twisting vines back onto the pieces that had been painted out. It was meticulous work, and it seemed to Catherine that he had dedicated himself to it like a religious mission.

"Do you know that there is a resemblance?" he had asked her, that very first morning they had been together. "She's just like you."

She'd turned to look at him. "I don't understand. What resemblance?"

"In the painting," he replied. He had kissed her; she had left, going into work. When she had come back to him that evening, he had a poster of *The Fairy Feller's Master-Stroke* on the table, weighed down at each corner with books.

"Oh, my God," she said, laughing as she came in the door. "For a second there, I thought we had another copy of an original." She had shaken her head, holding her hand over her heart in mock fright.

He took her hand. "Look at the girl with the mirror," he said.

He had pointed to the left-hand side of the picture. There in the center stood two women, directly to the left of the magician, whose open arms and wide-brimmed hat commanded the whole center of the painting.

Catherine leaned down to look closely. "She doesn't look like me at all," she murmured.

"She does," John countered. "The way she holds her head, the turn of her body. She's got your coloring."

Catherine smiled. These two women were famous for their eroticism, particularly the mirror girl's companion, dressed all in white, a hawkmoth on one hand, a broom in the other, a lady's maid straight out of a Victorian gentleman's fantasy; the kind of woman that every repressed schoolboy must have hoped would be hired for the house. Her calves bulged above tiny feet; her waist was nipped in to nothing; above it, her breasts strained at the bodice of her dress. The girl with the mirror looked toward her, but not directly at her; her eyes were downcast. She looked like a nymph ballerina, with translucent wings fanning out from her shoulders.

"I always thought she looked Spanish," Catherine said thoughtfully.

"Spanish?" he echoed.

"Yes," she said. "Look at her dark hair. She's got such a secret smile. She reminds me of those Spanish dancers. Their expressions. And her hands are almost clapping at her side."

"Except for the mirror." He took the books from the corners of the poster and held it up. "Look what's in the mirror," he said. "Look at the reflection."

She stared, frowning. "I can't see," she murmured. "It's just a plain green disc."

"Look closer."

She did. She could still see nothing.

"I always thought you could see the edge of her face," John said. "And it's a different version of her real face. Warmer."

She looked up at him, smiling. "Another girl living in the glass?" she asked.

He had put down the poster and put his hands on her shoulders. Then, with his right hand, he traced the line of her neck, the curve of her face. Electricity ran through her, a visceral, nearly desperate, desire to touch him. "You stepped out of the reflection," he murmured.

She took hold of his hand and looked at it. "What do you feel when you draw?" she asked.

"I don't draw."

"I mean your technical drawings."

"That isn't like this," he said, nodding in the direction of the picture.

"Why not?" she said. "You make something that didn't exist before. You imagine it in your head and transfer it to paper."

"You're comparing me with Dadd?" he said, laughing a little.

"I'm comparing the process."

"I never thought of it in the same way."

"You are creating something."

He frowned a little, holding her at arm's length. "I'm not a painter."

"Any more than I am a painter's subject," she said.

He considered it. "You are very like her," he repeated.

"Perhaps the two of us are the modern equivalents."

He smiled broadly. "You have something," he said. "I could paint you. Will you dress up as a ballerina, with wings on your back?"

She had returned to his hand, the one with which he had caressed her face and shoulders. She ran her finger down the center of the palm. "I'm not a girl in a painting," she said. "I'm real."

An expression almost like pain crossed his face. He pulled her close to him. "You think I don't know that," he said.

"You didn't answer my question," she said.

"Which question?"

"What do you feel when you draw?"

"Contact," he said. "Understanding."

"You feel an understanding . . . of what?"

"Of whatever it is I'm trying to see in my head. And then it's a matter of transferring it."

"The point of contact."

"The touch," he said. "Where it meets."

She moved under his hand. He started to smile. "You're making fun of me," he said.

"Like this?" she said. And lowered her eyes and turned her head, so that he was presented with the profile of the fairy dancer, springing into life. He began to laugh. "Real and unreal," he said. "That's what you are. Real, and . . ."

She put her fingers over his mouth.

He never finished the sentence.

She lifted her head now, in the half-light of the day.

"John, I can't sleep. I'm going to get up."

He made a movement as if to get out of bed with her, but she restrained him with a slow shake of her head. He watched her as she pulled on a pair of jeans and a sweater; at the door, she turned to say that she would call him when she had made breakfast, but he had already closed his eyes.

She went downstairs, looking up at the stained-glass window as she passed it. In the dawn light, the figure was filmy, picked out only in shades of bluish gray. She sat on the bottom step, wriggling her feet into her shoes. Frith eased himself grudgingly from his basket, looking up at her questioningly. She took the door key from the hall table, unlocked the front door, and went out into the garden.

Everything was perfectly still. The full moon that they had commented on last night—a swimming blur in the clouds—now sat low in the sky, almost invisible. The clouds had gone; the last stars showed in the sky. She tilted back her head and drank in the cool air. She walked through the heavy dew of the lawn, pulling a darker trail of footprints.

Most of the trees on the lawn had been planted, like the rest of the garden, in the year that the Lodge was built. Now 130 years old, they stood like a small army of green ghosts towering above her. A week or two ago, John had taken her on a guided tour, naming the ones he knew, guessing in a comical fashion at those he didn't.

Frith was way ahead of her. She could hear him skittering down the damp path toward the ponds and the stream.

"I want you to live here," John had said that first night. "I want you to stay."

"It's too soon," she'd replied. She had laid back on the bed. He sat next to her, looking not at her body but at her face. "It's too complicated," she added. "With Robert, and everything."

"You would rather be with Robert?"

"No," she said. "Of course not."

"You would rather wait for him."

"No!" She stared at him aghast. "How can you think that?"

"Yet you want to go and stay in that empty house, and you want me to live here without you?" He kept her gaze for a moment longer, then lowered his face, pressed his lips to her stomach, her breasts, her shoulders. His voice was soft, not insistent.

"John," she said, trying to lift him so that she could see into his eyes. "Tell me something. Aren't you afraid of rushing into this?"

He considered a moment. "No," he replied, perfectly calm.

"But you hardly know me."

He sat back, taking her seriously, holding her hand. "OK," he said. "Consider this. Tell me how long you knew Robert before you married him."

"Eighteen months," she said, frowning.

"And did you really know everything about him then?"

She thought about her husband, this man who had made her feel safe because he was so sure of himself. A man who rarely told her what he was thinking; who didn't seem to have dreams.

"I don't imagine he thought it was necessary to know everything," she said.

"But did you?"

"Oh, yes," she told him. "I wanted to be part of him. I believed in that." And she wondered again, the same thought, how she had come to be so connected to someone who was not connected to her in his heart. Her face clouded over.

"You loved him," John murmured.

"Yes." She remembered how driven she had been to get things right. To make things right between them. "It's peculiar," she said. "I always had this sensation that I was holding us together. Trying to knot us together, and all the time he was turning away. Not pulling away. Just—if anyone had painted us—I imagine him in the act of half-turning away, as if he'd been distracted."

"Did he have affairs?"

"No," she said. "Not until this one." And she tried to get her head round it: that she had always been trying to turn Robert back toward her. "I don't know why I did it," she told John now. "I just felt that that's how it ought to be. All or nothing."

"Swept away?" John suggested.

"No," she replied. "Because that sounds like losing touch. I wanted to be in touch. Inside his heart. But I don't think he ever gave it away," she said quietly, and nodded a little to herself, as if confirming a fact. "That's what it was," she said. "He kept something back."

When she looked back at John, she saw that he was looking at her with a strange expression: regretful, but also horrified.

"You can't be in love," he said, "and hold anything back."

She smiled at him, pulled his arms around her, laced his fingers in the small of her back, and put her own arms around his neck. "No, John," she told him. "No, you can't."

She followed the path that Frith had taken, down through the camellias and rhododendrons. There was one rhododendron, just where the path took a dogleg turn before descending steeply to the water, which was astonishingly beautiful. It must have been eighty feet tall and covered in startlingly pink flowers, almost too gaudy to be real; hundreds of miniature bouquets of densely packed cerise hung over the path. She stopped now and looked up through the branches at tier upon tier of color sandwiched between the glossy dark leaves of the tree. The pink had a blue tone, close to lilac, in this light.

She turned and looked across the fields below the weirs. She felt happy and released. As if she had been freed from a flat and unreal life, into one full of color. The wild garlic was in rank profusion by the water's edge; beyond it, the grass was growing higher in the nearest meadow. She glimpsed Frith running across the field, bouncing like a jack-in-the-box to get sight of the woodland.

"Frith," she called. But the dog didn't hear her.

She went on down the slope, to the water.

She walked round the far side, across the bridge, and sat down on the edge of the path. She looked past the shallows, to where the stream widened out into the nearest pool. In its undisturbed surface she could see the faint reflection of the pink rhododendron, and the fainter apricot and pink of the first light of day. The house was invisible behind its wall of trees. Nothing moved either there or in the fields behind. It was magical; a fairy-tale place.

Catherine stood looking for a long time, hugging herself. A fairy-tale place, and John the magician had made it, and brought her there.

She reached down and felt the temperature of the water. It was cold, but not icy. She took off her shoes and stood for a moment on the prickling gravel bed; then a secret smile came over her face. She had been eight or nine years old when she last stood barefoot in a river. There used to be a stream at the bottom of their road when she was small. The house that they had at weekends was ringed with oak trees, and the stream ran there, between the garden and the farmland beyond. As a child, she had always wished it were bigger. She entertained fantasies of sailing away, through the countryside to the sea, past all the sleeping churches and farms, plunging into the ocean, carried out on a blue-black tide.

Catherine jumped out onto the bank and, after glancing around herself with that same small smile of childhood pleasure on her face, eased herself out of her jeans and sweater. She paused another moment, wondering if she ought to, or could, swim; then she wriggled quickly out of the remainder of her clothes.

She stepped back into the water and made her way slowly across the streambed, feeling her way with her toes across the shingle, and walked on into the deeper pool. Soon the ground dipped away under her feet; she launched herself forward, gasping at the cold. Swirls of mud appeared in the pool, disturbed by her feet, twists of licorice curling in the green.

She swam for a few hurried strokes until the temperature felt warmer, laughing at herself, caught up in the strange secretive pleasure of it. She swam through the muddied picture of the rhododendrons, a brightening haze striped with ripples. Her hands brushed the stems of water lilies, their first leaves forcing upward to the light, scrolls of purple with pale roots extending sideways, catching her skin, touching her with blind fingertips. Turning back from the far edge, she lay on her back and stared up at the sky.

"Catherine!" cried a voice.

She heard the vibration vaguely, as if dreamed.

"Catherine!"

She turned onto her stomach. John was standing at the edge of the water, near the bridge. She laughed and held out her hands.

"What are you doing!" he shouted.

"Come in," she said. "It's amazing. It's warm."

"Oh, Christ," she heard him say.

He sat down suddenly on the bridge, his head bowed.

"John?" she called.

He didn't respond. He had crossed his arms over his chest, and was staring fixedly at the ground.

She waded toward him and got out. He was in the process of standing up. She ran along the herringbone brick border, naked, dripping. "What's the matter?" she asked, reaching him. "What is it?"

He shook his head.

"Did I scare you?"

He smiled. "Don't do that again," he said.

"But I was only swimming."

He took an enormous breath. She saw that he was very pale. "What did you think?" she asked. "I was just swimming. Look, I'm fine."

"In this," he said, not a question. He looked her up and down. "My God," he murmured.

She pressed herself to him. "I'm all right," she told him.

"I took Frith out of here four months ago," he said. "He nearly drowned us both."

"I'm not drowned," she said. "I'm warm." And she pressed his hand to her stomach.

He let it rest there. "I'm here," she said.

She took his hand and held it against her heart. He stared into her face. Keeping his gaze, she lowered his hand down the length of her body. The water drops danced in his head, on his tongue, in his throat. It was like relieving a lifelong thirst, the cold green rush of her, the water drops of the dream, the skin almost hot to the touch underneath.

"This is for you," she said, her breathing shallower, her lips parted. "This is all for you. This is yours."

He kneeled down, brought her with him, laid her on the ground, all the while thinking of the racing flood of needing her since that very first second he had seen her at the door to the house.

He closed his eyes, and the storm when he entered her was like nothing else he had ever known, would ever want to know; it flung him out of the day, the newly sunlit garden, the sound of her own ecstatic cries. He felt nothing: not the wet ground, nor the water anymore, nor the morning air on his back, nor even her hands on him. He had the curious and frightening sensation of traveling at ungovernable speed.

When he came back to her, he looked down at her closed eyes and parted mouth. He peeled a strand of wet hair from her neck; he listened as the pace of his heart slowed and the familiar dull ache in his chest returned.

"I want to live forever," he whispered.

She opened her eyes and smiled.

16

It was one o'clock when she got to the house.

As she turned the key in the lock, a small rush of warm air came out of the hall, the staleness of unlived-in rooms. Catherine put down her briefcase and took off her jacket, and went through all the downstairs rooms, opening windows. She got to the back door and went out into the courtyard garden. She hadn't looked at it in weeks, she realized. There were weeds growing up through the pots and containers; she paused for a moment, picking off the dead heads of daffodils.

Back through the house, the doorbell rang.

She checked her watch. One ten. Robert was early.

She opened the front door without a thought, not even with a tremor of nervousness. Yet when she caught sight of him, she felt suddenly sick. Like a small hard blow to the stomach.

He looked thinner, leaner.

"Hello," she said. "You're early."

"I've been waiting round the corner for half an hour," he said. "Is it all right?"

She stepped back to admit him, embarrassed that he would ask her this question. "You've driven down from London?" she asked.

"Yes?" he said, inflecting it like a question.

She nodded. "Eventually they told me where you were," she said. "After I went back to your office for the fourth time."

He had the decency to color.

"They were very loyal to you," she commented. "The first time I went, they denied knowing anything about it. They said you were on holiday."

"I'm sorry," he said.

"What an effort you took," she said. "It must have been complicated."

"No," he said, truthfully. Then looked up at her, realizing the tactlessness. "I'm sorry," he repeated.

She sat down on the sofa and looked at him, holding her hands in her lap. He looked around for somewhere else to sit, chose a chair, and dragged it closer to her.

"You're looking very well," he said.

"Thanks."

"Busy at work?"

She shook her head, dismissing the question.

"I'll come to the point," he said.

He shifted a moment and seemed to consider where to start.

From the initial jolt at seeing him, Catherine now felt curiously objective. Robert was an old-fashioned type. If she met him now for the first time, she would think just that. An old-fashioned kind of person, a little bit formal in the way he held himself. Had she once thought that, *ever* thought that before? Yes. He had been particular about things, meticulous sometimes. With a kind of studied look on his face.

How peculiar, she thought suddenly. *I'd forgotten him.*

"I want to buy a flat in London," he said. "I've seen a place." She wasn't going to help him, he realized. She sat regarding him with something like indifference. "It's not big," he continued. "Nowhere is, even for thousands."

There was still no response. His eyes went back to her face. She had started to smile. He found it completely unnerving. "Have I said something funny?" he asked.

"You and money," she murmured.

"It might have passed your notice," he said, "but that's how the world revolves."

"On money?" she said. "I don't think so."

It was his turn to smile.

"Say it," she said. "Say how naive I am." She felt a pinch of anger.

"Look," he told her, "you've no doubt worked this out for yourself, but we need to sell this house."

"Oh, yes?"

"We put a deposit down half-and-half, and we paid the mortgage half-and-half," he said. "You surely don't dispute that?"

"I'm not disputing anything," she said.

"Well, then this is half my property," he said. "There are no children, so we have to sell."

She looked at him coolly.

Strange, how much money mattered, she thought. If you had none, or you had plenty, it seemed to make no difference. Robert, whose salary had always been high, having married a woman whose wages almost matched his, had been inordinately careful when it came to spending.

She imagined Amanda rolling her eyes. "Mean," she would say. "Why don't you be honest?"

In fact, they had laughed about it over dinner. Robert good-naturedly protesting, Amanda pretending to raid his wallet, and flap her hands at the imaginary moths fluttering out of it.

On their honeymoon, she and Robert had gone to Rye. It was Catherine's choice; she wanted to see the antiques and art. She wanted to be by the sea. They had married in January, and any sane couple would have gone abroad. But there was something about the English coast in winter that she loved.

They had seen a bureau in a Saturday antiques market. It wasn't very expensive. Catherine had thought it a huge bargain. Robert hadn't exactly objected, but neither had he enthused. She had a perfectly clear memory of him slowly taking out the checkbook, taking the cap off the pen, arranging his check card just so on the counter-top.

Or in Paris. They went to Paris that first spring together. She recalled him standing at the gate of the Metro at Hotel de Ville, counting centimes carefully into his palm.

Robert leaned forward now.

"Why don't you share the joke with me?" he asked.

She blinked. "Sorry."

"Are you listening to me?"

"Yes," she said. "The house. I know."

"Well?"

She got up, suddenly feeling short of breath. He sat back in his chair with a wince, as if he had expected her to hit him. She looked at him in astonishment and walked past him, going into the kitchen. She picked up the coffeemaker, realized that it hadn't been used in weeks, and put it down again. "Do you want tea?" she asked him.

He had come to the door.

She turned to say something. Something about the house. And she was abruptly struck by how often they had stood in exactly this pose, she preparing a meal, he standing at the door. Telling her something ordinary. They had been ordinary, just ordinary. Not happy, maybe. But then not many couples that she knew were terribly happy.

"Why did you do it?" she said. "I mean, why just leave?" she persisted. "Just a letter, Robert. How could you do that?"

"Let's not go into this."

"It's a reasonable question."

"I don't want an argument."

"Neither do I. I just want to know." She held her breath, checked her breathing in an effort to control her temper.

He said nothing. He looked down at the floor, raising his eyebrows slightly. He looked disappointed, disapproving. As if the subject were distasteful.

"You're not sorry," she said.

He didn't reply.

She walked toward him. "You really aren't," she said. "Look at you."

He glanced up. "I'm not sorry to have left," he told her. "But I'm sorry at the way I did it."

She looked hard at his face. There was nothing at all there but a kind of patience, as if this was the price he had to pay to get what he wanted. He looked like man waiting in a bloody queue, she decided suddenly. Like a man waiting in a bank or at a petrol station, waiting to pay the bill. Bored a little, irritated just a little.

"Oh, my God," she whispered. "This is such a pain for you, isn't it?"

"There's no use going into it," he said. "Can we please just talk about the house?"

"No use," she repeated.

They were silent for a second, then she turned away from him.

"Look," he said, "this will get us absolutely nowhere. When all's said and done—love or not, or whatever you want to call it—I was a bloody good husband to you. I was the perfect husband."

She started to laugh again. "Robert," she said, "you should hear what you just said."

His color rose. "I never cheated on you, or laid a hand on you, or kept you short of money," he said. "I never stayed out late, or humiliated you, or let you down."

"And that makes a perfect husband?" she said.

"It makes a far more decent partner than thousands upon thousands of other people."

"I don't live with thousands upon thousands of other people," she retorted. "It's you we're talking about. Us."

He glared at her. "You've changed," he said.

"What?"

"You're different," he told her.

She stared back at him. "Well," she retorted angrily. "You're no different. You're still a smug, frigid bastard."

He recoiled. All she could think of was that she had done everything he wanted. If he could describe himself so perversely as the perfect husband, then she had been the perfect wife. She had given up her job in London to come and live where he wanted, given up the prospects of a potentially better career. Left her work colleagues and friends behind.

Yet she looked into his face now and realized that none of it was actually his fault, tempted as she was to make it so. He had taken what she had offered him; he had never questioned it. He had been loved. She had been faithful. All the things that he ascribed to himself could also be said of her.

It had been like one of those memos she had once seen on his office desk; the one that says: *I called, but you were out.* She had spent a vast amount of time calling him, trying to get his attention. But he had never actually really been there.

Whenever he had gone away on business, he had always dutifully sent her a postcard of the city where he was staying. She used to prop them up on the mantelpiece. Freiburg, Bruges, Munich. When he had come home, the cards that he had sent her would be lined up in a row, and he would be sitting right there in front of her, but he would be as absent as ever.

Once or twice, she had traveled with him on visits. But it seemed to make no difference. She had spent all her time waiting for him. She would wait in some bar, watching the barges in a place like Innsbruck slip like whales under the Deutzer Bridge. Or she would sit on the wall of the Hofkirk, under the shadow of Maximilian's tomb, and she would think that the expression, the smile on his face, would be different when he came to meet her in this foreign setting.

But it would be exactly the same. Always the same.

She understood, with a great thrust of realization—like dropping from a height, like stepping off a cliff into thin air—that she had been waiting all the time she knew him to see the reflection of her own feelings in his face.

She looked away from his inquiring gaze. "I'm no different," she said. And she waved her hand in his direction. "Take the bloody house," she said. "Have the lot. It doesn't matter."

"I shall take half," he said. "And you will have half."

She turned fully back toward him. In the corner by the door to the kitchen was the bureau they had bought on their honeymoon in Rye. She walked toward it and laid her hand flat on the top of it. "There's all the furniture," she said.

"We can meet another time to discuss it, if you like."

"This bureau . . ." And despite herself, despite her determination, she abruptly began to cry.

He tried to get between her and the desk. "Don't, Catherine."

"What do you bloody care," she said.

"But don't cry."

She pushed his hand off her arm. "Go away," she said.

"I'm not leaving while you're upset."

She started to laugh, wiping her face with her hand. "You really are fucking astonishing," she muttered.

He watched her with a critical frown. Eventually, she went back into the kitchen and tore off a paper towel. After a moment or two, she walked back to him. "I'm OK," she said. "See? I'm fine. I'm great. You can piss off now with a clear conscience."

He shook his head at her anger.

She gestured at the bureau. "You remember where we got it?"

"Of course."

"Well, do you want it? You paid for it."

He paused, looked at the floor. "I never liked it," he said. "You can have it."

He hesitated just a second longer, then walked away, through the hallway, to the front door. Opening it, he stopped on the threshold. She had followed him and was standing a few feet behind him. "You know, Catherine," he said, "before all this, if I ever did anything, said anything, that upset you, I apologize."

He was waiting for an answer. She didn't give one.

He stepped out of the house and she walked to the open door and watched him until he went out of sight. As he turned the corner, he looked back at her.

She closed the door.

17

That day, Mark was in the process of preparing the fine art sale.

The back door to Pearsons had been opened to allow for a delivery, an executor's sale. Mark was watching the unloading of an entire married life. He watched as it passed him, noting the details against the record: half a dozen mahogany bar back armchairs and an oak secretaire, a George III gilt-wood wall mirror. He glanced up and noticed a man crossing the parking lot, heading straight for him.

"Mark Pearson?" the man asked.

"Yes."

"John Brigham."

It took a second for the name to register. Mark took the proffered hand. "Ah," he said, smiling. "Catherine isn't here. She's due back any minute."

"Can I wait?"

"Please do," Mark said. He stepped back and ushered John into the salesroom. They made their way to Mark's office. Brigham stopped on the way to look at his own dresser, standing in the far corner.

"We thought it worth the wait," Mark said. "It's too good a quality to go in the fortnightly general sale."

Brigham said nothing. He looked at the dresser for some moments, then around at the rest of the lots. "You have a good selection," he said.

"Several deaths," Mark commented dryly. "Always good for business."

There was a beat, then Brigham walked on. They passed back out, through the double doors, to Reception and his and Catherine's offices.

"Come in," Mark said, opening his own door. He called back to the receptionists, asking for coffee; when he came in, Brigham had already seated himself in front of the desk.

The catalogue was in the process of final editing; reference books were piled on the rear cabinet.

"Researching something?" Brigham asked.

Mark smiled. "Medals," he said. "There was a whole stack of them in one of the chests of drawers. Burma Star, Africa Star. A First World War death plaque. Not my field. I had to resort to help."

"Is there always such a range?"

"Always," Mark told him. "Last fine arts we had a harp. Terribly posh, carved angels, winged beast feet. Then there was the polyphon, and a couple of train sets, and an elastolin set of a British Army band, the christening spoons, a trophy celebrating a tennis tournament in 1952 . . ." He grinned at Brigham. "Oh," he added, holding up a finger, "and the tazza with floral pierced and gadrooned border."

"A tazza?"

Mark spread his hands. "Search me," he joked. "Sounds brilliant though, don't you think?"

The coffee arrived. Mark took the opportunity to inspect Brigham in detail for the first time. Catherine had not given much away: all he knew was that she was practically living with this man. It disturbed him, what seemed to be the almost total submersion of her previous life into his; and yet, at the same time, it gave him some satisfaction to see her smile. She had not done so in so many months. If this tall, graying, handsome man was responsible for that, he felt that he ought to be grateful to him. But John Brigham didn't look too approachable at the moment. He was frowning to himself as he stirred sugar into his coffee.

"How are things at Bridle Lodge?" Mark asked. "I heard you altered all the waterways. Restored them."

"Yes," Brigham said.

"Must have been quite a project."

"It was."

"Have you anything else planned?"

Brigham glanced up at him. "No, nothing."

"I hear it's a fine Arts and Crafts house."

Again, another frown by way of reply. *OK*, Mark thought, *so you don't want to talk.* He stood up. "Would you mind very much if I carried on with the delivery?" he asked. "It's a busy day today."

"No," Brigham said. "Not at all. Please, go ahead."

As Mark came out of his office, he saw Catherine coming in the front doors. He waited for her; she said something to the girls at the desk and then came over to him.

Mark put a hand on her arm. "You've got a visitor," he said. "John Brigham's in my office."

"He is?" she replied.

"Cheerful sort of chap, isn't he?" Mark said. "Never stops talking. Is he checking up on his goods?"

She shook her head. "No. I shouldn't think so."

"He looked at the dresser."

"It shipped all right, didn't it?" she asked.

"Of course it did. It only had to come ten miles down the road." Mark pulled a face. "He looked like something didn't quite meet his standards," he said. He raised his eyebrows at her and walked back through the salesroom.

She watched him go for a second, then went into his office. John was already standing.

"I thought I heard your voice," he said.

She kissed him. "What's the matter?" she asked.

"Nothing," he said. "How did it go with Robert?"

She shook her head. "I don't know. He's getting a place in London . . ."

"And?"

"Nothing really," she said. "Nothing."

He regarded her closely. "Are you busy this afternoon?"

"A bit of paperwork," she said. "A few return calls." She looked at the piece of paper that the receptionists had given her. "And I have to call in on Mr. Williams. He wants to see me. Something urgent." She sat down in the next chair and put her hands to her face. "Oh, God," she murmured.

He sat down again next to her and she dropped her hands from her face.

"What are you going to do about Robert?" he asked. "Do you want to go back, do you want to stop . . ."

"Stop what?"

"Us," he said.

She stared at him. "Is that what you think?"

"Breathing space. Now that you've seen him."

She looked at him closely, thinking that he had come here, to this neutral ground, with a frown on his face, to find an excuse to stop seeing her. It washed over her quickly. *That can't be it,* she thought. *Surely that isn't it.* It couldn't be it, she reasoned improbably, because she was carrying an imprint of him: his hands, his thoughts. She wanted to be away from Robert, from Mark, from the salesroom, the noise of the traffic outside. She sat motionless in her chair and wanted John acutely, a physical necessity, like salt on the tongue dissolving, an acute dry heightening texture in her mouth. This peculiar longing, something like impatience; anxious at one moment to be out of his arms to breathe, to walk away; anxious in the next to be with him, to swallow the world in an instant, to obliterate it.

"Do you want the truth?" she asked.

He was holding her hand in his loosely, almost reflectively.

"I haven't given Robert a thought," she confessed. "I haven't given him half a thought for eight weeks. I ought to, wouldn't you say?

Don't you think that a newly abandoned wife should give the smallest little shit for where her husband is and what he's doing?"

He shook his head. She still couldn't read his face.

"Well, I'll tell you," she said. "I don't want to think about Robert, because for one thing he lives in a prison in his head, and for another, I can't think about him, because, since you, there isn't room."

At this, John glanced up. His expression relaxed and he began to smile.

She leaned forward. "I've just talked to a man who . . ." She searched for the words. "I got the same feeling, the feeling that I was dying on my feet. That I'd become invisible."

"You're not invisible."

She stopped for some time. "Walking around inside a maze," she murmured. There was a long pause. "What was it like with Claire?" she asked.

"Claire . . . ?"

"Did you ever feel that you were staring at a wall, a brick wall? That she didn't understand you, something you'd said, an idea you'd had, what you wanted?"

"No," he told her.

"Did you feel like two people?" she asked. "Two people with different feelings?"

"No," he told her. "Never."

She held his gaze for a second. "Did you know that it's a weakness to be like that?" she asked, her voice heavy with irony.

Abruptly, she stood up, dragging on his hand so that he got to his feet. "Let's go," she said. "Take me out of here."

They drove out to Sandalwood after lunch.

The journey took them through the river valley as it wound out of town, between the shallow hills. They turned off toward the village, and the river widened and the road narrowed. The water spread out into reed beds to the left; to the right, the land rose gradually. Barley had been planted; it was too short to ripple under the wind and stood in feathery green tracts up to the edge of the woodland. The road curved and twisted through other fields, over bridges. At last they came to the village and turned up the lane for the house.

"Did you ever come to this village at the start of the year?" Catherine asked.

"No."

She slowed down, nosing the car through the entrance, over a cattle grid. Lilac, with its first fists of purple and white, hung untended over the driveway.

"The churchyard is next to the house," she said. "In the spring, snowdrops come out on the graves. They've been planted on almost every one. They look like featherbeds." She glanced at him. John was looking out of the window at the grounds. She drove the car over to the side and pulled on the hand brake. "Why don't you tell me what's wrong?" she asked.

He looked at her. "There's nothing wrong."

"You've barely said a word to me. And Mark said that you hardly spoke to him."

He pursed his lips. "I don't think that I like Mark much."

She was amazed. "Mark?" she repeated. "He's the nicest man you could wish for. What did he say to you? Did he crack some sort of joke, or what?"

"Yes, he cracked a joke."

"Look," she said, "you don't take Mark too seriously. He has a black sense of humor. Are you worried about the dresser?" she asked. "The catalogue description is fine. It's exact. The dresser is unmarked. And insured."

"It isn't the dresser."

"What, then?" She was anxious; he had never cut her off like this before.

He shook his head. "Something I want to do."

She waited. He didn't elaborate. It was evident that whatever was on his mind, he wasn't prepared to tell her at this moment. She fought down the feeling that this was just like Robert; she had to tell herself consciously that this was not the case.

She lifted the hand brake and drove to the door of the house.

As she stood on the step after knocking, she looked around herself at the white wisteria that swamped the frontage; she saw that it had wound itself around the downspouts and was curling its way onto the roof.

John got out of the car. They waited. Above their heads, house martins were darting in their easy ballet and disappearing under the timber eaves.

Catherine knocked again. She stepped back and looked again at the upper floor. One window was open; the edge of a curtain fluttered from it.

"He rang me first thing this morning," she said. "I was talking on another phone."

"Perhaps he went back to bed," John suggested. "How old is he?"

"Eighty?" she guessed. "Eighty-five?" She looked doubtfully at the front door and again at the window. "I'll try the back," she said.

They went around the side, on a flagstone path in the shade of heavy conifers, so that it was greened over with moss and lichen. Bindweed grew up through the roots. They passed two huge bay windows, which must have been permanently overshadowed, even if the heavy curtains had not been drawn. Catherine noticed the whorls of damp on the linings, the encrusted paint on the frames, the rust marks running from the outdoor sills to the ground.

They came to a garden gate and opened it onto the back of the house. The whole terrace here was shrouded in a gloomy half-light, so thick were the trees alongside. In the deep shade was a garden potting shed, completely covered in some kind of thick, pale green climber with star-shaped white flowers. The padlock hung from the lock, open; the floorboards of the shed were rotted. No one had been in here for years, Catherine thought.

They got to the back door. It was open onto a back hall and kitchen.

"Mr. Williams," Catherine called. "Are you there?"

There was no reply, except for a cat that came down the hallway, mewing loudly. Catherine held out her hand to it, and it backed away.

"What's the matter?" she asked. "Hungry?"

By way of reply, it skittered past her, tail up. When it got to the terrace, it turned back and scowled, fixing them both with a yellow stare.

"Mr. Williams," Catherine called, stepping further along the hall.

John looked in the kitchen. It was old-fashioned, with its wood cupboards and a wooden draining board bleached to ivory and two iron taps over the stone sink, but it was clean and tidy. He stepped inside briefly, feeling the cold side of the kettle, noticing the empty table.

Catherine came back to the door. "John," she whispered. "Come and see."

She took him up the hall. This, too, was tidy, almost antiseptically so. It was the hallway that Catherine had seen before, with its antler coat rack and umbrella stand, and cracked Delftware on the walls, the plates that Mr. Williams said were not worth selling. She had always been shown into the room on the left of the front door: just like a waiting room, with a row of Edwardian hard-backed chairs and a small pine table.

She had looked in this room while John was in the kitchen; then she had crossed the hall, whispering Mr. Williams's name hesitantly. She took John now in the room; just a tiny space little more than a cupboard, the original clothes-drying and boots room of an Edwardian family. Coat hooks lined the wall; paneled cupboards were underneath. Green brocade cushions, flattened by use, faded by age, ran along the top of the cupboards.

"Oh, my God," John murmured.

The dim ocher walls were filled with photographs. They were all framed, and all but a handful of them featured the same woman.

Catherine put her hand gently to the nearest one, a studio portrait of a pretty girl in a soft-collared frock, her hair waved neatly to her cheek. She was smiling modestly, her chin dipped. The black-and-white print was so old that it was becoming sepia. She looked no more than eighteen, perhaps younger, holding a little posy of violets in her lap.

Next along was a wedding picture. Small and rather out of focus, it showed a large group of people on a set of wide-fanning stone steps, the front door of a country house that was not Sandalwood. This was far more opulent; the women were trussed in furs and fancily buttoned shoes, despite the glare of the sun. In the center of the front line stood the bride and groom; the same woman in the previous photograph, now in a long dress with a huge lace train, carrying a massive bouquet of lilies. The man alongside was Mr. Williams, uncomfortable in a starched collar and frock coat.

Farther still along the wall, the photographs and the country changed: the inscriptions were written diagonally across each one in black ink. *Jaipur 1946, Sandy and Denny Marshall, Col. & Mrs. Powell.* Here, among the wide-brimmed straw hats and the military fatigues and embroidered mess dress, were nameless dusty outposts and hillsides; camels around a water hole, knees buckled under them. Naked boys standing, arms crossed behind their backs, at the edge of the water. An army jeep drawn up at a crossroad that appeared to be in the middle of nowhere; a rocky promontory in a vast empty backdrop, the men swathed against the rising wind with cotton shawls wrapped around their necks and faces.

Here was an older version of the pretty eighteen-year-old girl; now obviously in her thirties, she lay full-length by the side of a pool, in dark sunglasses, holding a cigarette. Playing cards were on the small table next to her, and a mixing jug for martinis.

"Look at all this," John said.

He had opened a cupboard on the opposite side of the room.

It was fitted with hanging rails. Inside it were generations of clothes: coats, dresses, ballgowns, sweaters, skirts. There was rack upon rack of shoes, each carefully stuffed with tissue paper, as if the wearer might want them again at any moment. There were scarves, gloves, even handkerchiefs; underwear in separate sliding shelves, with small bags of lavender on each row.

John looked at her. "Have you ever seen anything like this?"

"Nothing quite the same," she said. "Not preserved like this."

"Do you know what it is?" he asked. "It's a shrine. He made a shrine to her."

They went back out into the hall, the gardenia scent of the dead woman clinging to them.

Catherine looked up the stairs.

They opened the door to the bedroom; the curtain halfway across the window, caught under the open sash, was the one that Catherine had been able to see from the front doorstep.

There was a double bed, with a red satin eiderdown and pillows with stenciled patterns of trailing roses. The wallpaper behind the bed was all roses, too: old English roses with double petals, red on white. It was an overtly feminine room, seemingly untouched from the early sixties. The curtains hung in elaborate swags and ruffles; yet more roses embossed on damask.

A large wing armchair stood facing the foot of the bed, its back to the door.

John stepped past her. He walked to the chair, looked at its occupant. Catherine heard the sharp intake of breath, but he didn't move for a moment.

"What is it?" she asked.

She moved to his side. He put out a hand, palm upward, to try and stop her.

As she walked, she noticed the photograph first. Another photograph of the fresh-faced girl of the studio picture, a copy, framed in gilt. It was propped on the eiderdown close to the chair. Then Catherine saw the hands, their papery thinness, the white knuckles shining. The tips of the fingers were blue; the hands lay curled in Mr.

Williams's lap, relaxed. All the space between the hands was soaked with blood.

Above the hands, Mr. Williams's face was white, expressionless. His eyes were open, gazing at the picture in front of him, blue eyes the color of faded ceanothus flower. He had dressed himself in his best suit. The collar, ill-fitting around his neck, was clean. He wore his regimental tie and a badge of some kind of charity organization in his lapel.

Only when Catherine had stared at him in horror for a second did she see the knife that Mr. Williams had used, a small penknife with a mother-of-pearl handle, resting on his knees.

He had cut his wrists and remained quietly where he was, waiting.

It was two o'clock in the morning when John gave up sleep.

He had been lying on his back staring at the ghosts of light on the ceiling, Catherine finally asleep beside him, his mind purposefully blank to the events of the day.

But it kept coming back, in rewind: the ambulance, the police. The body taken downstairs, the sound of footsteps in the hall. Cameras in the bedroom. He had been standing on the landing outside the room when they had lifted Mr. Williams and put his body into the mortuary bag. John just couldn't get over the plasticity of the arms and hands, even after the rigor had declined. The head had rolled just a little as they put the body on the bed, to put him into the rubberized sheet. The shoes seemed so pathetic, laced and polished, the effort to be well presented now gone.

John had turned away. It was so pitiable, such a wreck of an ending. But then all endings were pitiable, in their way. Dignity was a label attached by the living, he thought. Something to soothe us, like babies afraid of the dark.

When he had been a little boy, he'd been afraid like that. Terrified, in fact. Even when he was seven or eight, the lights had to be on outside his room. And even that didn't help very much. In the light cast by the twenty-five-watt bulb outside his door he saw wraiths crowding to catch a glimpse of him; he heard footsteps, he saw smoke stream along the floor. He couldn't be placated, even when it was explained to him that he had been dreaming. *It just seemed like you were awake*, his mother would say.

He wondered now, so many years later, in this dark room with Catherine breathing shallowly at his side, if he had ever put away the dreams of childhood. If he allowed himself, he could see them all now, massing silently at the edge of his sight. All the things he didn't want to look at.

He sat upright, swung his legs out of bed.

This was no good. This would get him nowhere. It wouldn't help him, it would only make it all so much worse.

He kept seeing Mr. Williams's face, the abdication in it.

He had his own choices now, he thought. Piece by piece, painting by solitary painting, Mr. Williams had sold his life over the years; hated selling any of it, according to Catherine. Each little bit was a wrench. Catherine had told him tonight that she thought that Mr. Williams's giving her the last portrait by the Scottish colorist had been nothing more than a sustained good-bye, his ticket out of the world. It was the last thing he loved, the last thing of all the pieces that he and his wife had bought together. Giving it to her had been like writing a suicide note: even more graphic, in its way, than the knife resting on his knees.

I have a room downstairs, John thought to himself.

He got up and walked to the window, pulled back the curtain a little, and looked down through the garden. It was a calm, starlit night. Looking up into the sky, he could clearly see the Little Dipper, resting on its side, almost directly above him. The Three Sisters of the Pleiades. In Spain, they had looked closer than this. He had learned all their names, once, watching their slow procession around the sky over weeks and months. The miracle of received light, the flickering messages from old worlds. Candles to light the way.

He had begun to buy in earnest in Spain. He had even sometimes come back to London specifically to make a particular purchase. Probably at some point he had even been to Bergens, and attended an auction, while Catherine had worked there. Strange, that she had perhaps been so close when he had been working so hard to fill the void.

Into the starlit candled dark he had poured objects. He hadn't even kept them in the house, but had hired a storage unit, a dusty flea-bitten place on the edge of Málaga. He would drive there with his precious buy, wrapped and boxed, and he would put it in with all the others. Just another box among the many. He couldn't have explained to a living soul why this worked. It was a kind of insanity, a mechanism of mourning. He put beautiful things into boxes and hid them away, and he would think of them under lock and key, in the anonymous yard on an industrial estate, among other people's furniture and stores. Hundreds of little lights under bushels, that only he knew about.

He just needed to know that they were in the world.

When he had come back to England and they had been brought with him, he had asked the movers to unload the boxes into the drawing room. Without unpacking them he had fixed the alarm system. And only then did he unwrap everything. It took him two days, because each thing carried a memory.

I made a shrine, he thought. *I made a shrine, too.*

And the thought now almost asphyxiated him. He dropped the curtain and stood gasping for breath, his hands on his hips, his head dropped nearly to his chest.

He looked back at Catherine, and kept looking, trying to discern her face in the darkness. As if in response to him, she stirred. There was a second or two of silence, then he heard her call him.

He came to the side of the bed.

"Can't you sleep?" she asked. She propped herself up on one elbow, pushing the hair back from her face. He reached out and touched her. She was so warm.

"I'm going to sell everything," he said. "Everything downstairs."

"What?" she said confusedly. "What do you mean? Why?"

He tried to think of a reason that would make sense to her. "I don't want to be like him," he told her; and she grasped his hand, pushing back some of the shadows that stood by the door, that stood in his way wherever he looked.

He wanted to trust her. He wanted to give it all away and turn his heart over to her, and he wondered—with the shapes of faces eternally at the door, their shifting selves getting closer now, smoke drifting along the floor of his memory—if he could trust Catherine Sergeant. Not just with these things, precious as they were, all the days of the past that they represented. But with everything.

Every priceless secret thing that he had been entrusted with.

18

John had forgotten what London could be like.

He stood at the corner of the Strand and Whitehall, in the unexpected heat of late May, waiting to cross the road. The traffic heaved, sweltering with impatience. There was some sort of work being done in Trafalgar Square and everywhere was a mess: pavements up, red-and-white barriers across each intersection, pedestrians jostling for position at each set of lights.

The sky was the kind of blue that he thought he had left behind in Spain; turquoise, rippling with humidity. He glanced across and saw Landseer's lions at the base of Nelson's Column looking impossibly vast in the human tide that ebbed around them.

When he finally got into the square, he could see that a new piazza was being made in front of the National Gallery: there were going to be steps running right to the entrance, sealing it off from vehicles. He stood and watched the work, feeling a kind of pang that he would never see a red London bus passing in front of the gallery again. He had that fixed in his head as one of the archetypal London sights, like guardsmen passing down the east side of Hyde Park toward Horse Guards, or the boat race sculls going under Putney Bridge.

He walked up St. Martin's Lane, passing the theater and restaurant where he once used to spend most of his time; he went on past the cacophony of Leicester Square, glancing at the tourists streaming out of the Underground station. London was sweating in eighty degrees; blasts of air-conditioning came out of every doorway. He shrugged his shoulders inside his coat, to loosen the fabric of the shirt from his skin. Helen would just love it if he turned up looking travel stained. She would have something to say about it the moment that he walked in the door.

He got to the restaurant late. It was just past one o'clock. He went down the stairs. The place was done out like an old picture house, thirties style, with gaudy columns and a brass handrail. At the bottom of the stairs, modern art flickered: neon in tangerine and red flashes. He had always hated it here, and it hadn't changed. Pretentious and cavernous. The faint chemical smell, like chlorine. Still, it was Helen's choice.

She was sitting at a table right in the center, wearing a tiny dress that was much too young for her. The lime green shoestring straps cut into her shoulders, he noticed, as he leaned to kiss her cheek. She smelled expensively overpowering; in fact, he thought, she was too much of everything—too much flesh, too much makeup, too many grimaces that passed for a smile. He knew that expression. His heart sank.

"How are you?" he asked as he sat down.

"Fine," she replied. She took a long drink from the gin-and-tonic that she was holding.

"Hot weather," he commented.

"Too hot," she agreed.

The waiter came and they ordered. He had time to look closely at her. She seemed older, but then in this sort of phase she always did.

"Are you OK?" he asked.

"I just said so."

He paused. "So," he said. "I got your message . . ."

She was looking down at the table; then without looking up she reached out and put her hand over his. It was a sad gesture, as if she were gripping him for balance, to feel stable. She made a great show of inspecting the menu, then looked back up. "Tell me about you," she said. "Have you sold the house in Alora?"

"No," he replied. "It's rented out."

"It's such a pretty place." She had visited him there just once and stayed for less time than had been planned. She had not been bright then, but subdued. If she had formed an opinion of the house, she had not shared it with him then. Rather, he had thought that she was uncomfortable, restless. It had been last summer and she had complained, in the last day, of feeling too hot. *I'm suffocated*, was how she had explained it. And left abruptly the next day, taking her rental car and, he had found out later, driving not to the airport, but farther north, deep into the mountains and beyond.

"And this place in Dorset," she said. "Is that a cottage, too?"

He smiled. "No. I went a bit overboard," he admitted.

She smiled at him. She could be so charming and so pretty when she wanted, he thought. "I must come and see it," she said.

"Yes," he told her. "Come whenever you've got a break at work."

She laughed softly. "Oh, I've had a long break," she said.

"Have you?" His stomach had turned over—a lazy roll—when he had heard the inflection in her voice. She had a pack of cigarettes by her plate and was turning the lighter over and over in the palm of her hand. The food came. He took his first mouthful; she looked at her starter, picked up her fork.

"Listen," she said, "this is a bit of a crisis, John."

There was no use anticipating whatever it was she had to say. It could be almost anything.

She had put her fork down and was looking at him. "I want to sell," she said.

He hesitated. He could feel the weight of this old battle descending on him. It felt as if the past with her had come up and pushed him, an old belligerence made flesh, like one enemy manhandling another, pushing him in the chest. "Why?" he asked.

"For the money," she said. "Why else?"

"You need money?"

He noticed her grip the lighter. She closed her hand right over it and clutched it, rubbing her thumb along the top.

"You need money because you've lost your job?" he guessed.

"Yes," she said. "And other things."

"Well, let me help you," he said. He had done so before. "How much do you need?"

"Look," she said, and her voice rose. "Are we going to have this conversation till the day we die?"

"What conversation?"

She put her hand to her head and laughed breathily in exasperation. "Oh, for Christ's sake," she told him. "John, please. Don't make me beg."

"I just offered you anything you want."

"But I don't want to take your money," she said. "I just want a piece of what is rightfully mine."

"Helen," he said, softly. "It isn't mine and it isn't yours."

"Of course it is," she snapped back, her voice rising markedly. "Of course it is!" She leaned forward across the table. "Keeping it at all," she said, "is just so irrational. It's more than irrational, in fact. It's criminal."

"No one knows."

She shook her head. "For an intelligent man," she said, "you can be very stupid."

He let a beat pass. "You're right," he murmured.

She registered surprise, mocking him with both hands raised, palms out.

"But not about selling," he said.

The waiter came and took the plates. Helen lit a cigarette.

They sat in silence for a couple of minutes. She asked for another drink; it was brought, and she made a prolonged show of turning the stick in the ice before discarding it. "Look," she said. She was flushed now. "I really need some money, John. I'm not joking."

"I can't—"

She pounded her hand flat on the table to cut his sentence short.

"Yes, you can," she said. "You must." He looked at her closely. She straightened in her chair. "There's no need to look at me like that," she said. "Why do you look at me as if I'm ten years old? I'm thirty-bloody-eight, John. I'm out of work. I want to buy a place of my own, for a start. Have something of my own. I need money." She sat back heavily and stared at him. Her voice had broken slightly in the last sentence.

"What's happened?" he asked.

"Nothing."

"Something's happened, besides losing your job?"

"No," she said.

He knew immediately that she was lying. He knew by the tone of her voice, the old lying, evasive tone. But he also knew by the look on her face. Something bruised.

"And in case you didn't know," she was saying, "property in London is expensive."

"Yes," he said. "I do know."

She spread her hands. Ash dropped from the cigarette onto the floor. "I need the deposit," she said.

"And you haven't got it?" he asked. "You've earned a fortune these last few years."

"And you're sitting on a fortune," she retorted. "Which we could sell, and make both our lives easier."

He felt a small tightening, like a cord being twisted, just below his collarbone. He took a sip of water.

"Tell me what's happened," he said quietly.

She stared at him, biting her lower lip. He waited. She held his gaze. "I lost a baby," she said.

"What?" And he immediately leaned across the table to take her hand, but, seeing the movement, she withdrew her hand from the tabletop and laid it in her lap.

"Don't be sorry for me," she said. "It was a termination."

"Helen," he said. "Heeble, I'm sorry."

It was his old childhood nickname for her. The reasons behind it were lost in the mists of time; neither of them knew where or why she had acquired it. The unconscious use of it now, though, brought tears to her eyes, and her guard dropped. The expression on her face, one of defensiveness, cracked.

"I'm thirty-eight." She began rubbing at the tears running down her face. "And so stupid."

"Who is he?"

"An actor."

John gave her the handkerchief from his pocket. "Have I met him?" he asked. "Would I know him?"

"It doesn't matter who he is."

"Was it his idea?"

"He didn't know."

John frowned. "Helen . . ."

She shook her head, picked up the packet of cigarettes, and shook out another, fumbling over lighting it. "I don't see him now."

"I'm so sorry," he repeated. "What can I do?"

She looked up at him again with a direct gaze.

"I can't sell the legacy," he told her.

"Yes," she said. "You can."

"It's a clause . . . not to sell . . . you know that."

"Who cares?" she demanded. "It was some bloody thing written over a hundred years ago. Nobody cares now. Some painter no one's ever even heard of, too. Nobody gives a bloody damn."

"I do," he said.

She leaned on the table, head in her hands, the smoke curling from the cigarette over her head. Through it, the neon art on the opposite wall flickered.

He had seen this attitude, this expression of defeat, this abandonment, before. He had seen it while she sat on the floor of her kitchen twelve years ago, knees brought to her chest, the empty brown bottle by her side.

What have you taken? he had asked her.

He had to edge on his haunches toward her then. She had been looking at him like a cat looks at a mouse, waiting. That terrible smile without humor in it. He had been convinced that she would lash out at him if he came within two feet of her, such was the caustic chill of that smirk. Yet when he took the bottle and read the label, she did nothing.

How many? he had asked. *Not all?*

Twelve years. So vivid that it seemed like just a few hours or days ago. The memory of it still frightened him. The shadow of despair had filled the small room. It was like being underwater, such was the shifting, light-refracting quality of it; a pool in which they both swam. It had been just eight months since Claire's death.

In response to his telephone call from outside John Soane's house on the day Claire died, Helen had taken him into her rented flat, a company flat in the old GLC building, looking out on the river. She had been up then, talking quickly. She helped him organize the funeral, and he always put the two together in his head, his dragging sense of complete helplessness and her staccato instructions, her agitation on the day of the ceremony. When the cars were late, she had been livid with anger. "I got this show together," she told him, when he asked why it mattered. "It's not a show," he had replied, stung. "You know what I mean," she had said, pacing the courtyard, watching the road. And then come back to him, all tears, all apology. "You must think I'm a monster," she said. "I didn't mean it how it sounded."

When the cars arrived, it wrecked him to see how many flowers she had ordered. Claire wouldn't have liked it. She liked things plain, not the multicolored show of this cortege. But he dared not say so; it would have sounded ungrateful. As it probably was, he had told himself at the time.

In the days afterward, he had noticed—but only through this same rippling drowned haze—that his sister hardly slept. Helen kept company with him through the hours he sat up. He would try to persuade her to go to bed, and she would claim that she didn't need to rest.

She told him that she was busy at work, putting together a series, and she would tell him of the disputes and meetings in the same repeated way: how she had prevailed over weaker opponents; how no one knew anything; how much the whole system depended upon her. Speaking to her, he felt as if he were on the tail of a whirlwind. She confused him. He followed her reasoning only slowly, as if he had been through an illness. As if he were still ill.

The down phase came with the accident.

He actually heard it. He had been sitting in the window of the flat. It was only ten days after the funeral. Trying to work that morning, his notepad and book of phone numbers were next to him. It had been raining, a fine drizzling mist blowing almost vertically along the water. He had found himself watching the dredger and the barges, thinking of when the river had been crammed with floating traffic.

He thought about the river and the docks: the tea wharves, sugar wharves, tobacco wharves farther east. There was a story someone in the office had told him, of a father who worked on the docks during the war, loading and unloading timber. About the smell of the pine-sap, camphor, cedar on his father's clothes. About being a small boy during the war, and hearing the drone of aircraft just before the air raid sirens, seeing the searchlights open their pencil lines of light in the sky, and feeling the almighty blast of the bombs. A rain of splinters, little black splinters of rain-forest mahogany, on the ground the next day.

You only had to hear the road names to hear the past: Plantation Wharf, Trinidad Wharf, Smugglers Way, Jews Row, Cotton Row, Ivory Square. Their history had vanished, crumpled down into the flat witness of street signs. He had been thinking of history torn neatly down the center like a piece of paper—London before 1950, London after 1950; one world barely related to the other. The time of dockers and lightermen now barely echoed in the dredger drifting opposite. He stood on one side of a neatly torn history, too: on the other bank of the river from him stood Claire, rapidly diminishing, the three-dimensional person fading into two-dimensional photographs and pieces of paper. All Claire was now could be summed up by the numbers that had identified her. Medical records. Bank statements. She had gone. Like the ships and cargoes, only faint resonances.

And he had been considering—this just a sonar echo down in the light-refracting pool, without any weight or seeming consequence, a pale thought—leaving the flat, crossing the road, and looking down at the water. He had felt a sudden clean and imperative need to put an end to the grinding wakefulness.

And then he heard the noise.

Apparently Helen, driving her little Fiat, had been making a U-turn in the road. There was no room, of course. The road wasn't designed for the maneuver. She had cut across one line of traffic and collided with a taxi racing along the inside lane. She wasn't hurt, but the passenger in the taxi was injured, and an ambulance was called. When John got to the scene, he saw Helen standing in the middle of the road, arguing with a policeman. The ambulance was next to her and the patient was being loaded into it. Helen looked almost ghost-like, dressed in a gray suit, the rain having plastered her hair to her head. She was drenched, but she carried on arguing, refusing to do anything about her car or even to give her name and address. It wasn't her fault, she kept saying.

He got her home eventually. They had spent half the night in the police station. She was so wired, so frantic, that he called her doctor. And that was when he had first heard the phrase *bipolar disorder*.

Unbeknownst to him, the older brother who was not at home when she was a teenager, she had had it—or at least had it diagnosed—since she was nineteen. The trace of it ran back through their family to their grandmother, a woman that John barely remembered. Helen knew what she had but had never told him, nor shown him her medication. He sat opposite the doctor in their high-tech minimalist kitchen, the symbol of Helen's success, her apparent achievements, and listened to how her life would be: the highs and lows, the mania and depression, that would make up her inner landscape. There was no cure. In the mania, she would be euphoric, extremely optimistic, with inflated self-esteem, poor judgment, and recklessness, and she would have difficulty sleeping. In the depression, she would have persistent feelings of sadness, guilt, or fatigue. She would find it difficult to concentrate and would have thoughts of suicide.

This last warning, delivered in the subdued tone of the doctor, had struck John with horror. He had the same, he thought. He had been feeling exactly like that today. Just before the accident, he had been planning to walk out, to answer the lure that rolled just a few yards away.

It took him a few days to persuade himself that this was not the case. That he did not carry the same illness as Helen. He made it his business to find out the names of her tablets, the regime that she was supposed to follow. And by this time, she was malleable, if not monosyllabic. She had plunged down the other side of the roller-coaster ride and watched him with disinterested eyes. She phoned in sick for work day after day.

Sometimes, in the down phase, she would make an effort to rally. He always thought that this was probably more poignant, sadder, than if she had just laid on the couch staring into space. In these rallies she would dress with care, put on too much makeup, and go out. He never cross-examined her as to where she was going. Just walking, she would claim. But she would come back drunk or worse, more strung-out, more tense than ever, with that horrible look of aggressive despair on her face.

He looked at her now. She was halfway down her third drink.

"Come and stay with me," he said. "I want you to meet someone."

She frowned. "Who?"

"Her name is Catherine Sergeant."

Helen began to nod slowly. "So, finally."

"Yes, finally."

"Who is she?" Helen asked. "What does she do?"

"She works for an auction house. A small local one. I met her when I sold a piece of furniture."

"An auction house?" Helen repeated. "So, what is she? A saleswoman or something?"

"She's an appraiser."

"Of what? Houses?"

"No," he said, "art."

The air froze. Helen put down the drink. "Art?" she repeated. She stared harshly at him. "An art expert!"

"Not just paintings," he said.

Helen started to laugh. "You're sleeping with some bloody art expert," she repeated. Diners at an adjoining table glanced in their direction. "Well, hip fucking hooray."

"Helen," he said. "Stop it."

"And I suppose we've had lots of cozy conversations about one painter in particular, have we?" she demanded.

"Helen," he warned.

"How old is she?"

"Why is that relevant?"

"How old?"

"She's nearly thirty."

Helen started to laugh in earnest. "Thirty?" she repeated. *"Thirty!"* She raised her eyes to the ceiling. "For God's sake, John."

"You might be happy for me," he said.

"Happy? You're sleeping with an art dealer twenty years your junior and it hasn't occurred to you that she might be interested in something more than your amazing youth and vitality?"

The remark stung him more than she could have guessed. She stared at his face, trying to read what she saw there. "You're in love with her," she said.

He didn't reply.

"Holy shit," Helen muttered.

"Stop it."

"Holy shit." And she smiled. He hated that smile; it made his blood run cold. It made him really afraid.

"Helen," he murmured. "Are you still taking paroxetine?"

"I don't take paroxetine," she retorted. "That shows how much you know."

"What, then? Olanzapine?"

She shot him a venomous look. "Why must you always do this?" she demanded. "Why do you always bring this up?"

"Are you taking lithium now?"

"Yes," she said. "I'm taking lithium now, all right?"

"You've taken it regularly?"

"I wish you wouldn't treat me like a baby."

"Have you taken it regularly this week, this month?"

"Yes, yes, yes," she responded. "What more do you want? Yes."

He waited a second. He didn't believe her.

"If you took an aspirin, why would I have to know about it?" she demanded.

"This isn't like taking an aspirin."

"It is to me," she said. "Now, for God's sake, change the subject. I didn't come here to hear your bloody memorial lecture on bipolar."

"It's important."

Her color began to rise. "I think I'm in a slightly better position than you are to know how important it is," she said. "And I don't need you or anyone to remind me."

He didn't reply.

Long moments passed. The people at the next table lost their interest in the conversation and went back to their own. John felt winded, as if he had run for a distance, or lifted some weight or other. He sat looking at his sister, torn between pity and annoyance.

"So," she said, eventually. "This woman. This Catherine."

He waited, wondering what was coming next.

"What does she know?"

"Nothing."

"Nothing at all?"

"She's seen things I've bought."

"But not the rest?"

"No."

"Are you telling me the truth?"

"It wouldn't matter if she knew or not," he said. "Catherine is a genuine person."

"Oh, it wouldn't affect how she thought of you?" Helen said. "Not one little tiny bit?"

He looked away from her. Helen had hit on the one fact that he had been hiding from himself. The fact that he had not told Catherine everything about himself—about this burden that lay between himself and Helen, about this secret that he had managed to get Helen to keep for so long—because he was afraid that it would change whatever was between him and Catherine. Just as it changed—affected, altered, poisoned—the relationship with his own sister.

"A genuine person," Helen was murmuring to herself. "You'd stake your life on it?"

He paused just a second. "I would, yes."

"And all the rest?" Helen asked. "You'd gamble all the rest?"

They glared into each other's faces. John said nothing at all.

"So," Helen whispered. "You'd trust her with your life, would you?" She smiled, pronouncing each word with elaborate precision. "I do *not* think so."

Long moments passed while John sat looking at his sister.

"I'm glad you've kept some of your sense, at least," Helen said.

He stared back at her. She lit another cigarette and called the waiter, asking for coffee. She complained about the food she had been given; there followed a long conversation, a further consultation with the maître d'. She was doggedly insistent; apologies were offered. John watched it all, feeling sickened at himself. He couldn't let go of it, and that was the absolute truth. He couldn't let go for Helen, and he couldn't let go for Catherine.

He was in prison, chained with a century-old promise.

He looked at the clock, feeling faintly sick. His chest hurt. His hands hurt. He realized that he had been clenching them. Slowly now, he unfurled his fingers.

"Come down to the house," he said at last, looking back at Helen. "I still want you to come down to the house."

She started to pick up her bag. "Oh, don't worry," she told him, pushing back her chair. "Wild bloody horses won't keep me away now."

Sketch to Illustrate the Passions: Anger

1854

It was thought that water could confine the anger of mania.

Cold water, of course; plunge baths from wooden bridges, into which a man could be precipitated, clothed or naked. Ice cold and pumped straight from the river, full of mud, it would leave him stranded up to his neck until the flood door was opened. The patient could then be retrieved from the floor, as often as not on his knees by the iron grille of the gate, trying to find his way out with the retreating water.

Shocking treatments would restore sanity to deranged minds; or, at the very least, calm a madman into submission even with the threat of them.

As the second half of the century dawned, Mr. Hood considered the new American treatments. He had an engraving sent to him of the Benjamin Rush tranquilizing chair, the patient being bound by foot and arm restraints and a shoulder brace. At the back of the chair protruded a rod, to which was fixed a head restraint, a box, which was lowered over the patient's face. It was said that this was calming to those who suffered mania, and, due to its efficiency, many were bound to it for weeks at a time.

There was, too, the Utica crib, a coffinlike bed made of latticed wood. In the New York asylums, those who raved worst were tied to the crib, and the lid shut upon them so that they remained incapable of movement.

Bedlam itself had few such modernities. But in one of the lower rooms was a gyrating chair, held in a frame very like a gallows. It was an eighteenth-century invention, and, as such, inappropriate to the most advanced in modern thinking. For that reason, Hood had never expressly prescribed its use. Nevertheless, it was rumored that some of the keepers had once excelled in it.

The patient was bound to the chair, which itself was bound to a large spindle, turned by a metal rod by an attendant standing on a flight of stone steps. As the rod was pushed, the spindle turned and the patient, consequently, spun round. Some of the oldest attendants took a pride in how long they could turn the rod; moreover, in the days before Hood came, the public would pay gladly to see the entertainment of those released from the chair, for none could walk except in circles. Such delights increased the ticket sales, taken at the main gate by a creature of indigo color, leaning upon a moneybox, like Cerebus guarding the mouth of Hell.

Naturally, the paying public had long since been banned from the hospital. It was not that it was inconvenient; rather the contrary. The amounts paid were a source of needed income. But eventually the walks of the wards of Bedlam became notorious for whores, plying their trade out of the rain. Amours of a kind inhabited every corner. It had been said that at any hour in the day, a sportsman might meet with game for his purpose, as great a convenience to London as was the Long Cellar to Amsterdam.

But that was long ago. The room that held the chair was locked; nor were any of the inmates now chained. Only the water treatments and the Rush chair remained, and now, in the 1850s, Bedlam instigated one of its greatest innovations, a treatment to calm delusions. Each patient upon admission was photographed, the purpose being to confront each man and woman with a true image of himself.

Dadd had already heard about the photograph. One of the Clique had visited him and brought him the news of the fixing of image by Talbot's calotype. They told him that in Regent Street, photographic establishments were set up, and that persons of quality attended them to record their faces forever in potassium iodide and silver nitrate.

Dadd had thought about it constantly, sitting alone, his eyes watching the slow progression of light across the wall.

This, then, was where the painter died, he considered. The reproduction of the face in art was obsolete; the painter's interpretation of the soul in the face was not required. Nor was it needed for landscape; in time, he thought, the monochrome plates would capture color. There would be no more need to paint mountains, or trees bent by wind, or bridges, or docks, or rivers. Sooner or later, the photographic plate would take hold of the rushing of water and paste it into chemical, and seal it forever.

Man had stolen time; he had placed it in a lens. He had command of the seasons, capturing them in every mood. And he had command of other men.

A chair was brought into one of the galleries, on the landing before the doors. It was an ordinary kitchen bentwood chair with a rounded back. One morning, Anna Mary Rivers was brought here, a girl of eighteen of good family. She sat with her hands clasped in her lap and her eyes raised to the ceiling. She refused to look elsewhere and was photographed in this attitude, her hair disheveled, a calico hospital gown barely covering her shoulders. She made no attempt to look at the photographer and it is to be doubted if she knew he was there. The records show her date of admittance—1st June 1854—and the date of her discharge, six years later. Nothing else is noted, and the years before and the years after vanished as if they had never been, and all that Anna Mary Rivers ever was, or ever became, was an eighteen-year-old girl on a cheap chair, her upward-looking gaze like some kind of prayer.

Others came that same morning. One William Wright was newly admitted. Fay Reynolds, an old woman of seventy, had been resident at Bedlam for twenty-five years. Wright, in a state of frightened shock, was a schoolmaster, and the only reason found for his despair was his involvement in a drowning the year before, when he had found a woman's body. Fay Reynolds had been perpetually in prison for prostitution before she refused to sleep, and sang to keep herself awake. They were treated with purges and water, and locked in calming rooms, and Fay Reynolds died and William Wright was released, without ever receiving their diagnoses of melancholia, or tertiary syphilis.

Dadd was brought to the chair just before twelve o'clock.

He did not know William Wright, but he looked carefully at him, thinking that he resembled his own brother. Wright was weeping as the photograph was taken, clutching at his chest. He was whispering to himself.

"Who is this?" Dadd asked the attendant.

"He is a fellow of St. John's College, Cambridge," was the answer. Dadd was nudged in the ribs. "There you are, Richard," said the steward, thinking it a joke. "You may talk to him in your Latin and he will understand you."

Dadd stared at his fellow inmate. "What is the matter with him?" he asked.

"He has basses and trebles in his head," the attendant replied. "That's my opinion, Richard. He is a musical scholar, and he has too many basses and trebles muddling his brain."

More often than not, Dadd would close his ears to this kind of reasoning. He heard it all around him every day. That such-and-such man had been driven mad by drink, or by visiting foreign countries, or by some kind of sin against religion. He knew that Brigham believed that his own illness had been brought about by sunstroke while he was in Egypt.

He did not know if it was the truth or not.

Lately, he had come to believe that Osiris had instructed him while his conscience was not awakened; that the murderous command had entered his head while sleeping, or distracted, and had solidified there, and made his brain its own wriggling, contorted, ungovernable place, so that he could never get the shape or size of it. And that if he slept now, or did not apply himself to concentration, the command would rise again.

And so for the last few weeks he had taken to awakening his conscience by trampling the floor of his sleeping cell. He stamped his feet until they were cracked and bleeding. They allowed him to do it for the first few days, and after that, they had called Mr. Hood. Brigham had suggested a straitjacket, of the kind that Dadd had worn when he had been admitted. But after watching Dadd for some time, and asking him what he was doing, Hood concluded that the straitjacket was not necessary.

"Richard," he had said, gently laying his hand on Dadd's arm. "You may rest from your labors. I believe you have vanquished the enemy. He is thoroughly flattened."

Dadd did not hear the humor. He leaned away from Hood's touch. "You had better go away," he said. "Or he will set upon you."

"Who will?" Hood asked.

"The Piper of Neisse," Dadd replied.

Hood did not understand at the time; only later, in his study, did he find the reference in papers removed from Dadd nine years before. Dadd had written a manuscript poem, The Piper of Neisse, a Legend of Silesia. In it, a young man is imprisoned for witchcraft, because he can make even the least agile of men dance. He dies there alone and rises up from his grave each night, rousing the dead in phantom dances through the town.

When Hood went back to see Dadd a week later, the stamping had gone. Dadd was lying on his bed, chest rattling with bronchitis.

"How are you?" Hood asked him.

Dadd had turned a perfectly lucid face to him. "I am inhabited by both the piper and the god," he said. "But they have taken to sleeping."

"Don't wake them," Hood said.

Dadd's eyes had filled with tears. "I have voices in their place," he said. "Voices that speak my thoughts out loud. What shall I say to them?"

"Tell them to leave."

"I cannot," Dadd said.

And so Hood had sat with him long after it became dark, listening to the silence that Dadd claimed was full of sound.

William Wright was taken away.

The photographer motioned that Dadd should be brought forward.

Dadd stood by the chair, looking intently at all the apparatus; a large darkroom tent had been set up adjoining the washroom. Dadd gazed at the black folds of material and at the darkroom plates.

"Is this calotype?" he asked.

The photographer smiled. "Do you have a knowledge of the process?"

"No," Dadd said. "But I have heard of it."

"It is not calotype. It is collodion."

Dadd put his head on one side. The photographer looked from patient to keeper: Dadd was tall and his beard was turning white. The hair was receding a little from his high forehead; the handsome eyes were piercing and intelligent. He resembled nothing more than an Old Testament prophet.

"Collodion," Dadd echoed.

"That is correct. Also called collodium."

"As in colletic, from the Greek, an agglutinant, a glue?"

The photographer paused. What little Greek he had once had was long since lost. Then, his expression brightened. "There is a kind of glue," he replied. "To be sure there is. Mr. Frederick Archer has perfected it. It is a solution of gun cotton in ether. It is a sticky liquid with which we cover the plates."

Dadd was silent for a moment. He was not used to conversation. He could hear his voices straining to interrupt his thoughts, and his body tensed.

The photographer had not noticed. "Collodion is more sensitive to light than calotype," he was saying. "It has reduced the amount of time in which the image develops. It was necessary to wait many minutes with calotype; now the image is ready in two or three seconds."

"It is sticky," Dadd murmured. "To capture the image."

"In a manner of speaking."

"On glass," Dadd said, looking at the glass plates.

"The collodion is spread over the plate. Then the plate must be sensitized, exposed and developed when it is still wet."

"To capture the image," Dadd repeated.

The photographer looked at him expectantly, still waiting for him to sit.

"I have captured images," Dadd murmured. "But they are not to be seen in the world. They are here." And he tapped the side of his head. "You cannot take your collodium to them. There is nothing to fix them but my own hand. And they travel . . ." He extended his arm and pointed with the other hand down from his head, across his shoulder, and down the length of the arm to his fingers. "They travel on thought," he said. "Which is not to be found in solution, or on glass plates, or in alcohol or water or with Pyro-Gallic." He stepped toward the photographer. "I have learned all your names," he said. "And yet you cannot fix me, nor my thoughts."

He refused to have his photograph taken.

He went back to the criminal quarters and was quiet for hours. He would not answer Brigham's gentle questions. Only in the evening did he begin to speak, ranting at the murder of portraits, of artists, of inspiration, by the collodion plate. When the rage was finished, he wept bitterly, hiding his face in the coarse pillow, drumming his feet like a child.

The next day, and the day after, he bore all the aspect of grief, unwilling to eat or to wash, throwing his food on the floor in what seemed to be desperate mourning.

He was locked in his room.

On the fifth day, he began to paint.

The watercolor was almost structural, sculptural, in its strong contrast. At the top left-hand corner was a house seemingly ablaze; in the bottom right, a forge. Two figures stood by the fire, their bodies and faces whitened by the glare. A third face was barely visible, in the shadows and staring into the flames.

In the inscription, winding under the heel of one of the figures, he wrote, "Sketch to illustrate the passions. *Anger,* by Richard Dadd, October 17th, 1854, Bethlehem Hospital, London."

He gave it to Mr. Hood, who kept it on the wall facing his desk, and stared, too, into the white-hot flames, and what they had consumed.

19

It was coming toward the end of the sale when Mark Pearson first noticed the woman standing in the doorway.

He had no idea how long she had been there; it could have been all afternoon. She was slight, but striking: cropped hair and swathed in an enormous velvet coat despite the heat of the day. The crowds had thinned a little since lunchtime; on the second afternoon of the sale they had now sold over nine hundred lots. The last was English and Continental furniture, John Brigham's dresser among them. Mark glanced at his watch; the final lot was number 983. He estimated that it would take another forty minutes.

The salesroom was very hot. They had opened the top windows but it had only served to increase the flow of sultry air; eventually they had opened the back delivery doors, and the bidders had a view out into the marketplace and the hills beyond. There wasn't a cloud in the sky.

Amanda had taken telephone bids all day; she had just finished and came over to him as the bidding for the last lot was completed.

"Robert is here," she whispered.

Taking his eyes from the woman in the coat, Mark followed the inclination of his wife's head. Robert was standing in the doorway, too, watching Catherine as she took the bidding.

"How do you think he looks?" Amanda asked.

"Indifferent," Mark said.

They looked at him together; it was true. Robert looked bored, leaning heavily against the doorjamb and loosening his tie. He stepped aside as the woman whom Mark had noticed earlier edged past him and began to walk slowly down the central aisle, looking from left to right for a place to sit.

Catherine was taking the bids. She saw the woman and the catalogue in her hand. Sitting down eventually, the woman began to fan herself with it. At first Catherine thought it was a bid; she glanced again toward her, then went on. After a moment or two, she was aware of her sitting forward occasionally to peer at various items. The woman's expression was noncommittal, but Catherine felt nevertheless that not only the items, but the whole salesroom, was under inspection.

It came to the final ten lots.

"Lot 972," Catherine said. "A Dutch walnut and floral marquetry bureau, inlaid with various woods and enclosing a fitted stepped interior. A thousand pounds?"

There was silence.

"Five hundred, then."

Five was bid; within a few seconds three or four dealers were bidding against each other. The pace slackened around three thousand.

"Three five?" Catherine asked the nearest man.

"Three two."

"Three four?" But there was no responding bid.

"For the first time of asking, at three thousand two hundred . . ."

"Three five," said the woman.

Catherine looked at her. "New bid in the center of the room," she acknowledged. "At three thousand five hundred . . ."

"Three six," said the dealer.

"Three seven," the woman responded.

A murmur went round the room. Some of those who had been

leaving turned back at the doors. The dealers, all familiar to one another, craned their necks to see who the bidder was.

The man paused. He was staring down at his catalogue. It was Stuart, the dealer whom Catherine and Mark knew well. He was glaring down at his catalogue, aware that he was up against a private bidder and annoyed that his own price should be forced higher. "Eight," he murmured.

"Three thousand eight hundred." Catherine looked back at the woman. She was met with a direct stare and a smile that surprised her. Then, a shake of the head.

"Staying at three thousand eight," Catherine confirmed. She saw that Stuart had colored. The woman seemed so laid-back that he had assumed it had been nothing more than a whim for her to bid, a whim that had just cost him six hundred pounds.

"Going now at three thousand eight hundred," Catherine said.

She glanced once again at Stuart's competitor. There was something vaguely familiar about her, she thought. The woman's smile suddenly broadened. "Four thousand," she said.

The dealer gave up, sighing loudly and returning to the chair that he had been sitting in.

"Any advance on four thousand . . ."

There was no opposition; Catherine brought down the gavel. "And the name?"

"Brigham," was the reply.

Amanda, standing at the rear, grabbed Mark's arm. "What did she say?" she whispered.

"Brigham," he repeated.

They looked at each other. "It's his wife," Amanda said.

"He hasn't got a wife," Mark told her. "She died twelve years ago. Catherine told me."

"Well, he can have remarried, can't he?"

"She could be anything," Mark told her. "A sister, a cousin . . ." He looked anxiously at Catherine. She had paused only for a second before passing on to the next lot. The woman was sitting back in her chair, apparently perfectly relaxed.

"She doesn't look bothered," Mark said.

"Is she supposed to?"

"Well, if she were his wife and had come here to find Catherine," Mark pointed out in a whisper, "you might expect her to look a bit more thunderous than that."

It took just half an hour to complete the sale; in all that time, the woman did not move.

When Catherine was finished, she left the podium and as she walked down the aisle, only then did the woman stand to meet her. She held out her hand.

"I'm Helen Brigham," she said.

Catherine smiled, returning the handshake. "I had just about worked it out," she said. "It's nice to meet you. John didn't tell me you were coming."

"I haven't told him," Helen said. "It's a surprise. Though he asked me the other day, of course. When he was up in town. When we met for lunch."

"For lunch," Catherine repeated. She frowned, confused.

"I'm just dying to see this new house of his," Helen said.

Catherine looked closely at the other woman. She could see no resemblance at all between this small, dark-haired woman and her brother. John was tall and ascetic-looking, thin, sometimes to the point of looking drawn; this woman was quite different.

"And you live in London?" she asked.

"That's right."

There was an awkward pause. Catherine was still silently trying to work out which day John had met Helen. He hadn't told her about it. "Well," Catherine said eventually, "you bought a lovely piece."

"You think so?"

"Yes, of course."

"But not as nice as anything that John has."

"Well . . ."

"I expect he's shown you the entire collection."

"I've seen . . . yes," Catherine agreed, confused by the pointedness of the question.

"All his secrets," Helen said. "Every one?" She lowered her voice. "My God, you must have been thrilled."

They were interrupted by Mark and Amanda.

"This is John's sister," Catherine said. She felt utterly confused suddenly. *All his secrets. When we met for lunch.* She gazed at Helen's profile as she turned toward Amanda; at the thick silk collar of the coat, the theatrical coloring of it; at the cruelly cropped hair and the pale face beneath it. "This is Mark Pearson, and his wife, Amanda. Amanda, this is Helen."

"Do you have a house down here you're thinking of furnishing?" Mark asked. "That is a lovely bit of nineteenth century you got yourself."

"No," Helen said. "The desk can go to John's for now."

She looked around her at the room, and at the customers, now gradually filing out. "You have quite a setup here," she said. "John said it was a small venture. But this is quite big." She turned back to Mark. "So, 'Pearsons.' This is yours."

"Not exactly," Mark said. "Catherine and I are partners."

Out of the corner of her eye, Catherine saw Robert coming toward them. He had grown tired of waiting; impatience was written all over him. She tried to signal that she would come and talk to him, but he was making his way past the last of the crowds and Mark had already turned. Politely, he held out his hand.

Helen looked from one to the other inquiringly.

"Helen," Catherine said. "This is Robert Sergeant, my husband."

There was a second's pause. "Really?" Helen asked. "How interesting. I'm John's sister. John Brigham." She extended her hand and Robert took it.

"Robert lives in London, too," Catherine said, lost for any other way to explain herself. There was an almost palpable tremor of embarrassment.

"Whereabouts?" Helen asked.

He named a street. Catherine had no idea of where it was. It was the first time he had even ventured the information that he had a flat, an address, rather than a hotel.

"Near the Cavenish?" Helen was saying.

"Not far."

"I know it."

"Robert's mother lives in Bedford Square," Catherine added.

Helen smiled, and nodded. "Does she?" she murmured.

Robert extracted his hand with a smile. "I need to have a word with you," he told Catherine.

They excused themselves, Catherine walking back to the podium and Robert following her. They stood between the wall and the display cabinet, where two customers were waiting to be given their purchases. The steward glanced at Catherine, holding the receipts book for her to countersign.

She turned her back, lowering her voice. "What did you want?" she asked.

"Should I know who John is?" Robert asked.

"He's a customer," Catherine said.

He looked acutely at her before replying. "I've been to the estate agents," he said. "They had two people interested before I walked out of the door. They want to see the house tomorrow."

"Tomorrow," Catherine echoed. "All right." And all the while, she was thinking: *all his secrets . . . all his secrets . . . you must have been thrilled . . .*

"Can you be there during the day?"

"What?" she said, distracted. "Oh, I don't know. I haven't looked at my appointments for tomorrow. I can be, I suppose. Are you going back to London?"

"Tonight," he told her. "Now. In fact, an hour ago if this sale hadn't taken so bloody long."

"I'll see to the house," she said.

He put his hand on her arm. "I went back there today," he said.

"They wanted all the stuff about council tax and water rates. I couldn't remember. I went back to check in the study."

She held his gaze.

"You aren't living there," he said. "Are you?"

"It's nothing to do with you where I live," she replied.

"I was thinking . . ." he said. And he laughed a little to himself and shook his head. "I was thinking how much I had hurt you. I was feeling guilty. You alone in the house."

"You should," she told him.

The steward touched Catherine's shoulder. "I'm sorry," he said. "If you would just . . ." And he held out the receipts book. She signed; he returned to the cabinet; all three standing there looked at the couple alongside them.

"I'm not talking to you here," Catherine whispered. "And I'm not discussing something like this."

She made to turn away from him. He caught her elbow.

"You didn't waste much time, did you?"

She pulled her arm away, furious. "You've got a bloody nerve," she hissed. "What does it matter to you? You don't want me, Robert. You left me for someone else, remember?"

"There isn't anyone," he said.

There was a beat of astonishment. "What?"

He stayed silent, his lips pressed tightly in a kind of grimace. Then he seemed to take hold of himself; he straightened, pushed back his shoulders, looked around the room. He put his hand in his pocket, took out a business card, and gave it to her.

"This is the estate agent," he said. "Ring them."

He turned away, and went back to the group in the center of the room.

Helen was in the process of writing out a check, leaning on a table. She signed with a flourish and handed it to Amanda. Catherine watched Robert talk briefly to Mark; then Helen touched him on the arm. He lowered his head to listen to her and eventually nodded.

They went out of the room together.

20

John drove down into town that evening.

He had been waiting at Bridle Lodge for Catherine; when she didn't come home after the sale, he paced the house for a while before ringing Pearsons.

Amanda had answered the phone.

"Hello," he said. "It's John. John Brigham. Is Catherine there?"

There was a pause. "No," was the short reply.

"Is she on her way here?"

"No," Amanda said. "At least, I'm not sure. I think she went home."

"Home?" he echoed. "To her house, you mean?"

"Yes."

He stopped, trying to make out the expression in her voice. "Is she all right?" he asked. "Her cell is switched off."

"Do you want me to give her a message if she rings here?"

"No," he said hesitantly. "No, that's OK. Thanks."

He had tried her house phone. It just rang and rang. For a while he thought that she must be out. Then, after the sixth or seventh attempt, he began to get a conviction that she was there but just not picking up. He got into his car.

When he pulled up in the quiet street where Catherine lived, he was surprised to see that the house was in darkness, yet her car was parked in the drive. He walked up to the front door and knocked. Getting no reply, he kneeled down and tried to look through the letterbox. The hall was just a blur of gray. "Catherine," he called through the box. "Are you there?"

A premonition ran through him. It was like being doused with cold water. Getting up, he looked around the side of the house, went to the gate, and opened it. There were no lights here, either. The little garden was empty. He knocked on the kitchen door. "Catherine," he called.

He tried the handle and found to his surprise that it was open. Stepping through, he saw her belongings scattered on the work surfaces: her jacket, the car keys. A cupboard door hung open.

He looked to his left, to the little dining room, and was shocked to see Catherine sitting bolt upright in a chair, perfectly still. She was sitting with her eyes closed and her head tilted slightly backward, in an attitude of wariness or aversion. It was only when he took a step toward her that she suddenly stirred herself.

"Jesus Christ," he muttered. "What on earth's the matter? Why are you sitting here in the dark?"

She shook her head slightly, getting up and walking toward him. "I must have fallen asleep," she said. She ran a hand through her hair. "What time is it?"

"It's nearly eight," he said. "I've been ringing this number."

"Have you?" She spread her hands. "I came back to check on some things Robert said we had to have on hand for the house sale, some papers . . . I was up in the study . . ."

She paused.

"What's wrong?" he asked.

"I . . ." She looked about herself, then back at him. "Helen came to the auction," she said.

"Helen?"

"She walked up and introduced herself," Catherine continued.

"I had no idea she was here."

"Hadn't she rung you?"

"No."

"She said that you had asked her." She remained immobile. He tried to read her face. "When you met her in London."

He didn't reply.

"Was it a secret?" she asked.

"No. Of course not."

"But you didn't say that you were going."

"She rang me last week and asked me to meet her."

Catherine was frowning. "You didn't mention it."

"I wasn't sure if I should go," he told her, finally. "Helen . . . Helen can be very difficult."

She moved to the other side of the room and switched on the light. In her face, when she turned around, was the one emotion he never wanted to see written there: doubt.

"There's no secret," he repeated.

She gave a small, tight smile. "That's funny," she said quietly. "Because that's exactly the opposite of what Helen told me."

"About what?"

"Secrets," she said. She glanced back at the chair in which she had been sitting. "In fact, I was trying to remember exactly what it was that she told me," she continued. "She said something about the collection. Your collection. And then she said 'all his secrets.' And she asked me a question. She said, 'Every one?' "

He put his hand to his head. "Helen is . . . there is this thing about Helen . . ." he began.

But Catherine's voice had risen slightly. "And then she looked at me, and she said, 'My God, you must have been thrilled.' In a whisper. That I must have been thrilled." She was staring directly at him, a questioning inflection hanging in the air. "I wonder what it was that was supposed to have thrilled me so much," she murmured.

"Catherine . . ."

"Why didn't you tell me that you were meeting for lunch?" she asked. "What was so private about it?"

"Nothing," he said.

"You went all the way to London. You must have been gone all day. You must have been gone the day that Mark and I were cataloguing until eight or nine o'clock."

"Yes," he said. "Wednesday."

"But . . ."

"Catherine," he said. "Can we go home? Can I talk to you at home?"

"Is it so serious?"

"I'd rather be at home."

He lifted his hand and held it out to her, but she didn't respond. She didn't even look at the gesture. She had kept her gaze on his face. "What was so private about it?" she repeated.

"I just didn't want to worry you with it."

She frowned. "And why would I be worried?"

He sighed exasperatedly. "You're right," he said. "There's no reason why you would be worried. It's me that's concerned."

"Why?"

"Because . . . you have to know Helen." He held out his arms to her.

She looked at him, and turned her head slightly, still frowning. "I'm missing something," she said. "I don't understand what's going on."

"I want to tell you," he said. "Let me tell you at home."

She sidestepped him. Catching a reflection, he glimpsed an empty tumbler on the table next to her. Now that he was near her, he could smell the whiskey on her breath. She didn't drink. She barely touched a glass of wine, let alone spirits. "How long have you been sitting here?" he asked.

She turned away. He came up behind her and wrapped his arms around her. She twisted in his arms and slowly pushed him away. He stared at her, suddenly aware of more than just a few inches of space between them. He felt the gulf open as surely as if he were standing on the edge of a precipice. "Oh, no," he murmured. "Don't think that."

But she voiced his fear. "You're keeping something from me," she whispered. "Something important."

She walked past him, out into the kitchen, the way he had come.

She opened the door and went out into the courtyard. Following her, he found her taking deep breaths of air. The pain in his chest was thin, tight, like the tip of a blade wriggling between his ribs. He tried lifting his head, pulling back his shoulders. He was breathing, but not getting air. As he listened to Catherine's breaths, it felt strangely as if they were sunk in water, in half-lit depths; if he put his mouth to hers, she could breathe for him. He tried not to think of this strange image, the image of himself as a parasite taking the very air out of her throat. He looked at her profile—arched neck as she tipped back her head and gazed up at the cloud-strewn humid sky—with the ivy of the fence behind her, variegated patches of shade—and felt her stepping away, through a door, through a skewed perception of him.

"I'll tell you everything," he said.

She looked at him. "I thought I could trust you," she murmured. "I thought this was different. That *we* were different."

"Tell me what you want to know," he replied. "I haven't a secret from you." He corrected himself. "I won't have a secret from you."

She crossed her arms and looked at the ground, giving an almost imperceptible shake of the head. "Family secret," she said. "Helen was talking about some sort of family secret. Did you hide it from Claire, too?"

The pain become more refined, a single hot line from the base of his throat to the center of his chest.

"Helen says a lot of things. She doesn't see the world straight. She—"

"What is the secret?" Catherine persisted.

The garden pressed in on him; he could smell the copper taint of a shrub close by, something with ink-dark leaves. Somewhere nearby, a street away perhaps, a dog was barking intermittently. He saw a window light in a neighboring house.

He felt the world flicker and the images and sounds compact, as if everything had suddenly been caught in some vast net and pulled upward, and Catherine's face and body swayed toward him. He put his hand to the wall and dropped his head to his chest. The collapsed darkness became a minute tapestry of detail: the ragged arc of a lichen under his fingers, the grit of the brick, the shuffling of the stars between clouds.

He saw the magician under Dadd's fingertip, extending his arms to hold the mottled wings and clasped hands; he felt the touch of dancers' feet, little more than drops of rain, over his shoulders. The girl in the green glass mirror stayed where she was, looking into the glass with disappointment.

"Why can't you tell me?" Catherine asked.

"I can," he said. "I don't want it." He straightened up; the garden rebounded like a flexed photograph, a piece of celluloid. "There isn't anything I wouldn't give you," he said.

She drew back from him suddenly. "Give me?" she repeated. She gasped audibly. "I don't want anything from you."

"I didn't mean . . ."

"You think that I want to take this thing from you?" she said. He heard the deep hurt in her voice. "You think that's what I'm interested in?"

"No, no . . ."

"Don't you understand?" she said. "I don't want anything from you. Nothing. Nothing!"

"Catherine . . ." he said.

She put her hand to her head, a fist against her temple. Her voice fell, for a moment, to a shaky whisper. "This is so like Robert."

Panic was rushing through him now. He tried to catch her arm, but she stepped quickly out of his reach. "Don't you think I'm sick," she said, "of people and the way that they hold on to objects, their bloody possessions?"

"This is different," John whispered. "Only you would know how different. Even Claire didn't really know. I told her. But I never actually showed her."

Catherine dropped her hand and shook her head. "I don't care," she said. "Don't you understand? I don't care what it is. I don't care if it's the bloody Crown Jewels." He saw, to his horror, that she had begun to cry. She wiped her face with the heel of her hand. "I just wanted you," she said. "I wanted the world the way you saw it. I wanted the seeing . . ."

And the word *seeing* cut a piece out of him.

She was still talking.

"But now I find that wasn't right," she said. She walked past him slowly, scrupulously getting past within an inch of him without touching. "And . . . you know what?" she asked. "I was thinking just now, when I was sitting here, I was thinking that you must have talked about me to Helen. And you all must have discussed me, and you let her come to this conclusion, that I couldn't be trusted . . ."

"No!" John interrupted. "Catherine, it wasn't like that."

"Well," she said dully, defeated. "Whatever it was."

"Please don't do this," he said. "Please."

But she had stepped onto the threshold of the house and now turned half toward him, her hand on the frame, her face obscured by shadows.

"Catherine, come home with me," he said. "Please."

But she shook her head. "I'll ring you tomorrow," she said, her voice heavy and dull with disappointment.

She stepped inside, and he heard the key turn in the lock.

Lucretia

1854

Two women were in his mind.

It had come to him through the gossip of the prison that there had been a murder in the women's cells.

He had been thinking of Lucretia, the martyr, the heroine, the faithful partner whose virtue had been taken, and he started to paint her in browns and purples, taking the knife from the folds of the cloak across her shoulders, and pointing the tip at her breast.

They said in the prison that the women had not known each other, that they had been brought in separately and merely formed an alliance through others who knew them both. The tongues that wagged then told of a jealousy, sprung from their knowledge of a man and his possessions, to which they both felt claim.

He took his mind from their degradation and into Lucretia's bare shoulder, her eyes lifted to heaven, her hair streaming over her neck. He painted the skin very white, luminous, the background dark, the folds of her garment intricate. Strength in the posture, determination of death in her expression.

"What has happened to the murderess?" he asked the steward one morning.

"She is confined," was all that he would say.

And confinement it would remain forever, for the rest of her days, unless it could be proven that the woman was not so mad as cunning in her intention. He heard the whispering, as though transmitted through the very brick, heard it flowing in the random utterances that passed for conversation in the darkened hallways. They muttered that she had come into the prison only to find her mark. Only to rid the world of her enemy and reclaim her inheritance. He began to dream vividly of the point of the knife, and he painted Lucretia's knife very pale against the dark cloak, her left arm that grasped it almost floating and she unaware of its intention. He painted her boldly, like a man, so caught up was she in her husband's imagined disgrace, so oblivious to his forgiveness.

He closed his eyes as the paintbrush lay on the folds of the garments.

He was trying to recall the other female faces of his family. His mother, now faded into obscurity, so much so that he could not recall a single detail of her face. Yet he remembered Mary Anne, elder to him by three years. It had always been said that she resembled her mother, and perhaps there he could keep the memory of them both, two coins pressed from a single mold, with her intense and sympathetic gaze, the curls at her temples, the lace cap that covered her head. There was an anxiety in her look, he thought. Was that a manufactured recollection, her anxiety for him reflected in his memory? He wondered if she ever thought of him.

And then Maria Elizabeth, who had married his friend John Phillip. Or so they had told him.

Phillip was a painter; would he have painted Maria himself? Would he have painted them together? Would John Phillip have perhaps painted Catherine, his brother's wife? Was there an image of them all somewhere that he might be allowed to share?

Dadd opened his eyes and gazed on Lucretia. He knew in a passionate instant that he wanted to see his sister. And his sister-in-law. He wanted to see Catherine. He wanted to know if there were children. No one told him of his family. He was set off in a parallel world to them, and yet he yearned to hear them and see them, and he sat still in front of the painting now for more than an hour, until the steward came to disengage the brush from his fingers.

"I would like to see my sisters," he told the man.

"Your sisters, sir?"

"My sisters," he repeated. And seeing no reaction other than a smile, he began to shout. "Are you deaf?" he demanded. "Are you as raving as those you pretend to shelter? My sisters! My sisters!"

It was late in the evening when the senior steward came to him.

Dadd was sitting quietly, having taken the laudanum.

They told him then that Maria Elizabeth, the youngest, the sweetest, the most untouched of all the family, had been committed to an asylum in Aberdeen.

His sister had tried to strangle her youngest child.

It was likely, they told him, in softest tones—what, did they think he would leap up and strike them, did they think that he would strike the walls, injure himself?—he had no strength to do such a thing, he had no strength at all—they told him that, like him, like her older brother, she would never leave the place where they had sent her.

21

Two days had passed.

Robert had spent them in Manchester on business; now, as he got out of the Tube at Bank station, London in the rush hour hit him. He stood looking up Cheapside while the crowds surged past. His clothes stuck to him; he felt as if he'd been sleeping in his suit. It had been a long day; the train, as usual, had been delayed. He had been sitting for two hours this afternoon in a stifling carriage, watching Newcastle-under-Lyme pass at a snail's pace. He was miserable, exhausted, and a headache was beginning far back behind his eyes. It was too hot to be in the city, he thought. Far too hot.

Leaning on the black railings, he tried his cell, but there was no reply from his office. Only voice mail. He left a message, to say that he would make the early morning meeting. When he had finished, he stared at the handset morosely for a few seconds before shoving it back in his pocket. He looked across the traffic; diesel hung almost visibly in the air.

Just at that moment, he badly wanted to be back in Dorset, driving out of Dorchester South station, the way he had gone a hundred times after a business trip. It seemed like some sort of distant paradise now. There were just two sets of traffic lights to get out of town and up onto the long straight drive toward Beaminster, out onto the breezy tops with green valleys stretching down on either side of the road. He wanted to be back in his hometown, with its sloping square. But that route was forfeit.

He wouldn't pass the black-on-white 1940s signposts hooked crookedly up on the verges any longer, or take the left-hand turn down the hill toward Pearsons, its roof showing red among a haphazard jumble of sandstone and slate tiles. He wouldn't pass through the great-banked edges of the lane, with its cow parsley and beech trees, braking carefully at the dogleg turn where the frost always lay in winter, and the rain could collect in one of the field entrances. He knew only too well that it had been his own decision—a premeditated, careful decision, or so he had thought at the time, at least—to come back to London. But he missed the past; he missed the peace. He missed looking at the patterns of things: leaf shade on the road, the peculiar chalk ridges and circles in the crops, the quiet of his own back garden.

For some unfathomable reason, the corner of the garden came into his head in vivid detail now. He propped his briefcase on the railing and leaned on it. A whole line of taxis drew up alongside him, rattling, panting like dogs, waiting for the lights to change. He shook his head at himself. Like dogs. Beset by dogs. Where the hell had that come from? What a thought. He closed his eyes and withdrew to the garden, where he had made a seating area last year, just wide enough for one bench. He had put up a little fence and painted it. His first practical project; he had been proud of it. Catherine had planted a climber; he tried to think what it was. A kind of clematis with a magenta flower. But the pleasure of having made it, of having completed the work, had been disproportionately huge to him.

He felt a pang of territoriality. It didn't belong to him anymore, not in any real sense. They had an offer on the house already; the estate agent was keen to let the completion go through quickly. Someone else would sit in the corner by his fence. He felt suddenly ridiculously, almost childishly, cheated. He wanted to go and snatch that part of his life back; take the turn on the downhill lane and the garden seat and Catherine planting the climber in the rain.

He stared at the traffic a moment longer, then pushed himself away from the railings and walked down Lombard Street.

The flat was in a marble-faced block at the back of Bishopsgate. It was functional. That was the best that could be said of it. It hadn't been designed to be lived in long-term. Reaching it now, stepping out of the throng of the pavement crowds and into the little foyer of the building, he walked up the three flights of stairs.

Letting himself in, he went through to the bed-sitting room. He took off his jacket and lay down on the sofa, sighing with exhaustion, feeling the smothering stuffiness of the room, and staring at the ceiling. He began to think of Catherine as he had seen her two days ago. She had been different, he thought; there was no doubt about it. Very different in the way she held herself. Quieter, calmer. There had been an air of confidence about her that he did not quite recognize. And then, closer to her, he had seen that his leaving had, after all, left a mark on her. It gave him no satisfaction to see that she had a direct, assessing look on her face when she talked to him, as if any preconceptions that she might have still carried about him had been swept away. She looked at him as one stranger might look disinterestedly at another, and he saw that she was also older. She had always looked rather childlike, but now that look had gone entirely.

He looked at his watch. Five forty. There was nothing to eat in the flat. He lay wondering what he could do. Go down to the Greek sandwich bar on the corner before it closed. Cross back over the bridge and sit in one of the pubs south of the river, one of the ones he used to drink in before he got the train at Waterloo. Sit near Tate Modern and watch the river go by; go in and eat there, perhaps.

He smiled to himself. If Catherine had been here, there'd be no doubt where they would eat. It was always galleries, galleries, galleries.

When he had first met Catherine—on the least beautiful, least painterly platform in London, Liverpool Street on the day of a train strike, and later in the crowded queue for the phone, before either of them possessed a cell phone—she had struck him as rather fey, something to be protected. On that first meeting, she had been wearing a black coat with the collar pulled up around her ears. He had noticed her thin wrists and pale skin. She had been shivering. He had bought her coffee, and that had been the beginning.

She had hardly spoken about her work at first. Indeed, it would be quite fair to say that she had kept it from him. She had said that she worked at Bergens, and let him imagine that she was some sort of receptionist. She seemed exactly like that; some girl from the suburbs who was good at looking attractive and being polite. He liked her modesty.

She had barely a word to say about herself; they spent most of their first few times together talking about him. She would draw him out; it was not that he wanted to monopolize the conversation. But then, he had seen her do that with other people, clients. She would let them speak and glean whatever she wanted from them in the process. She was a careful, pragmatic listener. And when you had finished talking, she would know all about you. And you would know nothing of her. Or very little.

That had been the attraction for him in the start. She had struck him as unknowable, distant. The princess in the tower. He supposed that he had barely given her any credit; he had been flattered by her intense gaze, her questions. He courted her. An old-fashioned word. But he liked it all. This quiet girl. Buying her roses. Her face had absolutely flooded with pleasure when he had given them to her that one time. She wasn't used to being looked after; she had been alone since her parents died. She had gone through university alone.

For some reason—it turned out to be inaccurate—he had imagined that this was the same as his loneliness, the withdrawal he had experienced because he didn't want to be near his mother. Not wanting to be near, and not actually being near at all—he had thought it was the same thing. Alone for the same kind of reasons.

Of course, it wasn't the same at all. He had isolated himself from the incessant amateur dramatics of his mother; Catherine had been separated from a woman she adored. They were both alone, and he had thought they were of the same mind because of it.

He knew within a couple of weeks that she had fallen in love with him.

"I can't think why," he had told a colleague at the time.

The woman had smiled at him. "You're a handsome chap," she had said. "Very clever. Very reliable, Robert. Women like that."

Had Catherine liked that? Perhaps. Everything had been all right at first. It was only after six months or so that he realized—a realization that had a terrible misgiving in it—that Catherine was much more than he had supposed. That the fey and fairylike exterior he had fantasized about actually hid a vein of steel. She was fixed and intent. She knew what she wanted. She was deeply a part of her job; she was visual, she had a perfect memory.

And it was then—probably just then, just before they were married—that he had realized that he had not paid enough attention, while Catherine was paying so much. He had gone on in his straight line, doing his work, being a dependable partner, earning a vast salary that he thought she admired, when it had hit him, quite suddenly, that Catherine was his equal. More than his equal. For she had something that he did not and would never possess.

It was not, in fact, a quality that he envied.

She gave everything. She handed her whole self to him, to the whole steadily growing edifice of their being a couple. She gave it concentration. She wanted to get to the heart of him. And he felt that acutely, as if he were under some insidious form of attack.

He suddenly realized that this was a woman who would inhabit him, colonize him, turn him over to her rule. She would want to *know*. She would want to *see*. And it was this curious, persistent, undermining *seeing* that he couldn't stand. He resented it hugely. More than resented it, in fact. He feared it. He feared handing himself over to her. He feared her intensity. And the very thing that had first drawn him in began to repel him.

He had told himself that fact too late, when they were by then married, had been married a couple of months: he recognized that she would always want what he didn't want to give. There would always be some way in which he would not defer to her. She would always feel herself held at arm's length. He couldn't help it; he did not even really feel that it was his fault.

He felt, if he were perfectly honest about it, that he had been artfully suckered into giving, or being asked to give, what he would not relinquish. He felt that she had somehow lied to him.

There had been one night when they had been sitting together—there was nothing remarkable about that night, he had said nothing, they had only been sitting together, each reading a book—when she had looked at him with such a glance. More than loving; it was a look of complete happiness, of utter happiness. A smile like that ought not to worry anyone—it sounded odd, now, to say that it could—but it had done just that, worried him like hell. That surrendered, complete abdication of herself. That amazing ability. He knew he'd never master it. He'd never feel it. More important, he would never want to feel it. To give yourself over like that. It made his blood run cold.

He thought of her like one of her paintings, one of those detailed Victorian canvases, the large ones that she knew so much about. The ones with a whole host of characters. She admired painters that had devoted so much care to such detail. He hated them. He hated the very idea that one person would consume another like that, every particle of her, each inch of cloth, every fleck of skin, every strand of hair. And paint the patterns of the carpets under her feet, and the flowers on the wallpaper behind her head, and the reflection in the glass that she held in her hands. It was almost cannibalistic, this greed to precisely replicate another human being.

Sighing, he got up off the bed and began to take off his travel-stained clothes. He folded the suit jacket and the trousers, putting them aside carefully for dry cleaning. Then he walked to the shower and spent several minutes standing under the hot water, feeling the pounding of the needlelike stream on his shoulders and back. He put his head under the hot water and let it douse his face. And all the time she was in his head, in the pictures that played there.

He had seen his mother the previous weekend; felt that he ought to at least see her once, take her out once, now that he was down here. He had offered to take her to tea at Fortnum's, but had got little thanks for his trouble.

The moment that his mother had sat down she was complaining. "Jesus Christ," Eva had muttered, rolling her eyes in the direction of a group of young women at a neighboring table, who were laughing loudly. "It all gets worse."

He had ordered tea. His mother had sat back in the chair. She was wearing a rather absurd fifties-style shirtwaister with voluminous skirts.

"I remember that dress," he told her.

"It's like me," she had said. "Moth-eaten."

Above them the ceiling fans whirred. Their noise and movement increased Robert's sense of disjointedness with the afternoon. He was not where he wanted to be, even now, even after all his efforts to break free. He realized with dulled disgust that he would probably never break free of his mother, and through her, his wife. Both of them clinging to him like webs.

As if reading his thought of Catherine, Eva spoke up. "Have you left her finally?" she asked.

"Yes."

"Good," Eva commented. "She was no fun at all."

He couldn't look at her. Eva had taken a long sip of her tea. "Paintings," she said. "All she ever talked about. I should like a bit more than that, myself."

"A bit more than that?" Robert asked.

"A bit of fun," Eva said. "Like your father and I had." She smiled to herself and fingered the material of the dress. "Nine years in Singapore," she mused. "A party every night. Every hour a happy hour. That was when the British knew how to live."

He had stared at her, at her cruelty and selfishness. At her cruelty now over Catherine. At the elaborate necklace she wore, which he had given her for Christmas. It had originally been a gift for Catherine, a surprise. Until the realization had come to him that he was going to leave her, and the giving of such a necklace suddenly seemed absurd.

Seeing his mother wearing it now was uncomfortable, as if she were wearing a trophy of her daughter-in-law's demise.

Getting out of the shower now, he suddenly heard his cell phone ringing.

He walked back to the bedroom and picked it up, expecting to hear his office returning his earlier message.

"Hello," said a female voice. "Remember me?"

He knew it, but he couldn't place it. "I'm sorry . . . ?"

"It's Helen," she said. "Helen Brigham."

He raised his eyebrows. He had taken Helen Brigham to the station the other day, and given her this number when she had wondered if the train would run on time. She had seemed so distracted that he had reassured her that he would help her if she were stranded; although what exactly he could have done, staying in a local hotel, or why Helen Brigham wouldn't have rung her own brother, had not occurred to him until afterward.

"Hello," he said now, still puzzled.

"Well," she said. "I'm standing on Cheapside and I'm looking down Bransgore Street. Which number are you?"

He paused. She was here in London. But then she did live somewhere to the east.

"Is there a problem?" he asked.

"No," she said. "But I need to talk to you." There was a pause. "If that's convenient."

"Yes," he said. "Of course. Yes." And he gave her the number of the flat.

Five minutes later, she knocked on the door. He stepped back to admit her and led her into the tiny sitting room. "A drink?" he asked.

"A glass of wine would be nice," she said.

He brought it from the kitchen a few moments later. She held up her glass in a joking gesture of celebration, to clink his. "What shall we drink to?" she asked.

"I've no idea," he said.

"Life and its strange twists," she said. "Life as a footnote."

"I'm sorry," he said. "A what?"

"A footnote," she repeated. "You know, the little bits they put as a backstop to text. A sort of afterthought."

"Why would you think of yourself as a footnote?" he asked, perplexed.

"Don't you?" she asked. "Left behind while they move on."

"Are you talking about Catherine?" he asked.

"Yes. Catherine."

"But she didn't leave me behind," he said. "I left her."

Helen lowered her glass of wine, which was already half empty. She considered him. "You left her," she repeated. "Why was that?"

He frowned. She smiled.

"She's living with my brother," Helen said. "I would like to know what sort of person she is."

Robert took in the information "living with my brother" slowly. He took a drink of his own wine. "What difference does it make?" he said. "They're both adults."

"She's very young," Helen commented.

He thought about it. Catherine was three years younger than he was; this woman, conversely, was probably six or seven years older than him, nearing forty. Although it was hard to be sure. She looked very pale. Her hands were veined, the skin dry, the knuckles unpleasantly prominent. If she was coming home from work, he thought, she was dressed in a very casual manner: jeans, T-shirt, sandals. He noticed that her feet looked dirty, as if she had been walking a long way. And the jeans, too, were not very clean. She looked like some sort of aging child. Rather sad, too; he had seen that the other day as she sat beside him in the car.

He realized that he had been inspecting her, and blushed a little.

"Is she good at her job?" Helen asked. "This . . . art appraising. This auction business."

"Yes," he said.

"Does she specialize?"

"Yes. Victorian things."

"Paintings?"

"And sculpture."

Helen Brigham stood up. She put down her drained glass, walked to the window, and gazed at the office space visible below them.

"Is there a problem?" he asked.

He realized, then, that she was crying. There was a second of frustration—exactly that, not sympathy, but frustration that she should come here and burden him with it—before he walked over to her.

"Can I do anything?" he asked. "What is the matter?"

She had her hands over her face. "She'll take it from me," she whispered. "It's all I have for the future."

"Take what?"

She dropped her hands. "Does she have any money?" she asked suddenly.

He was lost for words. Helen had been to the auction rooms. She had heard Mark Pearson say that Catherine was a partner in the business.

"You see," she said, "I have to protect my brother from fortune hunters."

Robert laughed out loud, taken by surprise.

"It isn't a joke," she said.

"I'm sorry," he told her. "But I don't think you need to be worried. Catherine wouldn't be interested in that sort of thing."

She made a disbelieving, sardonic face. "Everyone is, at some level or another. Everybody wants what they can get."

"No," he replied. "Not Catherine. It wouldn't occur to her."

"It might," Helen said. "If she found something worth keeping."

She turned away. She crossed her arms over her chest, hugging herself rather than crossing them.

"Did you ask your brother this?" he said.

She shook her head. "It's very hard to explain. He would think I was overreacting. You see, I asked him a while ago . . ." She paused, putting the knuckle of one fist to her forehead, and rubbing the skin. "I think it was last week," she murmured. "I asked him . . . I am worried . . . I can't sleep . . . I needed money . . ."

Robert felt embarrassed. He could see the tears slowly descending, tears that seemed to have more life than the papery skin beneath them. "I'm sure that he wouldn't deny you help," he said.

She glanced at him. "He wouldn't?" she asked, as if Robert had more access to John's motives than she did. "He wouldn't keep it back, because of her?"

"I don't know your brother," he reminded her.

"Neither do I," she said. "I don't know anyone anymore." And she dissolved into real sobs. There was nothing he could reasonably do but put his arms around her. "You can't trust anyone," she said, her voice muffled against his shoulder. Then she raised her face to his. "Isn't that true?"

"I don't know," he said, disconcerted by the desperate expression on her face.

"Did you love her?" she said. "And she loved you? Once, I mean. You loved her once, and she loved you?"

"Yes," he said, feeling uncomfortably that it was not quite the truth.

Helen Brigham's fingers tightened around his upper arm. "But you can't trust that," she whispered. "Not even that."

She moved her hand up his arm, along his shoulder, and then pressed her mouth to his. He was taken aback; yielded for a second or two to the insistent pressure, was almost tempted to respond; until he felt her fingers exploring his face and the intimacy of it jolted him backward. For a moment he caught sight of her, eyes closed, mouth slightly open. Something about the fleshiness of the mouth, the slightly stale smell of her, had suddenly overwhelmed him. She opened her eyes.

"I'm sorry," he said. She looked disoriented. "Come and sit down." She did so, looking intently at him.

"Are you all right?" he asked. Because it seemed to him that there was patently something not right about this situation, about this woman, but he couldn't fathom what it was.

"Yes," she said. "I'm all right."

"Do you think," he ventured, "that perhaps you should go and see your brother and talk this over with him?" He cast about for something positive to add, some piece of useful advice. "And perhaps Catherine," he added.

"You want me to go and see Catherine?"

"To set your mind at rest."

"You want me to go and see your wife and my brother," she repeated.

"It's only a suggestion."

"Can't you help me?" she asked.

He was thoroughly confused now. He felt that he wanted to wash the taste of her from his face, but couldn't think of a reason to excuse himself. "I'm sorry?" he said. "But with what?"

"Can't you speak to Catherine?" She put her hand on his knee.

"To say what? . . . I don't understand. What would you want me to say to her?" He moved slightly back on the couch, gently disengaging himself from her reach.

She saw the movement and abruptly stood up. "I can see you don't want me here," she told him.

"Helen, I—"

"I'm sorry to have wasted your time." He tried once again to speak: she held up her hand to stop him. She went to the door and paused there, hand on the latch. He hesitated at her back, embarrassed and dismayed.

She looked back at him. "You talk to Catherine," she said softly. "You talk to your wife, and you tell her." She stopped, inspecting him, his expression. "Are you listening to me?"

"Yes," he said.

She opened the door. For a second, she paused on the threshold, one hand lingeringly caressing the other, stroking the back of her own hand, smoothing her own fingers and wrist and forearm.

"I'll talk to her," he promised.

She looked down at her arms, and then slowly around herself at the almost empty, anonymous room.

"Tell her to keep away," she murmured. "From my brother."

Songe de la Fantasie

1864

Richard Dadd was transferred to Broadmoor Hospital, a purpose-built criminal asylum in Berkshire, on July 23, 1864.

He had been in Bedlam for almost twenty years.

They had anticipated that there may have been some difficulty in persuading Dadd to move, even from his familiar cell. But he had taken the news calmly, almost without reaction, and spent several days filling the portmanteau that had been given to him, asking for small lengths of cotton in which to roll his paintbrushes, and that he also used to wrap his volumes of poetry.

Brigham had noticed that on the morning of the day of departure, when he went earlier than usual to check his charges, Dadd was sitting on his bed, with a book open on his lap.

The painter looked utterly benign. It was hard to believe that he was a fantasist, a schizophrenic, a murderer. Dadd was forty-seven years old, and yet he looked very much older. He bore little resemblance now to the photograph that had been taken of him only five years previously. After his prolonged weeks of grief he had finally relented to let his image be recorded, and had been shown at his easel, working on his painting Oberon and Titania; an imposing man, broad and bulky, his eye fixed on the photographer and not the lens. His hair had been still dark then, *with only a few traces of gray. Now he looked as if shock had overtaken him. His hair was almost completely white.*

The physician's opinion was that Dadd had reached a sudden—if delayed—acquiescence to his circumstances. After his photograph had been taken, Dadd no longer raged, or took to violence, even of argument. He is improved in temper, *his notes ran.* Though still holding his old convictions.

"What are you reading?" Brigham had asked him that last morning in London.

"Resolution and Independence," *Dadd said, holding out the book.*

Brigham read the page out loud. "William Wordsworth. My whole life I have lived in pleasant thought . . ." *He smiled.* "Well, sir, there's an idea for you."

"My old remembrances went from me wholly, and all the ways of men," *Dadd read.*

"Well, that is good. Old remembrances are no use to us, sir."

"Are they not," Dadd murmured. He picked up the last piece of cotton sheet, closed the book, wrapped it, and held it to his chest.

They brought the carriage that was to take Dadd and four other inmates at eleven o'clock.

Dadd was silent until he reached the last flight of stairs and could see the patch of yard, and the rims of the wheels, and the horse's hooves on the brick driveway. He held on to the handrail and stopped.

"We'll move on now," Brigham said. "Last few steps now, sir."

But Dadd would not move. Tears were in his eyes; as he stood rooted to the spot, they began to fall. Slow, heavy tears.

"There's nothing to be frightened of," Brigham said. "Come, sir. There's a fine new building waiting for you at the other end. A fine view of woodland. And there are terraces to walk upon. It is a better place than here, Mr. Dadd."

"I have had to leave it," Dadd whispered.

"That's right, sir," the man encouraged. "That's right. You must go."

Dadd turned to him. The tears were splashing on the fustian jacket. It was the same one that Dadd had worn twenty years before when he had been admitted. "You will have it," he said.

"Have what, sir?"

"The canvas they will not let me take."

There were more than forty paintings in the locked storeroom next to the physician's office.

"You have seen me working on it," Dadd said.

The attendant nodded. He took out his own handkerchief and wiped Dadd's face. Suddenly, Dadd started searching in his pockets. He took out a piece of paper. "I wish to write," he said.

"There's no time," Brigham said. "The driver is waiting. You must take the train in forty minutes."

"Give me a pencil," Dadd said.

Looking into his face, Brigham felt nothing but pity. What a life wasted, he thought. He had sat and watched him many times working on his drawings. Sometimes Dadd would spend all day producing a little thing, a face, a hand, a branch of leaves. And then, at the end of the day, he would screw the paper and throw it away. The attendant had picked up many of them. He kept them at home, carefully smoothed out and held flat under a traveling trunk that his wife filled with linen. One or two had got damp, and the children had taken some; but he still had a good number. He had got an affection for the peculiar chap; he thought his drawings very fine, even if he threw them away. Sometimes in the morning, if the man had had a poor night, Brigham would sit with him and listen to the horrors that had inhabited the dark.

He took a stub of pencil out of his own jacket and gave it. Dadd scribbled hurriedly for a few seconds. He handed the note to him.

"You take this, Edward," he said, using the attendant's Christian name for the first time. "You give that to Mr. Neville and tell him that it is to be seen to." His hand closed on his wrist. "You take it for me," he said. "You have been kindness itself to me. You are a fine stirring fellow. You are Polyphemus."

"Indeed, I am not, sir."

"From the idylls of Theocritus, the lover of Galatea."

"I don't doubt it. But I am not he, sir."

"It has taken me nine years," Dadd said. "It is called The Fairy Feller's Master-Stroke. I have nothing else to give you."

The attendant smiled. "I cannot take that, sir," he said, "for you have given it already to Mr. Haydon."

Dadd stared at him, baffled. "The Master-Stroke?" he repeated.

"Yes, sir."

Dadd shook his head. He looked down the stairs, to the splashes of sunlight dancing on the road. "I shall paint you another," he said. "I shall paint you a copy. And you must have some of the others that they have here."

"It doesn't matter, sir."

"Oh, yes," Dadd murmured, pressing his fingertip into the center of the piece of paper that he had already put into the attendant's hand. "I shall certainly paint you another, Mr. Brigham."

The carriage pulled out of the yard. It rattled slowly down the long driveway and out into Lambeth Road, toward the oldest settlements of London, at Lambeth Palace.

At first the blinds were closed, pulled down so that the patients would not be disturbed; but after less than a mile, it was thought that the noise from outside, which could not be drowned or lessened, was more disturbing if no sights accompanied it. And so the blinds were raised, and Richard Dadd saw London for the first time in two decades.

They went down to the river, to Westminster Bridge. It was thought that the horse ferry across at Lambeth would be too slow, and so they passed in a roaring slew of carts, carriages, and foot passengers over the span. Halfway across, Dadd leaned forward, looking to his left-hand side.

"What has happened to Westminster Palace?" he asked.

"It is burned down," he was told. "They are rebuilding it. There will be a great clock tower on the bridge."

Dadd stared at the half-raised Pugin and Barry edifice, hidden behind its scaffolding, on which men were antlike dots working between the beams. He saw the empty gaps of windows, the horses drawn up with loads, dozing in the midmorning heat. Dust drifted across the Thames, the surface of which, muddy and churning, was clogged with every kind of river traffic.

The carriage turned right, along Horse Guards; left again along the Mall and Constitution Hill. Dadd showed no interest in the street to the right of them, Pall Mall, where he had first exhibited at the British Institution, a young man of twenty-two, a coming talent, a genius, a person to be courted. Only two years later he would produce Titania Sleeping and Puck, both bought by Henry Farrer, when Henry Farrer was the dealer with the most commercial eye, and forecast great things, a place in the public eye, fame and fortune. But all that past had vanished; Henry Farrer would not recognize Dadd now.

The carriage emerged onto Hyde Park Corner, where the traffic ground to a halt. There was some sort of hold-up along the road; the driver called down that they could not pass. After ten minutes or so, one of the attendants got out and negotiated a pass for them along the Serpentine Road through Hyde Park, people shrinking back to let them through.

Dadd sat forward on the edge of his seat for the first time. He had drawn the Serpentine, that sinuous stretch of water, more than once. He caught sight of the Long Water and, beyond it, the pretty little dogcarts and broughams passing along West Carriage Drive. He blinked rapidly; his sight was not what it had been. He had been looking for too long at paint only six inches from his eye. He simply could not focus on the rolling waterfalls of color. Two children were running alongside the carriage, each with a handful of gravel, which they were throwing at the wheels; he tried to lean out of the window to look at them, at the liveliness in their faces. He was pulled back, into the shade.

They passed out of the Marlborough Gate and into the morass of traffic again; the green was left behind; ahead, new buildings shone white, faced with Isle of Portland stone. Beside himself, Dadd began to breathe *heavily; the impact was too much. Yet he had to remember. It was all he would see before he was locked away for the rest of his life. It was all he would have to paint. He must remember the way it looked, so much busier than before, so many more people. He must remember. It would vanish in a matter of minutes. He tried to place the perspective of the sky against the city, the people against the pavements, the jolting motion of the broughams, the fluttering of pale dresses of the women within them, the dancing of horses' movements, the writhing blocks of humanity in the street; it almost choked him.*

And sound more than anything: the wall of voices, the echo of the trees and water, the hollowness of the park, the stagnation of the street, the blackening circles of the chimes of churches . . .

They were at the railway station. Dadd was given a small cup of water, in which was dissolved drops of laudanum. He was helped down the steps and out into the baying mass of Paddington, into Brunel's massive terminus for the Great Western Railway, running from London to Bristol: a hugely vaulted iron-girder roof with decorative iron ribs, held up by cast-iron columns.

The noise now was more than mere volume; it was a living monster of sound, another Bedlam. Men dragged luggage on wheeled carts; racks of leather, bands of brown. The iron wheels of the luggage carts assaulted him, smothered him, the awful metallic clanging of them next to him as he was half walked, half dragged, beside the train. Dadd dared not look up at it; already the glittering windows, the brass on the finishing, the open sash glass where here and there a body hung out, calling to him, waving at whatever was behind him, laughing, had frightened him beyond belief.

Dadd tried to look upward instead, disoriented and nauseous: he had never traveled by train. The sight of the engine at the front, on the very point where the track began to curve, out into the light, sent him into a paroxysm of terror.

He was bundled through the smoke and steam; they were late, the train was about to leave. Strangers sidestepped him and grimaced. He could not bear it. The world was a blazing star; he had been swept up in switching parallels of light, of dark. The crowd howled at him; he moaned as he was bodily hauled into the belly of the beast, and sat in the corner of the allotted space, shivering, weeping, his hands over his face.

When he reached Broadmoor, Dadd showed no interest in his new private room; no interest in his belongings that were brought to him. Even a violin had been purchased and was waiting for him on a little writing table.

It was remarked upon that he was quiet and peaceable with his fellow patients; but the diagnosis did not touch him. It was not calm at all. It was retreat. It was indifference to the ordinary world. He was an exile.

In time, he was roused to sit up, and dress himself, and eat. He sat with others, in the day rooms, hands folded in his lap or placed exactly on his knees. He said very little, because he knew that he could not communicate what he knew, or that it would not be accepted. Life did not exist in what his senses told him, in what was received in the lies of sight and hearing.

The real world, a thing of beauty, had to be guarded, he knew; shut up firmly against its parody. The real world existed not outside himself but inside, gifted to him by old gods. The real world vibrated under glass; he could hold a magnifier to the paper, and see it. Just the smallest slender door through to that world, the real world hidden in the invisible grains of cotton and wood, flattened and processed into paper and canvas. The real world hid there, in between the strands of fabric and grass. Somewhere deep in its heart was the truth.

He sat next to the window, with its view of the woodland, but he did not look out at all.

He kept his promise. He painted a copy of The Fairy Feller's Master-Stroke, *for Edward Brigham.*

And called it Songe de la Fantasie, *his place of safety.*

22

It was ten o'clock in the morning when Catherine found him.

John was sitting in a corridor outside the cardiac care unit, his cell phone in his lap. In the process of dialing a number, he suddenly stopped when he saw her walking toward him.

She halted in front of him. Her expression was one of frustrated fury. "Peter Luckham told me," she said. "He rang and asked how much longer he should look after Frith."

John switched off the phone.

"You weren't going to tell me?" she said. "Nothing? *Nothing?*"

He looked up at her. She was flushed and out of breath from running. "I have to wait to hear from somebody else," she said. "I have to have Peter ring me! How could you!"

"I'm sorry," he said. "The last time I saw you—"

"You've been in the hospital two days, and Peter Luckham gets to tell me." She spread her hands in appeal. Almost to herself she muttered, "God, *God.*" And to him, "You really thought that I wouldn't want to know this?"

"Catherine," he told her, "you said you would ring me. When you didn't ring . . ."

"I know what I said," she whispered. "I know what I said." She was beginning to catch her breath; she looked up and down the corridor. "What are you doing sitting out here?" she asked abruptly.

"I'm about to leave."

"They're letting you go? Have they finished?" she asked. "What tests have they done? What did they say?"

"Catherine," he said. "This is something and nothing."

"Peter said you rang an ambulance two nights ago!"

"Yes, I did."

"When, exactly?"

"About three in the morning."

"After you came to see me, that same night?"

"Yes."

"Oh, God," she repeated, more softly now. "And that's something and nothing, I suppose?" She shook her head and passed a hand over her eyes. "You could have just picked up the phone to me. You think I'd not try to help you? What, that when I finally heard"—there was a flash of sarcasm—"I wouldn't give a damn?"

"I didn't know if you'd want to hear from me."

She gave a gasp, and tears came to her eyes. "You fool," she said. "You bloody, bloody idiot." He stood up, still unsure of her. She looked away from him, collecting herself. "Look, if nothing else, tell me. What have they said? What have they told you?"

He looked away up the hall.

"Aren't you going to say?" she asked. "What is this, a state secret or something? Tell me!"

"It's angina," he replied.

"Angina," she repeated. "Like . . . what, stress?"

"Not really."

"What then?" He didn't reply. She saw the small valise at his feet. "Is this yours?"

"Peter brought it."

She sat down next to him, two seats away, and twisted in the chair so that she faced him. "John," she said. "Please tell me what they said."

He was trying not to give in to the relief and fear that had dominated the past forty-eight hours. He always felt so horribly vulnerable in a hospital ward. He just wanted to go home—had made himself very popular this morning, in fact, demanding to be discharged. In the end he had signed a form to say that he was discharging himself. They had put him here to wait for the refilled medication.

He tried not to look into Catherine's face directly.

"Intractable angina," he told her.

She shook her head, repeating and whispering the words to herself. "I don't know what that means."

"It's . . ." he paused, looking down at his hands, massaging the fingers of his left hand with his right. "I've had it some time."

"You have?" she said, aghast. "Since getting back to England?"

"Before that."

"But for how long?"

"Several years."

She was scanning his face closely. "Is that why you came back?"

"Mostly."

She looked down at his hands, following the persistent movement. "All the time since I met you?" she asked. "All the time I've known you?"

"Yes."

She stared at him, horrified, trying to take it in. "But you could have an operation, surely?" she said. "Something to help. There's loads that they do, isn't there?"

"I had an angioplasty in Spain," he told her. "But the condition's called refractory angina."

"A bypass," she said. "You could have one of those? Somebody I used to work with knew someone who had a bypass. He had diabetes, but it worked like magic."

John still hadn't looked at her. "You can't operate on this kind," he said. "Some people called it stubborn angina, and that's what it is. Fucked-up angina. You put a stent in one place to open up the flow, and it closes down somewhere else."

She tried to take it in. "I've never even seen you take a single tablet."

"I have beta blockers, calcium blockers. I used to take statins. Sotalol. I still take nitrates."

There was a long silence. She looked him up and down, baffled at his offhand attitude. She had heard of beta blockers. Not statins. Not Sotalol. She couldn't even guess what they might be. Over John's head, a luridly colored poster on the wall extolled the virtues of exercise and healthy eating. It wasn't as if he were overweight, she thought. He didn't smoke. It didn't make any sense.

A volunteer passed with a trolley of drinks and turned into a side ward. They listened to her talking to the patients, a good-humored banter passing back and forth.

"What did you think I would do?" Catherine asked him. "Why didn't you tell me all this? Did you think that I would run off, leave you, what? Did you think I couldn't grasp it or something? That I wouldn't understand?"

"I don't think about it," he said. "I hate these places. I hate the whole subject. That's why I didn't tell you. I just don't think about it."

"It's not a good enough explanation," she said. "It's rubbish."

"It's my problem," he said.

"Well, thanks," she replied. "For that vote of confidence."

She looked up the corridor. The ward sister was walking toward them, holding a pharmacy package. She gave Catherine a little nod of acknowledgment and handed the parcel to John. "I don't suppose that I need to tell you about these," she said.

He stood up. "No."

"You need to come back to see the consultant."

"Yes, all right."

"I rang his secretary," the nurse continued. "She said you didn't attend last week."

Catherine looked accusingly at John.

"I will," he said. "Thanks."

They walked out, he holding the door open for her. It was a blustery day, clouds scudding across a patchy blue sky. On the hospital steps, John took a deep breath, stowing the medication in the pocket of his jacket.

"I'll give you a lift," Catherine said.

"I can get a taxi," he said. "I was about to ring one when you arrived."

"You bloody won't," she said.

He started to walk away. She watched him for only a moment in astonishment before hurrying after him. "What is it with you?" she demanded.

"Nothing," he said.

"Look at me," she told him. "Look me in the eye. You haven't looked in my face since I got here."

Reluctantly, he did so.

"What is it?" she said.

"I don't want you involved in all this. I'm not such a good bet, Catherine. It's not fair to you."

He turned away and started down the slight slope toward town. He walked with a curious crooked gait, shoulders hunched, as if he were warding off a blow. At the very next junction, he waited while several cars negotiated the narrow entrance into the public parking lot; the last one was a private cab. He hailed it and bent down to talk to the driver.

She ran down the path, snatched his arm, and pulled him away.

"How you bloody dare," she said, "to do this! You're not getting away that easily. You wanted me to live with you, and you wanted me there every moment of the day . . ."

"I thought it was what you wanted," he said.

"It was," she told him. "So what did I do? What was so bad that you shut me out? You can't tell me that you're ill, you can't tell me whatever it is, this thing with Helen, you just . . ." She cast about for the words. "Just cut me off." And she gestured at the taxi driver to drive away.

"I've been alone a long time," John said, as they watched the car go.

"And that's a reason?" she replied angrily. "OK, that *is* a reason. It's a reason to want someone with you, to want to be loved, to never be alone again, not to slam the door in my face."

"I didn't want to load you down with it all," he said. "It's my problem."

She gazed at him, utterly frustrated and confused.

All round them the busy access road moved, awash with people, patients and visitors, delivery trucks. They stood on the corner, a small oasis.

He looked at her, thinking that if he had just one more year, or two years. A man his age might expect twenty-five. What would two years be? It hardly rated as a miracle. Not for a man of fifty. Two years with Catherine. Two years, eight seasons.

Eight seasons with Catherine.

He pressed his mouth tight shut; but it turned down despite him and all his efforts to control it. He could feel himself standing there with a face like a frightened little boy with this clown's-bow grimace of shame. *Fuck it*, he thought. *Don't start crying in front of her.* And he made himself laugh in the same second with the stupidity of it. "Jesus," he muttered. He felt in his pocket for a handkerchief, realized he didn't have one, and closed his fingers inadvertently on the packet of medication.

"So what are you going to do about it?" Catherine asked. "There must be something. Some operation."

He opened his mouth to repeat the constant thread, arteriosclerosis, inoperable refractory angina. Then thought better of it. He hated the words. They were stuck inside his head. He wished that he could somehow climb inside there and get them out. Once heard, never forgotten.

He looked at Catherine and she saw the reply written in his expression. She lost color.

He had asked his GP for a prognosis two months ago.

"You need to rest," he had been told.

"Is there any other treatment?"

"A form of gene therapy is being tried in the U.S. A growth factor injected into the heart."

"Can I get it here?"

"I'll look into it."

They'd regarded each other, John trying to read between the lines of what he'd been told. "Can I walk any distance?" he'd asked.

"Yes, of course."

"How far?"

"However far you feel is OK."

"Play sport?"

"Perhaps not wise."

Well, he wasn't wise. Being wise was as good as being an invalid. It wasn't what he wanted. It was a long, long way from what he wanted. And so he'd worked on the weir gates, hauled the timber into trailers. He had walked four miles one morning before he met Catherine, hoping that, on the frosty day in March, with the first sun through the trees, and the first thin green inches of the bluebells showing above the soil in Derry, while everything looked so promising, so good, the first bright day of the spring, that the nagging, exhausting ache would shut just his heart down there and then. He couldn't be wise and sit and wait. He would rather put a gun to his head and be done with it.

And then Catherine came to the house. And it wasn't an easy decision anymore. It wasn't the same choice. It was no longer a matter of walking the pain down in Derry. He had started a little deal with himself. Take his medication, and not walk too far or do any heavy work anymore. He decided to restore the stairway in the Lodge; a small, intricate job, not too taxing. All the time lying to her by not telling her. He bartered being wise against loving her, and prayed to God that he wouldn't die in bed.

He looked at her now. At her paleness. And felt a shitty, guilty regret.

"I'm a selfish man," he told her. "I wanted you."

She put her arms around his neck.

She didn't cry at all, but her breath was a shallow flutter against his face. After a minute or so, she drew back from him and took her keys out of her bag. "I'll take you home," she murmured.

He took her hand. "Don't take me," he said. "You'd take a sick person. You'd help them. But I don't want your help. I don't want nursing. I just want you to come back to the house with me."

She looked at him, and then nodded. "All right, John," she said. "All right."

23

They had got back to Bridle Lodge at midday. John had got out of the car, unlocked the front door, and walked straight to the alarm panel outside the drawing room. He had turned and looked at Catherine, and held out his hand.

"Come here," he said. "I want to show you."

He'd keyed the alarm; they went in and closed the door behind them.

John went to the desk on the far side near the windows. He opened a drawer and brought out a sheaf of papers.

"These are all the invoices I could find," he said. "I went through it all when I got back from you the other night. They go back about ten years." He looked around himself. "Other things I can guess where I bought them, the time," he said. "But some of them . . . the little bits, some of the Bow porcelain I don't know . . ."

She'd walked over to him. "Let's take it to London," she said. "If you really want to sell, you may as well get the best price you can. And it wouldn't feel quite ethical to put it through Pearsons."

He'd taken her hand in his, lifted it to his face, and pressed his mouth to it.

"Or you can think about it some other time," she said. "If you really want to sell, if it's what you really want to do, there's no hurry . . ."

"Yes, there is," he had replied. "I want all this to go."

She paused a beat. "It's such a lot, John. You'll want to keep some of it."

He'd dropped her hand slowly. "Helen wasn't talking about this when she talked to you about secrets," he told her. "She was talking about something else."

He took her to the window seat and positioned her there, facing into the room. He watched her for a second over his shoulder, then walked back to the center and lifted aside the gateleg table, moving its contents to one of the sideboards. Then, getting down on his hands and knees, he rolled back the edge of the rug. The floor looked smooth; oak floorboards with an almost black patina.

"This took me a hell of a long time," he was saying to her as he got onto his hands and knees. "I almost gave the game away the first day I saw you, talking about lifting floorboards." He began to run his hand over the floor. "I wanted it really invisible," he murmured. "I took up the board and cut it. It was January. Those weeks when it never stopped raining. When I'd eventually made the compartment, the board had expanded. I had to wait until it dried. I put it in the kitchen near the stove . . ."

She was staring at him, mystified.

"Here," he said. He tried prying the board with his fingertips. It wouldn't budge. He got up, cursing softly, went back to the Jacobean chest, and took a small screwdriver from it. Catherine leaned forward, her elbows on her knees.

A few moments later he had removed two boards; from out of the cavity underneath them, he took a metal box. It was about two by three feet and shallow, an architect's steel drawer from a plan chest that had been fitted with a steel lid. It took some maneuvering to get it out and, when he had done so, he laid it flat on the floor in front of her.

"It used to be in the bank."

"What is it?" she asked.

He looked at her and said nothing.

The drawer was divided into two compartments: one small, one large.

He opened the smaller one of the two, and one by one, put plastic file covers on the ground. They were an ordinary letter-size. Inside each folder was a brown paper envelope.

"I've wrapped them in a couple of layers of acid-free," he said.

He stood up and brought the folders to her. There were about twenty, she estimated. Next, from the same drawer, he brought her a pair of cotton gloves. She put them on, her eyes fixed on his.

"Open them," he said.

She laid the pile next to her on the window seat and took out the first. It had words and a date on the left-hand corner, *Night and Day, 1864.* She gave a sharp intake of breath, and looked back at him.

"Open it," he repeated.

She took out the acid-free paper, and the drawing wrapped inside it.

A penciled sketch lay in her lap. The half-circle, looking like the template for a stone carving or plinth, was inscribed on the bottom right-hand corner: *Richard Dadd, 1864.*

"But this is in the Ashmolean," she said softly. "They bought it just before the war."

"This is a copy," he told her. "Dadd made a copy."

She stared at it for some seconds in astonishment, then looked at the pile of folders next to her. He held out his hand to take the first; wordlessly, she picked up the next one and opened it.

"*Port Stragglin,*" she said. "Oh, my God."

She had written a seminar paper once on this watercolor. It had been painted in 1861. On the original, Dadd had written a poignant inscription, *General View of Part of Port Stragglin—The Rock and Castle of Seclusion / and the Blinker Lighthouse in the Distance / not sketched from Nature.*

She turned the envelope over again and looked at the date on the outside, *1865.* "He redrew them?" she murmured.

"Everything he had to leave behind in Bedlam," John said. "Or gave to anyone else."

She looked again at the drawing. "Not sketched from Nature," she murmured. "He used to draw such beautiful things, his flowers and trees, like pre-Raphaelite paintings, or Surrealist . . . and that phrase, 'not sketched from Nature,' because he was out of sight of a garden . . ." She shook her head.

She held up the drawing. "I always thought this was perfect," she said. "The rock and the town, the ships in the harbor, everything perfectly done. The chimneys on the houses, the rigging on the ships. The towers that follow the road up the rock. When you first look at it, it's impossible. Nowhere on earth is made like that. To get a whole world like that on a little piece of paper just seven inches by . . . I don't remember, seven by four inches?"

"Five," John said.

She shook her head. "So this is exact," she said.

"Exactly the same size."

She sat back. "My hands are shaking," she said. She closed her eyes for a second. "This is what you were talking about, this is what Helen wants."

"No," he said. "She hates them. She wants to sell them. She wants the money."

"And she thinks I want to sell them, too," Catherine murmured. She frowned suddenly. "You're not going to?"

He was watching her. "What do you think?"

"Well, this alone . . ." she hesitated. "What would they make, if you sold them? I don't know . . . it's impossible to say. Ten thousand? Twenty, thirty? They never come on the market. I think the British Museum has the original of this. There are some private owners," she continued, thinking aloud. "In America. There's one in Connecticut . . . the Tate has some, and the Victoria and Albert Museum . . ." She looked back at the drawing, and again at John. "But mostly," she said, "when you see a catalogue, it just says, 'Whereabouts unknown.'

There might be a picture, a copy, or a photograph taken years ago, but no one . . ." She took a breath. "No one knows where they are now," she said. "They vanished."

John had replaced the first drawing in its envelope.

She gazed at him. "John, how many have you got?"

Not answering, he inclined his head toward the next folder. She opened it.

It was *Mother and Child*. "Oh, God," she whispered.

"It's the clothes," John said. "The incredible folds. Just too much material, and too much shadow."

"And the bird in the background," she said, smiling hesitantly now. "Such a strange, strange bird, with its puffed-out feathers." She turned her head to one side, looking carefully at it. "It's peculiar to see it so small," she said.

"He almost miniaturized this one."

"It's quite a big painting," she said. "Oil on canvas. It came up for sale in the 1950s."

"The 1960s," he said.

She glanced from one to the other. "How could he remember them all?" she wondered. "Everything's the same. Every single thing in them. It's as if they've been photocopied."

She sat in silence for a while.

He took *Mother and Child* and gave her the next.

Within ten minutes, she had picked them up, taken them to the empty table, and spread them out on the top. John said nothing else, waiting. Only after some time did she turn and look at the metal container.

"There's nothing else?" she asked.

"I have eighteen paintings," he said. "And fourteen miniatures on enamel."

She said nothing. She didn't move.

"*The Child's Problem*," he said, "*Bacchanalian Scene, Cupid and Psyche, The Pilot Boat, The Flight of Medea* . . ."

"Oh, shit," she said. "John."

He stopped, then burst out laughing. "That's not an academic response, Mrs. Sergeant."

"Oh, yes it is," she retorted. "You've got a copy of *Bacchanalian Scene*, in miniature?"

"Yes."

"On enamel . . ."

"He tried out all sorts of things in Broadmoor," John said. "He painted a drop-curtain for the theater, and scenery for their plays, and lanterns, and he engraved glass . . ."

Catherine had gone back to the window. She stood with a hand over her mouth for a long time, gazing at the garden. Then she turned back to him.

"Eighteen paintings," she said.

"Yes."

"Copies?"

He smiled at her. "You're doing a great job of keeping calm," he said.

"Copies or not?" she repeated.

He went to the metal container and opened the larger compartment. He took out a canvas bag.

"These were always rolled," he said. "My father said they were never framed. So . . ." He paused while he pulled the drawstring of the canvas. "Some have cracks. They all need attention. They need restoring and frames and . . ."

He pulled a painting from the bag and held it out to her.

"What is it?" she asked.

"Unroll it."

The first thing she noticed, in all the other faces, was the magician.

Dominating the center of the picture, he sat with his arms outstretched.

Catherine gasped, then leaned forward. She looked hard at the magician's face, and then back at John.

"He's different," she said. "Look at this . . . look at him."

She got up from the seat, tilting the painting so that it caught the light. Her eye ran over the whole. It was like *Songe de la Fantasie*, in that some of the flowers were in bloom where they had only been in bud, or were invisible altogether, in the original painting. The grassheads that trailed across the picture now were in seed, their minute petals open.

"They're all different," she murmured. "Every one of them."

The Fairy Queen of *The Fairy Feller's Master-Stroke* was standing directly above the magician, and now looked out of the picture, instead of turning her profile to her partner. The dragonfly trumpeter now was walking straight for the viewer, wings outspread. Every face in the picture was looking straight out, some with the fixed stares of *Bacchanalia*, others merely curious.

Catherine's fingertip brushed the two girls at the magician's side. John had come to her side.

She dropped the painting slightly and stared at him. "It's you," she whispered. "The magician is you."

He glanced at the portrait. Even the colors were changed; the grays of the original had become powder blue, the ground under the Feller's feet was bright yellow. The people in the picture were flourishing, growing, moving. There was light in their eyes; it was as if the artist had caught them in the act of dancing, running; the skirts of the girl with the mirror floated outward, her feet were lifted. She was flying, for a moment, on the wings that extended from her shoulder blades.

"Look in the mirror," John said.

It was her. It was Catherine's face. Someone else was leaping out of the reflection, close enough in coloring and dress to be the girl who held the glass, but not close enough. She was someone else. She was someone transcending the mirror, passing through it.

Catherine didn't take her eyes off the painting. "This is what you meant," she said. "When you told me to look at the girl in the mirror, you meant that you had seen this. You had seen who was in the mirror."

"You," he said. "That's what I couldn't get over when I first saw you. You're in the mirror. He saw you in the mirror and painted you."

She looked at him. "You're serious."

"Of course I'm serious," he said. "Why not? He saw other worlds, vast enough to be *Port Stragglin*, and so small that even today you'd have to find them with a magnifying lens."

"But it's impossible," Catherine replied.

John stepped so that he was behind the painting she held, looking straight at her. "Of course it is," he said. "But then again, is anything truly impossible? Where are the boundaries?"

"You cannot seriously believe that he saw me," she said.

He paused. "No, I can't say that I believe it," he answered. "But I believe he saw a version of the world, something that runs alongside us. Another reality." He nodded at the painting. "They used to call them fairy pictures," he said. "As if they showed something that wasn't actually there, wasn't alive. But"—he shrugged—"there were people all over the world saying that they saw these images, just as he did. A whole industry grew up on the back of paintings like this. It was the fashion for years."

"But they didn't really exist," Catherine said.

"Maybe not," John told her. "And you can look at a picture like this, and say that nothing that Richard Dadd painted really existed. After all, what was he? A madman. A man locked up for most of his adult life. A man who could take a knife to his father's throat and think for the rest of his life that he had done the right thing. A man who heard voices . . ."

"But you think it existed?" Catherine said.

John smiled. "If you're asking if I believe in fairies . . ."

She smiled back. "You do."

"No," John said. "But I believe that someone like Dadd knew a world we couldn't begin to imagine. What's to say what's living in that world? Right next door to us. Right inside us, the things we never acknowledge, or we learn to ignore."

"Otherness," Catherine murmured.

He looked up. "What?"

"The otherness of things," she said. "I've heard it described that way."

He looked down again at the painting. "What else do you see?" he asked.

She was shaking her head rapidly, though slightly, from side to side. "I see your face in the magician," she told him.

"Ah," he told her. "But that's not magic at all."

"Why not?"

"Because this painting was made for my great-grandfather, Edward Brigham."

Her mouth dropped, then a light dawned in her face.

"He was Dadd's attendant in Bedlam," John said. "He looked after Dadd for nine years. And in those nine years, Dadd painted *The Fairy Feller's Master-Stroke*."

"Which he gave to the senior steward at Bedlam, Mr. Haydon, who liked *Oberon and Titania* so much that he asked for something similar."

"And when Dadd got to Broadmoor," John said, "he painted this copy, a copy that isn't a copy, because it's better."

"And put Brigham's face into the picture."

"And yours," John said.

She laughed a little, too amazed to do anything but still stand clutching the painting.

"Don't you think it's a better picture?" he asked.

"I don't know," she said. "I can't really string a coherent thought, John."

"I think it's better," he said. "It's more optimistic."

"I can't think," she murmured. "Take it off me."

He did so; she sat down again abruptly. "This isn't happening," she murmured. She looked around at the table, and at John. "You've got the eighteen watercolors," she said, "And the miniatures, and this, and . . ."

"Eleven others."

"Eleven other oil paintings, in there?"

"Yes."

"Copies of ones I'd know?"

"Five copies. Six originals."

She put a hand to her forehead. "You have six Dadd originals?" she said. "Oils?"

"Yes."

"How do you know?"

"What?"

"How do you know that they're originals? You mean they've never appeared in any catalogues, any references?"

"They're mentioned in his journals of Syria," John replied. "They're all paintings of Egypt, Syria, Greece."

She said nothing at all. She watched as John carefully, slowly, replaced the painting in its weatherproofed canvas.

"They have to be kept better than this," she murmured.

"I know." He stood by the container. "Do you want to see the rest?" he asked.

"Tomorrow," she said. "Can we look at them all tomorrow?"

"OK." He replaced the container, put back the floorboard, replaced the rug and the table. He eyed her warily. "Are you all right?" he asked. "You don't look so good."

"Are you surprised?" she said. "I can't believe you've got them under your floorboards," she said. "Under the bloody floorboards."

He came and sat next to her and took her hand.

They walked up to Derry Woods that night, starting across the fields from the weirs on the river when the dusk was so deep that it was almost dark.

The paths were dry underfoot, with chalk showing through as the path rose. It was warm, humid, the heat of the day still hanging in the air. Under the beeches, the gloom deepened as they followed the route, Frith gone far ahead of them, thrashing a way through the undergrowth, until they could only hear him, and lost sight of him altogether.

They had last walked here three weeks before. It had been the first week of May then, and the new leaves on the trees had been a high, bright color, dazzling, and closer to yellow than green. The beeches, strung out in a long line down the hill, formed one unbroken green tunnel; below them, just above the water, under a haphazard mixture of hawthorn and scrub, wild garlic had been completely covering the ground, its waxy leaves open in a peeled-back display, giving a powerful, almost rancid, wash of scent.

They looked back now the way that they had come, over the tops of the trees now, to the hills beyond, now just a line of darker shadows on the far side of the valley. Bridle Lodge had vanished from view; they could only guess at the line of the river. All was silence in the upper reaches of the valley. Only in the land below, probably somewhere in the Lodge's own garden, blackbirds were in competition in the twilight.

They stood in silence, his arm on her shoulder.

It was fully dark now.

And yet there was still a kind of light in Derry; they sat on the dry, warm ground, and waited for Frith to come back. In a few minutes he appeared, running full pelt through the trees, catching scent of them as he was almost upon them.

"Where have you been?" John asked him, as the dog lay down beside them and rolled luxuriously on his back.

Catherine looked up at the sky, empty of cloud. She had the same sensation she'd had when a child, of rushing upward. Falling upward through the stars.

She reached for John's hand.

"I want to give Helen something," he murmured. "She needs money."

"Why don't you sell them all," Catherine replied. "You would make a lot of money, John. Perhaps a million pounds. Perhaps more. Helen could have half of that."

"Is that what you would do?" he asked.

"They aren't mine," she said. "It isn't my choice."

"But is that what you would do?" he asked.

"If I were desperate for money I'd have to."

"But imagine that you weren't. What then?"

"I don't know."

"Keep them?"

"I really don't know," she said.

"Pass them on to your children."

"If that was what had happened before, then . . . yes."

"But I haven't got any children," he pointed out. And he was silent for a while. Then he said, "My father kept them all his life. He never told us about them. He left them in his will. It wasn't as if he didn't need money in his lifetime. But there was an instruction not to sell them in the bequest. Dadd gave them to Edward Brigham on the understanding that they would never be sold."

"But you said the other week about selling everything," she said.

"I meant all the porcelain," he told her. "I suppose, then, that I meant the Dadds, too. But now . . ."

"Now what?" she asked.

"It doesn't seem right," he said. He sat forward, knees drawn up, arms crossed over his knees, letting go of her hand. She could just about make out his profile and the frown on his face. "I have to think of these things," he said. "Helen, and the paintings. I can't just leave them. They have to be sorted out. I've been living with my head in the sand, trying not to think about it, for too long. I have to decide."

"Not just yet, though," she said.

He only squeezed her hand by way of reply. She had a sudden crushing longing to stay in the dark. To never go back to the house. Things were not the same in the light. They were clearer, more cruel. In the dark, you could pretend you were invulnerable. That the world would stay away from you.

"Helen's never with anyone for long," John was saying. "She's had a lot of relationships, all ending badly."

"I'm sorry," Catherine murmured.

"Nothing lasts for long with Helen," John said. "She has a lot to hide."

Catherine shifted forward, too, so that she could see his face a little better. "What do you mean?"

"She has bipolar disorder." John turned to look back at her. "Dadd would have known it as mania," he said. "A few years back they would have called it manic depression."

Catherine looked at him in the shadows. "Oh," she said. "Oh, I see . . ."

"She hides it," John said. "Even hides her medication. When I lived with her for a while in London after Claire died, she had an accident. She took time off work. The firm's medical officer came to see her. It transpired that she had never told them about the bipolar. She was asked to resign."

"That doesn't seem fair," Catherine commented.

"People aren't always fair when it comes to psychiatric illness," John said. "But she hadn't disclosed it. They called it a breach of trust."

"What did she do then?"

"Got a job abroad for a while. Moved around. Then came back to London after a few years. But I don't think that she ever really got over being fired," he said. "She bore a grudge about it." He looked down at their joined hands. "She does bear grudges," he said quietly. "You may have noticed."

They were both silent.

Somewhere down the hill, they heard a noise. Next to them, Frith sat up, ears pricked.

"Don't you dare," John warned him, hand on his collar.

"What is it?" Catherine asked.

"Deer, I should think."

She waited a moment; a breeze had picked up, carrying the sound of more than one animal moving slowly through the land below them. They listened to the steady progress, moving from west to east.

Catherine closed her eyes now. The noise of the deer was receding slowly. The scent of the woodland rushed up toward them on the heavy night air.

"Isn't that strange," she murmured. "I can smell something citrus. Oranges."

"It's Douglas fir," John replied. "There's a little copse of them about a mile away, up on the top toward Bere Regis. Their needles smell of oranges and lemons."

"It must remind you of Spain."

"It does," he said.

"Why don't you go back?" she asked. "Put the paintings back in the bank, go to Alora. Lie in the sun."

"Would you come with me?" he asked.

"Of course."

He smiled, though she couldn't quite see it. He had turned his face slightly away from her again. "I can't ask you to do that," he told her. "And I can't put the paintings back in the bank."

"But why not?"

"Because Helen is co-trustee," he said.

"What difference does that make?"

"Why do you think I took them out in the first place?" he asked. "I was afraid she would just take them out and sell them one day."

"But she can't do that!"

"I did it. I took them out, anyway. I considered selling them."

"Does she know?"

"No," he said. "And she's not going to."

"But what if she went to the bank and found they were gone?"

"She won't," he said. "At least, I hope she won't. She's never been there in all the time we had them. I only took them out in January, when I spoke to her after leaving Spain. She sounded very hyper and destructive." He paused. "I think she must have been having problems with the man she was seeing."

"If she finds out now," Catherine said slowly, "she'll kill you."

They stopped, Frith was whining pitifully, desperate to plunge after the deer. John clipped on the dog's lead. He stood up and held out his hand to Catherine.

"You still haven't answered the question for me," he said.

"Which question?"

"What would you do with the paintings, if you didn't have children?"

She paused, feeling the whole texture of his hand in hers, the precious warmth of his skin, the pressure of his fingers. "If Helen had children," she said, "they would have to pass to them, to your nieces or nephews."

"They would never get that far," he told her. "They would be sold before her children were ever born."

"You can't be sure of that," she said.

"I'm certain of it."

She looked back down the hill.

"Then donate them to someone," she decided. "That's all you can do."

"To lie in storage for the next hundred years?" he asked.

"No," she told him. "To be loved. To be seen, to be loved."

The Crooked Path

1886

They told him strange things that year.

Dadd had many visitors, encouraged by the stories that he had become calm. They brought the world with them, the teeming world with its myriad complications, its populous thoughts, the taint of its cities.

They told him that, flooded with migrants, London was now twice the size that it had been when he was first confined to Bedlam; its immensity was famous the world over, by far the largest city on Earth.

It had more Irishmen than Dublin, more Roman Catholics than Rome; it had spread out into Highbury and Hornsey, Brixton and Balham. Places that Dadd would have known, in his youth, in the time of his initiation into the Clique, as elegant and a place for gentlemen were now slums: Holloway, Islington; Soho and the Strand. Holloway had become a wasteland of marshaling yards for the railways, and on the empty grounds between the lines Hell was reenacted daily; here, bones were boiled, rags sorted, and contractors brought their piles of dust.

The railway, thought a great blessing, was also the city's blight. Until ten years before, the fields of Gospel Oak and Kentish Town and Chalk Farm were cattle pastures and watercress beds; but then came the North London railway, the Tottenham and Hampstead Junction railway and the Midland railway, turning all the fields into shunting yards drifting with steam coal smoke. Primrose Hill, which Dadd had known as secluded from a city as anything in the distant reaches of the countryside, had a huge cutting for the Euston railway slicing it in two.

Dadd listened to the pictures his visitors painted. He had not liked the railway on the one occasion that he had ridden on it. It was not simply the noise, after the silence of his life. It was the surrender to all things mechanical, physical and seen. It seemed to him that each man put his faith in only what could be quantified. God had become a Gothic mockery. There was no more room for the small and uncelebrated detail. He preferred the retreat of his own world, and was glad that he was not forced to take part in the other, which men called reality, outside Broadmoor's walls.

The one story that he had been told that truly haunted him was that of the underground rail. The new District line in London ran from Paddington to South Kensington; then east to Blackfriars. Then it began to burrow. They were beginning to start what they called deep-hole boring, where the carriages would be cable cars. Already they had gone beneath the city and Stockwell, like rats in drains and sewers, running greased along their tunnels, silent under the feet of those swarming above.

There was one particular feature, one particular horror, that invaded Dadd's sleep.

It was the single tube tunnel under the Thames between Tower Hill and Vine Street, on the south side. It had already been open for fourteen years when Dadd came to hear of it; 1,400 feet long and only seven feet in diameter, lined with cast-iron sections. When it was opened, a small passenger car ran on a little two-foot track, hauled on one endless cable by a steam engine on the south side of the river.

He kept thinking of the little car, crammed with passengers. The car would rattle, straining at the weight of its load over the narrow track. A man could reach out and touch the sides of the shadowy tunnel. There would be a sensation of being encased in a long iron pipe, the rivets passing within eighteen inches of the body. Rivets and sections that kept out the enormous width and weight of the water above.

This was Hell alive in the world. This was the place of the wide-eyed demons that he had seen for years. A man-made coffin, stinking of wet and smoke and the sweating bodies of others.

But the funicular carriage had only lasted three months. After that time, the car was removed and the tunnel opened to pedestrians. Lit by gaslight, and having to step between the still-existing train tracks, one million people a year crossed the river underground.

He thought of those people. The million faces lit by the gas; the hundred million breaths exhaled in the fetid air. He thought of descending the timber staircases every day, with barely room to descend with any ease. He thought of what might happen in the case of fire or flood. Water filling the iron pipe; flames rolling along its length, and only the timber staircase left as a route to the daylight.

In an effort to climb out of the thoughts, he began to paint precipices. Mountains soaring above water; paths curling between breathy heights. He began to dream of standing on the very top of the highest mountains, where even the colors had dropped away.

He painted The Crooked Path in September, a dry month after a dry summer. Vertical lines ran down the right-hand side of the picture, sheer rock faces. On the highest, balanced somehow on the narrowest of ledges, two soldiers from different millennia were engaged in a life-or-death struggle. Directly below them, three figures sat gazing away from the battle, out across the open country. Two were hunched and veiled, the third seemingly indifferent.

He wanted to show that they did not care about the struggle happening above them; enclosed in their stony corner, there was nothing to show how they had found their way to the spot. He called it The Crooked Path but there was no path. There was no route or road through. Those that battled above had nowhere to go with their eventual victory; those who sat below would never make the attempt to go on, or go back. Isolated, stranded, every figure was in the prolonged act of breathing his last.

Two visitors came from the Chalcographic Society. Dadd did not remember their names.

"Where is the path leading?" one asked him. "I should say that the crooked path is a rather inaccurate description. There is no path to speak of."

Dadd bore the comments with indifference; they did not see, despite their inspection. Perception was a craft. Opinion was a facile pretender.

"How many people have you drawn below?" the second man asked. "I count three bodies, but five faces."

He looked at the man. The fifth face was well hidden, peering from the folds of the garment. The year before he had painted Fantasie de L'Hareme Egyptienne, and he had put a face there, just to the left of the center; shrouded in a cloak, the dark skin and eyes peer out, mere finger-nail cracks in the whiteness of the scene, touches of charcoal in the gouache.

"There are witnesses in grains of sand," he said. And he smiled broadly at them, waiting for their response.

But they did not see. In between the rocks, under the empty ledges, next to the feet of the soldiers, under the hand of the waiting travelers below, in-scribed on the sheer faces of the mountain, were hundreds of eyes.

This was what came at the end of a journey: the watchfulness of the gods.

He took himself out of his room and asked to be allowed to walk on the terraces. There, for the rest of the day, he walked backward and forward, feeling the watching eyes upon him, looking at the earth as it dropped away.

24

All the windows of Catherine's house were open; it was the first thing Amanda noticed as she parked the car in the drive.

Catherine answered the door to her knock.

"What's going on?" Amanda asked.

"I'm cleaning," Catherine said.

Amanda pulled a face. "Never take it myself," she replied. She stepped inside. "What's the occasion?"

"We have a buyer," Catherine told her. "I'm clearing my things out."

"Everything?"

She indicated the piles of towels and bedding. "Yes."

"Clothes, furniture?"

"I'm stealing one of the firm's vans. They're coming after lunch."

"Ah," Amanda said. She put her handbag down on the couch. "Stealing. I must remember to tell Mark."

Catherine, in the act of switching on the kettle, put her hands on her hips and stared at the floor, thoroughly preoccupied. "This seemed like a good time," she murmured eventually. She started making up another cardboard box, taping the edges in place. She looked around her, picked up and folded and packed a couple of towels.

"So," Amanda said, "you're really moving in with John?"

"Yes."

Amanda watched her friend. "And are you OK, really?"

Catherine glanced at her questioningly.

Seeing that there was going to be no immediate answer, Amanda went into the kitchen and came back out with the tea. "Tell me all about it," she said. "Or not, as you wish."

She poured the tea into the mugs and stirred two spoons of sugar into her own drink. "I've eaten two bars of chocolate and four biscuits in the last hour," she mused wryly. "There's not enough sugar in the world for my system. I'm coming back as a man next time." She glanced again at Catherine. "Do you think you might be rushing all this with John?"

Catherine paused a moment. "You think I'm making a mistake?"

"Just because you have to leave this house doesn't mean you have to move in permanently with John," Amanda pointed out. "You could come and live with us."

Catherine looked down at her hands for a moment, then back up at her friend.

"You *do* think I'm making a mistake."

Amanda shrugged slightly. "He's a lot older than you. And you're in a fragile state of mind."

Catherine laughed shortly. "Oh?"

"Come on, darling," Amanda said. "Your husband leaves you without a word . . ."

"And then I meet John."

"Exactly," Amanda said. "And his deranged sister, not forgetting." Catherine paused a second at the word. "Oh, you don't know," Amanda said, seeing the pause. "The check that she wrote has bounced. So I don't think we'll ship that bureau up to John's house, if it's all the same to you." She looked at Catherine narrowly. "You don't seem surprised. Has she done this sort of thing before?"

"John told me she had little money."

"Well," Amanda observed dryly, "he might have told us before we accepted a bouncer from her." She sighed. "But back to a more important subject," she said. "You and her brother." She finished her drink and put the cup down on the table. "You're a bit too old to go off on one like this, all starry eyed."

"You're wrong."

"OK, I'm wrong. If you like."

"My head's not in the clouds. In fact, it's anything but."

"Ah," Amanda said, raising an eyebrow.

Catherine looked at her for a long moment. "John's ill," she said.

Amanda took this in slowly, looking at the expression on Catherine's face. "But not seriously, surely?"

"Yes. Heart disease."

"Is he waiting for a bypass?"

"No."

"Not a transplant?"

"No," Catherine said. "He's not a good candidate."

"Jesus," Amanda breathed. "I'm sorry."

Catherine had sat down, and she now slumped back in her chair, looking past Amanda, through the window to the garden.

"Is this why you're moving up there?" Amanda asked.

"It seems pointless being anywhere else."

Amanda bit her lip, touched. "Look," she said. "Isn't there anything he can do?"

"No, not much," Catherine said quietly. "Some sort of gene therapy in the USA possibly. He seems resigned. It's as if he's waiting."

"For what?"

Catherine said nothing. Amanda stared at her. Eventually, Catherine took a deep breath and rested her head on one hand. "You know that my father died when he was forty-six."

"Yes," Amanda said. "But not a heart attack?"

"No, no." Catherine paused. "The funny thing was," she said, "I mean, the peculiar thing, was that he used to have this recurring dream. I've been thinking about it. He used to dream that he was standing on the top floor of a building, outside. He would be standing at the edge. He used to say that he could see the stone coping running round the edge of the barrier. It was four or five feet high, and he had climbed up on this stone wall, and was looking down."

"How horrible," Amanda said. "Sounds suicidal."

"Except that he wasn't," Catherine told her. "He was the most cheerful man, and I always used to think it was strange, to dream of exactly that—what seemed to be a suicidal drop. But that wasn't the most peculiar part."

"What was?"

Catherine smiled faintly. "He used to say that one day he would jump," she said. "He would *have* to jump."

"And that's not suicidal?"

"No," Catherine said. "He said that he knew it was something he would have to do. Like a routine task ahead of him, a project of some kind. An academic exercise, almost. To see if he could do it." She tilted her head, looking past Amanda, remembering. "And on the day he died," she said, "I thought, *He jumped. He jumped.*"

"Perhaps it was a premonition?"

Catherine paused. "I had the same dream last night," she said. "I was standing on a precipice. And I stepped off, and fell. I woke up falling."

Amanda shuffled forward in her seat so that she was closer to Catherine. "It's not the same as with your father. You're worried about John, it's linked in your head with John, and your brain produces that image—the jumping into thin air image. It's just association."

Catherine was silent.

"Catherine," Amanda said. "It's association, not premonition."

"OK." Catherine looked up from her clasped hands. "I'm sure you're right."

"You've been here by yourself, thinking this?"

Catherine nodded. She put her head in her hands.

Even the act of reciting the dream had brought it back. The dreadful, skin-crawling sensation of stepping from the height into nothingness; the vertigo, the rushing of air. The rock faces gathering speed past her face. She had woken up with her hands and face tingling fiercely.

She had got up in the dark. Scrambled, horrified, out of John's bed. It had been very early; just after five. She had gone over to the window and stood leaning with her hands on the sill, catching her breath, and waited for the first light to touch the garden. She must have stood there for almost an hour, because she was too frightened to turn back and see that it was not her dream of falling, but John's.

She was afraid that she had dreamed it for him. The more she thought of it, the more likely it seemed to her. Once imagined, it wouldn't rest.

Straining in the darkness to hear, she wasn't sure that she could make out his breathing. She became more panicked with every passing second; she became convinced that she would turn and see him lying immobile. Go over to him. Find him cold to the touch. It happened to people. She had read about it. Most heart attacks happened in the middle of the night. She had dreamed the dream, the terrible dream, because he had put it into her mind as he left her.

The dawn came up imperceptibly. At one moment it was pitch black, and then it seemed that in the next second she could see the filmy outlines of the trees, the terrace. In the next, she saw the water meadows, the mist moving through them from the river. A tawny light, somewhere between gray and russet, made the fields full of autumn for a while instead of summer. Then—only five minutes of watching—the grass was that pale, pale green when it first grows, almost translucent.

She had turned back then and looked at him. He was lying on his side facing her. Looking at his hands, she saw them flex slightly. Then he had sighed. She had felt absurd, stupid and absurd. This longing and fear, this complicated feeling, went so far beyond the thin words she could ever use to describe it. And she knew that there was never going to be enough time.

And yet she needed no time at all, because she already knew him. It was nothing to do with age, even the man he was, even the Dadds. Even those points of contact and understanding. It was something else. A recognition. The second—perhaps the third—time that she had seen him she had recognized him. A surprised and sudden conviction, utterly unlike what she had felt for Robert. She had been committed to Robert, but it had been mechanical compared to John. There was no effort in being with him, no compromise, no matter what Amanda thought.

She knew that if she looked up at Amanda now and told her all this, she would be met with some ironic comment. Amanda was a lot of valuable things, but she was not in the least romantic, or even very imaginative. Catherine could never tell Amanda, or Mark. Probably never tell anyone at all what she felt. That she simply had the satisfaction of being in the right position, like an actor moving to cue points on a stage. She already had her prompts; she was already in the action of the play. The lines were already written; they had come into character.

And when John had looked at the girl in the mirror, she had understood what he was saying, and the relief was tangible. She had found the place, found the other world on the right hand of the magician.

She felt Amanda's hand on her shoulder. She looked up to see her friend gazing down at her.

"Darling," Amanda said, "nothing will happen to John."

"No," Catherine said. "No."

"You must get him to go for this gene therapy, whatever it is."

"I will." Catherine rubbed a hand across her eyes.

"Get him on a plane," Amanda insisted.

"Yes, I will," she said. And she returned Amanda's smile.

But she already knew that she wouldn't.

Because they had already stepped from the edge. They were already falling. Through the air, through the glass.

25

"I need to talk to you," Robert said.

Catherine had answered her cell as she had pulled into the drive of Bridle Lodge that afternoon in the Pearsons van. John was waiting for her; the door opened and he came out, dressed in paint-speckled jeans and T-shirt. He had waved; she had picked up the phone, gesturing to him that she would answer it.

"Where are you ringing from?" she asked Robert.

"The motorway," he said. "I'm just at the services near Ringwood."

She was surprised; he was only forty miles away. "What are you doing down here?" she asked.

"It's Saturday," he reminded her. "And I need to see John about Helen."

Catherine stopped short in surprise. "Helen?" she said. "Why?" She gazed at John through the windscreen. "He's right here."

"And I need to speak to you."

Catherine's heart dropped as she watched John walk over to her. Behind him, the gilder who had been helping him with the final stages of the stairway, the restoration of the panels, came out, easing his back, shading his eyes to look across the drive.

"I'm busy right now," she said.

"I wouldn't ask if it weren't important."

"Robert, I'm unloading my half of the furniture from the house."

"Where?" Robert asked.

"At Bridle Lodge. John's house."

There was a long pause. John had come up to the side of the van. She opened the door. "Hold on a minute," she said to Robert, and covered the handset. "It's Robert," she told John. "Something about Helen?"

John shrugged, puzzled. "Tell him to come here."

He arrived within half an hour. In the meantime, there had been a flurry of rain, hard and swift, splattering the windows of the house and darkening the grass. They had rushed to bring the furniture in, and the van was half unloaded; the rest of the furniture was temporarily stacked in the hall. As Robert got out of the car, Catherine watched him look into the van. He walked across to her stiffly.

"Robert," she said. "This is John."

John held out his hand; looking at it for a second, Robert briefly returned the handshake.

"This is about Helen?" John asked.

"Is she here?" Robert asked.

"No," John said.

"Have you seen her in the last week?"

"No, not at all. I haven't seen her for a while."

"What's happened?" Catherine asked.

Robert looked at John and back again at Catherine. "She came to my flat in London," he said. "And she's been ringing me."

"About what?" Catherine asked.

Robert ignored her question and looked directly at John. "She's been ringing me every day this week. Sometimes five or six times a day."

John was silent. He looked at the floor.

"I have only met her twice," Robert said, laying heavy emphasis on each word.

"She isn't well," John murmured.

"That I had gathered," Robert retorted, giving John a look that plainly demonstrated that Helen was her brother's responsibility.

"I've asked her to come here," John murmured. "She hasn't returned my calls this week."

"Come inside," Catherine said.

She had indicated the house; Robert looked up at the furniture, just visible through the open door.

"Can I speak to you alone?" he asked. And he began to walk away, across the gravel, away from the cars, slowly, pointedly, his hands in his pockets.

Catherine looked at John.

"Go ahead," he told her. "I'll wait."

Catherine followed her husband, finally catching up with him at the edge of the terrace. Robert had stopped and was looking down at the view.

"Doesn't he care about her?" he asked.

"Of course he does. You don't understand what's gone on."

Robert laughed shortly. "Well, she hasn't much time for *you*," he said.

"Me?"

He inspected her face, her reaction. The fact that there was not much surprise in her voice. "You shouldn't be here," he said, abruptly.

"What?"

"Getting in between the two of them."

"That's my choice."

"One you've made very quickly."

He turned away from her and looked again down the slope. There were a few seconds of silence. "Lovely place," he commented.

"Yes, it is."

"You've landed on your feet."

She stared at him, affronted, feeling the color rise to her face. Behind her, she heard John go into the house and close the door. She looked at her husband. The same old Robert. Neatly dressed.

Scrubbed and polished, like a clean floor. He was always so tidy; everything kept in its place. Every emotion battened down in case of storm. And she saw that he was neater, tidier, more closed off than ever.

"A cage of a face," she had told John.

He had laughed. "That doesn't make sense."

"Doesn't it?" she had asked. She had laced her fingers across her own face. "Like this," she had explained to him. Then she had dropped her hands. "His whole body is like . . . a fence, a barrier. He gets solid. Literally immovable."

John had shaken his head. She perceived that he thought she might be exaggerating. She wished he could see Robert now. In profile, he looked unnaturally still.

"This must take a lot of looking after," Robert was murmuring. "A proper estate."

Catherine was silent.

He made a move to sit on the terrace wall, then realized it was still too wet from the rain. For a second he stood staring down at the soaked lawn and pathways; then he turned his inspection to her, looking at her with the same flat expression. "Is he like her?" he asked.

"In what way?"

"In . . . temperament."

She shook her head.

Robert was standing very upright, his chin lifted. He looked rather like a man who has been insulted in some way; some subtle way that had only just occurred to him. She turned away from him, running the tip of her shoe along the bottom of the wall, and then leaning down to pick up the few stray leaves that had collected there. She held the damp leaves in her hand, folding them into a ball.

Robert took a step toward her. "He's twenty years older than you," he said. "And looks thirty years older. What's the matter, waiting for him to keel over? Good strategy. Whole bloody estate falls into your hands. Don't suppose he's left it to Helen?"

She turned away and started walking back to the house. Watching her go, he saw her raise her hand to her face, and rub her eyes with the heel of her hand. He started after her.

"Catherine," he called. "Catherine."

She had got to the doorway. She turned to look at him. "You'd better go," she told him.

"And he's so very different from Helen?" Robert demanded suddenly. "You'll find him difficult, I can guarantee that. Do you suppose that a character like Helen's doesn't run in a family?"

"Oh, no," she warned. "Don't begin on John. He's nothing like her."

"He'll become like her. He'll show his true colors."

"No," she retorted. She found that one hand was fisted against her chest. She took a breath.

"You'll see that I'm right," he said.

She looked at him, then turned away from him, choked with fury, hand on the latch. She stared at it, at the brass of the lock, and the dim and distorted reflection of her face reflected in it.

Robert turned on his heel. He went to his car and reversed it savagely out of the drive, spraying up gravel in his wake.

As she stood and watched him, there was a sound of footsteps in the hallway, and John opened the door.

They said nothing to each other.

She stood trembling; he took her hand.

Then they walked away, through the rain-drenched garden, down between the trees, picking their way finally past the heads of the peonies that lay flattened, drooping their dark red bodies out of the border and down against the pale brick of the path.

Flora

1882

The visit came late in 1877; an art journalist from London who had been paid to see the once-genius at work.

Dadd had seen him standing in the hall of Broadmoor, looking about himself at the dining areas and the view of the gardens. He had been standing in a rectangle of sunlight that turned his black clothes sepia, rusty; round-shouldered, portly, his hat held in his hands, he seemed deep in thought.

When Dadd was introduced to him later in the superintendent's office, it was obvious that this man was not a gentleman. His collar was yellowed, the bands of satin on the coat lapels were worn. His demeanor was all turned down, a down-turned mouth and down-turned eyes, and hands clasped one across the other in an odd posture.

Dadd had painted a man like him once, nearly thirty years before—the little man who scrapes his shoe outside the drawing-master's door. He had called it Insignificance *or* Self-Contempt—Mortification—Disgusted with the World. *And it was the world that bore down on the little man's shoulders, the enveloping cloak of the rusty sepia-black world that hung over his shoulders in the sunlight.*

And so the first question he had asked him was "How is the world?"

The journalist had snatched a glance at the attendant; he did not know if any information could be given.

"The world is running apace," he said at last.

"After what?" Dadd asked him.

The little man smiled. "Oh—all kinds of miracles."

Dadd leaned forward. "Have they a name?"

"The transmission by telegraph . . . the phonograph . . . the light globe."

Dadd inclined his head. "What is a light globe?" he asked.

"A filament . . . a vacuum . . . that creates an artificial light."

"By what means?"

"I am not sure," the journalist confessed.

Dadd's eyes ranged over him.

"I hear that you have painted wall murals," the journalist continued. "And the theater curtain, here in the hospital."

"Yes," was the reply.

"You have painted on cloth, for the curtains and scenery?"

"The stars, the planets," Dadd said. "The rising of the sun."

"I have never seen a sky of yours," the journalist said. "I have seen very many figures, and landscapes."

Dadd considered this truth. "I have looked for another world under my feet," he murmured.

When the article was printed just after Christmas that year, the little man in the rusty-colored black coat had called Dadd's paintings "melancholy monuments of a genius." It was better than the last review, in which the interviewer had called the paintings "curious freaks of fancy." However, Dadd was not troubled by them; he never saw them, never read them. They were kept from him in case the diagnoses disturbed him.

He thought for a little while about voices transmitted by wires, and preserved in wax, all which seemed to him to be the product of sickness, a worse sickness of mind than he possessed. And the names were so curious. The phonograph. The telephone. How did a man press a voice into wax, or thread it along a wire?

Birds hung on wires. Sometimes, in the fields when he was a boy, farmers had killed and hung crows on wires at the edge of woodlands, or on field gates, as a warning. He thought of the world's voices hung on gates, hanging head-down in air, strangled and rigid, knotted and tied.

Flight was harnessed this way, and the same with voices and light. A voice, or an illumination, a man-made sun or star, compressed into the hand, balled into a chemical. It was odder than looking in a mirror and seeing a familiar room reflected, printed backward. All the world was going in the same direction, encapsulated, imprisoned, reduced.

It seemed that man's sole intentions were to tie creation to a gate. Put the sun in a glass globe; put a symphony on a wax cylinder. But it made nothing. There was nothing extra gained, except perhaps a little space, an empty space that used to be filled by the actual persons that owned the voices, the actual musicians that played the instruments. It provided a space where once an audience sat in a symphony hall, or a man sat reading aloud in his own room. It prolonged and extended a single moment, making it both small and rootless, no longer identified with a particular place.

Music went hurtling around in the sepia reproduction of the world, the photographed and recorded world, losing the value of the actual moment, because it could be seen and heard over and over again. There was no more advantage in being present. It was of no particular use anymore to be present. The moment could be preserved and played back to you. The experience of passion could be replicated and shared a hundred thousand times, exactly the same in the hundredth telling as it was in the first. No progression, only replication.

He wondered if they had taken the men who created the false miracle into confinement; if they, too, languished into old age. He did not know. He had not asked, so astonished had he been that such a sad little man could create such fantasies, or believe them if they had been told to him.

He imagined his own voice encapsulated and then played back to him. It was simply the expression of what his mind had been telling him for decades; that there were voices let loose in the world that clung to false bodies and inhabited minds. Voices that took on the sound of a man's own.

Soon, he thought, sitting before a blank wall and staring at its face, the world would believe its own bodiless, formless ghosts; it would hear them. It would transmit them to others, and every man would allow himself to become convinced of their reality. Soon, the whole world would be barred and caged, and the asylums would be opened, because there would be no distinction between the lunatic and the rest of mankind.

There was not so much difference then, after all, between the madman and the sane. There was not so much difference between the artist and the lunatic. They bled into each other.

A month later, Dadd was told that Rossetti had died.

Dante Gabriel Rossetti, named after an angel who had, in turn, painted angels. A man who did not need platinum or iridium, zirconium or magnesium, to illuminate his faces. And yet even Rossetti had been tormented in his way. The man had exhumed his own dead wife to retrieve a book of poetry that he had written, and thereafter retreated into an addiction to chloral hydrate. Rossetti, who had painted the same beautiful face of his model over and over again, and called it Proserpine, *and* La Ghirlandata, *and* Venus Verticordia.

Dadd resolved to paint his own beauty.

He called her Flora; and she was as real as Elizabeth Siddall, Rossetti's muse. His own model was called Florence, and she was the wife of the medical superintendent, whom he saw at daily intervals. He asked if he might paint a fresco of her, in the way of the old masters. She was a kindly woman, of a sweet nature, and implored him to paint in her own hallway, so that she might see it as soon as she came into the house.

He painted her on a large space, six foot by ten, directly onto plaster, using the fresco techniques he had learned forty years before; color mixed with water onto fresh plaster.

He painted her like a May queen, garlanded, crowned.

When it came to her face, he had more difficulty than he had ever known. He could no longer recall the exact contours of the faces of women he had known. He had not seen them in a lifetime. He tried to remember Catherine, but no image came. Eventually, he painted a fairy's face with his own striking dark eyes.

She sang out of the picture, calling, calling, the sun rising at her back, the fields filmed with promise of heat, the trees dark with full leaves, the river running through the fields behind her.

The fresco took eight weeks. When he had finished, Dadd retired to his room, lay down on the bed, and stayed there. He called it an idleness; he told his physician the same.

"I am very idle," he said to the doctor who was summoned.

His heart and chest were examined.

"There is some congestion in his breathing," was the doctor's verdict. "Nothing more or less than I might expect in a man of sixty-five."

Dadd lay on his back, hands crossed at his waist, eyes closed: an icon of sleep, a prophet in stone.

In his dreams, he saw himself astride the echoing Earth, painting the planets and stars on the backcloth of the sky, with Catherine at his side.

26

Helen pulled her car over to the narrow patch of ground alongside the road. She looked ahead for a while, to the few flint-and-cob houses on the lane that climbed the hill. Then, getting out slowly, in labored movements, she walked down to the bridge.

Beyond the span, the course of the river spread out into water meadows and became shallow and fast running; here, by the bridge, it was much deeper. She leaned on the parapet and looked down into the four or five feet of water. It was clear above the chalk and pebbles, and looked cool. She watched the eddies, the ripples, the bright green strands of weed lazily streaming from their roots. Running her hand along the stone, she felt the cracks with the tips of her fingers, passed her flat palm along the lichens, feeling their corrugated edges.

As she stood there, a family came along the river path. She heard their voices first and then saw them between the trees, a couple and three children. All three were at the water's edge, where the weeds were thickest. They had a dog with them, a Labrador. It quivered on the bank before plunging in after a stick that the biggest boy had thrown. Helen watched the tableau for some time; all five following the swimming dog, waiting for it to return, framed by the trees, the low-cut hedge, the flat fields beyond beginning to turn to hay.

She let them pass her, smiling at them. The sun beat on the back of her neck; she went down onto the path and into the shade.

She was deathly tired; tired from the driving, the miles of road. So tired that she would have willingly laid down right now; she looked at the river and wondered how much of a relief it would be to be swept downstream, gliding like Millais's Ophelia between the reedy banks and shallows. She wanted, at least, at the very least, to dip her body into the cool and the cold, sink her head under for a second, feel the water in her mouth, on her neck, running over her eyes and through her hair. She was so exhausted. The oblivion would be beautiful, if just for a minute. Or an hour. An hour in the Millais painting.

It was twenty-four hours now since she had gone into the merchant bank at the top of Walbrook. Her heart had been beating so fast from nervousness that she thought she would faint. The last time that she had visited the place had been twelve years ago, when Claire had died. When she and John had transferred the paintings here from their father's bank, into somewhere more central for them both. She only vaguely remembered the interior, a gilt-and-black mausoleum that had been partially modernized, combining the Corinthian marble with smoked-glass security screens.

She had given her number and references; shown her identification. Nothing in the way that the staff looked at her had prepared her for the truth. They acted as if they didn't know. And this fact had struck her with venom, with utter cruelty, when she had come back out into the foyer after visiting the vault. They were smiling at her, the wicked smile of the conspirator.

She had broken back out onto Walbrook livid with fury, and randomly turned south. When she had got to Cannon Street station she had found herself walking toward the Embankment, and from then on, she walked for miles. In the sweating heart of the city, all the way along the river, all the way across Bloomsbury, up Kingsway, until she had stopped on the steps of the British Museum, sitting down among the crowds there, feeling beaten by deception, betrayed.

John only had to tell her. That was what she kept thinking. John only had to speak to her. He needn't even have asked if he had her permission; he simply had to say. But he hadn't. He hadn't even bothered to ring or write a letter. That was what devastated her the most, that he didn't trust her enough to even let her know his decision. He had taken every single painting, every single drawing. He hadn't even left the miniatures, and she had once told him that, even though she hated all the rest—my God, how she loathed them, the eerie and ugly little fairy world, and all its grotesque detail—she liked the little pictures, the ones on enamel, some of them no bigger than a thumbnail. She liked looking into them. It was amazing how deep they looked, how three-dimensional. You could look into them forever and still see something new.

But he had taken even those, pocketed them like a thief. That was exactly it, she had thought, sitting between the ranks of students and families spilled over each other, buffeted by the noise and the unremitting sunlight. He had stolen from her. He had taken them all away, and hidden them, and never said a word.

She never went back home. She had hired the car and got out of London, and driven down here, to the green south with its endless open downland, its chalk flanks. And it was here, last night, in the dark, that she had stopped the car in a pullout, and almost crawled to the shoulder, and was sick into the grass, pressing her hands to her face, her palms hard into her eye sockets, blinded by white flashes, black broken lines.

The day had broken into this dancing, streaming ribbon. She heard them talking to her, not loud enough to distinguish the words, but just talking. That rambling soliloquy in the background that she had learned to tune out came down, a mothy blanket bubbling with sound.

She never took lithium anymore. Lithium, the great healer. All the medication was pointless. It cracked her teeth, it thinned her hair, it made her put on weight. More to the point, it made her—that, and everything else they prescribed her—truly suicidal.

There had been one time. A time in London, after the accident with the car. She had been going somewhere—some interview for an employment agency. She had been standing on the platform at Chancery Lane. It was supposed to be one of the deepest stations on the Underground, and she remembered almost feeling that, the depth of it, how far down she had come. She could feel the oppressive atmosphere in the air. She had waited for a long time for a train. There had been a delay posted up on the electronic board. And then she had felt the train coming, felt the rush of air along the tunnel, and she had been seized by a sudden thrill of release. She could jump. She could fall onto the line. It wouldn't take much. Practically no effort at all. And the realization that she could do this, that she had the power to stop the weight, the unbearable weight of dread and nausea, just by taking a step or two forward and falling . . .

She had glanced up the line. The rails were so uncomplicated. It would be blissful to feel the push of the metal, the almighty crush. Just a second's impact.

The train rushed past her. The noise of it charged through her. She had stood and waited, and then stepped inside the carriage with everyone else.

But it had been so tempting. So tempting. Flooded with desire to cut herself free, she had sat quietly in the seat and fixed her eyes on the floor.

She had never told John, or anyone she knew. After the experience of being fired for not disclosing bipolar, she never mentioned it again in any conversation, let alone a job application. She let people think that she was moody, if that's what they wanted. She let them think that she was difficult. It worked in business; her staff retreated from her. No doubt they talked behind her back, but she didn't care about that. At least it made them do what she wanted. They were wary of her. Careful not to offend her. Careful not to light the fuse. She saw it in their faces.

By the time she met Nathan, she no longer cared. She had accepted that she was shut up in her own world, where she made the rules. And in her manic phases, she had been to bed with whomever she wanted; men she had only known for a few hours, even a few minutes. It was in a manic phase that she had started the relationship with Nathan, in a flurry of desire and possession that she could barely now remember.

Since the termination, she knew that she had gone down like a stone, farther down than ever before. Some days she didn't get up at all. She had wanted it to be so different with Nathan. She had wanted to be a different person. She had firmly believed—my God, she had believed it, trusted it with her whole being—that she had turned a corner; that she had control of it. Because she loved him. She allowed herself the picture of the family, the house, the future; the picture of herself at the center of an ordered life. She would be a picture of calm. She would change. Nathan had been her last chance to change.

It had been now or never. She was in her late thirties; time was running out. Her options were shrinking. She had wanted to give up what she had been before, the way that her life had habitually run. She had wanted the whole idyllic scene, the children, the home, the neatly made beds, the cupboards full of linen, the fresh flowers in the hall, the whole picture she had painted in her head. She had wanted that world, her imagined world, her particular sweet fantasy where she had control of the characters.

She could master the illness; she would conquer it. And for a long time—it seemed like the longest time of her life—she had fought the familiar plucking fingers of the lowering mood, pulling her back to the misery of the drop, the siren call of the abyss, the stroking seduction of the dark.

She sat on the ground by the river now and stared ahead without seeing.

It hadn't worked. In a down phase like this, the world was a slowly rotating carousel, getting ever slower. She would be the only rider, and everyone else, and everything else, stood outside the ride, just gradually passing slurs of shape.

John was less than a mile away now, she knew.

If she walked straight up the lane past the cottages, she would come to a crossroads. Turning left would take her back into town; going straight on would bring her to the edge of the woods. And there would be a gate in the lane, and the beginning of a long drive. That was the entrance to Bridle Lodge. She knew, because she had driven this way the night before, at midnight, and parked her car in the driveway entrance, and looked for the house between the trees. There had been no lights. She had toyed with the idea of walking up there in the dark, a shadow among shadows. Breaking in perhaps, through a door, a window. Finding what he had hidden from her.

But, in the end, she had decided against it. She would see him in the daylight. She would face him. She would ask him why he had done it. She would get her explanation.

And so she had turned the car around and driven aimlessly, eventually stopping in a picnic area—just a rough wood table and a clearing—in the hills above the Frome valley. She had slept in the car.

"Are you OK, love?"

She jolted at the sound of the voice.

A man was looking down at her. He had his little terrier by the scruff of its neck, so that it wouldn't run past her.

"Yes," she said, shading her eyes. "I'm fine."

"You're feeling all right?" he persisted. "Anything I can do?"

She got to her feet, brushing herself down. Why was he asking her such a thing? Did she look out of place? She hadn't considered it. Standing there, the quick-flowing river reflected in the canopy of the trees, the reflections crossing over the man's face, the little dog dancing in his grip, she swayed momentarily.

He put out his hand as if to steady her.

"Is there anywhere nearby to stay?" she asked.

The man was frowning. She looked back at him, puzzled. Surely that was not an unusual question to ask. They were here in the heart of holiday country. The county was dotted with hotels and guest houses. Was it such a ridiculous question?

The man gestured over his shoulder. "There's a bed-and-breakfast just up the road," he said. "House with a yellow sign, on the left. You'll see as you go up toward Derry."

"Thanks," she said. She reached down to pat the little dog, then turned and walked back along the path. Behind her, she knew that the man was watching her every step of the way.

The guest house was just where he had said it would be. They had a room. Helen brought in the only luggage she had—a carrier bag that held a hairbrush and a few toiletries she had bought that morning.

As she mounted the stairs behind the woman who showed her to the bedroom, she felt her feet drag. Fatigue swept over her; her knees buckled at the effort of climbing. Everything went gray: that old familiar gray she recognized, as if all the vibrancy had suddenly washed out of the world.

She found it hard to listen to what was being said to her. She just wanted to lie down. She said something to the woman—she couldn't remember what—thanked her, probably, said the room was nice—something. It didn't matter.

When the door was closed, she laid down on the bed, fully clothed.

And she was sound asleep when, half an hour later, the brief rainstorm scattered its heavy drops against the window.

Tlos in Lycia

⚬⚬⚬

1883

It *was dark; he was trying to remember the route that they had taken when he had been a traveler forty-one years ago.*

He took himself back to the journey, to the warmness of the long-lost day. Lycia, on the edge of the Mediterranean. They had come through Greece, Caria, Rhodes, and passed south, in a country whose name was like a whisper, a lover's endearment. He had been a young man then, barely twenty-five. A young man of promise, whom the whole world now had forgotten. Whom the whole world now believed was already dead.

Dadd stirred in his bed, turning his head toward the window. His eyes opened briefly and looked at those assembled in the room: he thought that he glimpsed Brigham, whom he had left behind in Bedlam. The physicians Munro and Morrison. Even Sir Charles Hood seemed to stand behind them, although that was impossible. Hood had died in 1870; Dadd had been told that even his paintings that Hood had owned had been sold at public auction. They had been dispersed, as the man himself had been dispersed, as he himself would soon be dispersed into the grains of sand and strands of grass that he had painted as his own memorial.

He did not even know who had bought the paintings. He had been told that someone had paid 136 guineas for Oberon and Titania, *and that at least had amused him. He had often thought, since, of his ghastly Titania forever glowering on a stranger's drawing-room wall.*

Dadd closed his eyes on the company. They were ghosts, all.

His mind ran back, over mornings when the sun barely crept into the Bedlam cell; of days, later, when more light was admitted. He remembered the window being altered. He remembered the birds in their cages. He remembered the year when he had at last allowed his photograph to be taken, and the time he had spent looking at himself, an image within an image within an image, for he was more than the man in the picture, and the painting behind him was more than strokes on a page. They thought that they had incarcerated him, but in fact they had freed him; he had traveled much farther than the average man, by virtue of what Munro and Morrison and Hood were apt to call insanity.

He had been freed to walk through his own subtle paranoias, to illustrate his own hell, to design his particular paradise. He thought of Port Stragglin with its parapets and mountains, its physically impossible gradients and fortresses that he had conquered in his mind. He was a landscape of impossibilities and triumphs. He had done the impossible; held the world in his hand, created others, crushed what he did not need.

He was the purveyor of magic, the sorcerer, the Medusa, the Tiresias, the father of demons. He was delicate and kindly; he had spent a year painting the tracery of insects' wings. He had painted a dragonfly, a satyr, a bower of roses. He had painted murder. He had painted knives within the reach of a child's hand, and nightmares on that same child's face. He had drawn tiny gardens of Eden, and populated them with horrors. He had been king and emperor, soldier and thief. He had made empty canvas bleed and sing; run with music. Score a line on flesh; leap with seething ingenuity.

He felt his hand being lifted.

He opened his eyes and looked at the doctor who leaned over him.

"Will you take a little of this?" the man asked. And he held up a glass to his lips. The liquid was a little cloudy. He drank it.

"Laudanum, for sleep," the doctor murmured.

He watched the man's fingers on his wrist and looked with objectivity at the hand splayed beyond: his own right hand that had made so much in life, now inert.

It may have been hours later when they had lit the gaslight in the corridor, and he could no longer see their faces, that someone asked, in a quiet voice beyond the door, if he were still alive.

He dropped his body, weightless as it was, lighter than air, and walked away. The wall crumbled, and he was standing in a crowd of familiar faces. He looked around himself, the grasses leaned across the whole picture. He reached up and touched the nearest, coarsely twined in the stem.

He began to smile. He began to laugh with delight. The sound bubbled out of him, and the whole community in front of him turned: the king and queen and all their courtiers, the pirate, the woodsman, the scholar, the insect trumpeters, the fairy feller himself who, for the first time, turned his face on his creator, and dropped the axe to the ground.

It was real, after all. Everything imagined was real.

He had not lived in darkness; he had not died in fantasy, or been in prison, or lost his reason. He had been alive. He had seen it. He had heard it. And it was not false, but thrived. He had touched them. They had come to him. Universes in thought, multiplying souls. He had known, always, that they had been there, and that he was not out of the world but within it, on that threshold of light and dark, on the invisible meridian.

He leaned back, letting them course through him; galaxies burning in a filament of thread; voices singing through wires. Every impossibility, every possibility.

When he looked back to them all, the girl in the green glass mirror was already smiling.

She stepped down from the shelter of the magician and walked toward him, holding out her hands.

27

There was nothing else to do but go forward.

John took a step across the insubstantial divide, a faint filmy border between this world and sleep. He had woken when it was still dark, and stayed awake, listening to Catherine's breathing and to his own. He had matched the two sounds for a while, copying the cadence, watching her barely visible face in the darkness, intending to get up and go to the window and open it. He wanted to feel the fresh air on his face.

But as he turned on his side, the room looked different, peculiar; it was like looking at a shoreline, the soft little waves breaking at his feet, a humid mist clinging to them. The room, the window, had receded. A kind of softly humming exhaustion came in with the tide; he closed his eyes.

As he moved away, he saw his feet on the water's edge for a moment; then the flickering of passing lights, like reflections. There was a dazzle that reminded him of a long-lost journey; the train ride that he sometimes took across the river into work in London. There had been a bank of poplars planted next to the railway line, perhaps two or three hundred yards of trees. And on sunny mornings, if he closed his eyes, he would see their images flickering on his closed lids; and the effect would be strange, hypnotic and disturbing, a kind of computation that his brain couldn't manage. He had heard someone on the train say one morning that it was the kind of effect that triggered migraine, a strobe dancing behind the eyes. He felt that now; a moment, no more than a single moment, of cinematic frames rushing across a lens.

Then the water was gone, and he was standing on solid ground.

He saw a central patch of red first, pale rose red, almost pink, describing a long slow arc. It was a piece of cloth falling to the ground. He looked beyond it, narrowing his eyes, straining his vision; out of a moss gray bank appeared shapes first, then faces. Eyes turned on him, eyes with incredible intensity. He saw a hand raised in the foreground, and the flash of metal, touched by the sun and turned gold; gold, too, in a strip across the ground as the light intruded on the gloom.

Then, one by one, the flowers were illuminated like lesser suns, all the way along the bank and stretching upward. He saw that it was a dense hedgerow, and the flowers were dog roses and daisies, the petals intricately picked out so that he could almost feel their texture just by looking at them.

Stillness; then the picture fell apart as everything began to move. It rotated and changed; out of the bank emerged figures of all shapes and sizes; a sea captain, staff in hand, a cloak across one shoulder; a woman with a ruff collar of thick lace above a scarlet coat; working men, countrymen in smocks and gaiters, a boy in a green jacket, a man with a grizzled face and a cap crushed far down over it. They had all been posed stiffly between the leaves, and now they moved, walking over the green, the grasses, the remains of nutshells, scattered in thousands of pieces just beyond the strip of sunlight.

He stared harder into the center, where the cloth had fallen, and he saw the magician looking at him, one hand raised as if in warning, a smile on his face.

The man began to stand up and John saw how tall he was, how broad, overshadowing all the other eyes and faces and figures that were now running toward him. And then the figure in the bottom center of the picture turned, holding the axe over his head. It caught the sun again, and flickered once, twice, as dazzling as the disjointed images from the past, the poplars from the train window, jumbled on the blade. John saw him coming, the axe weaving in the air.

The man was smiling, the magician's hand was upraised, and, as he watched, rooted to the spot, he saw, through the dancing racing lights, the magician's hand fall.

He woke, gasping.

Catherine had hold of his arm. "What is it, John?" she was saying. "What is it?"

He turned to look at her, still seeing the rushing crowd of faces bearing down on him.

She got up out of bed and ran round to his side. She opened the drawer in the bedside table, took out the medication.

He put his hand over hers.

"You must take it," she told him.

She gave him a glass of water, and he obediently swallowed the tablet. They waited together, she now sitting on the side of the bed, and he half sitting, half lying, hand fisted against his chest. When his breathing had slowed, she took his hand in hers, closed her own fingers around the fist.

"What was it?" she asked.

"A dream," he said. "It was *The Master-Stroke*. They were all moving. They were all coming toward me."

She sighed. "You're worried about the paintings."

"Maybe."

"Do you want to go to London? Talk to someone?" she asked. "Or, you know, we could just take them, if that's what you wanted."

He looked down at their joined hands.

"John," she murmured. "I want you to do something."

"We'll go," he murmured. "And take them."

"I'm not talking about the paintings now," she told him. "I want us to go to the U.S. I want you to see this doctor . . ."

"No," he murmured.

"It could make a real difference," she said. "You don't have to listen to anyone in this country. There are other options."

"No," he repeated.

He looked up and saw the tears in her eyes. In the same instant she looked away from him, trying to hide her feelings.

He wanted to explain to her about the light. How he kept dreaming about it; standing in between light and dark at first; then the rushing changing light of this morning's dream; but most of all about the sensation that had first swept over him that morning, that he had felt now several times; the sensation of drowning in the hazy sea, softly, without struggle.

"I can't understand you," she was saying.

He turned her face back toward him.

"They'll just try another angioplasty," he said. "Or cut me up with epidural catheters. Do you know what they call those things? Subcutaneous ports for medication. A kind of hole open in my chest. No thanks."

"It would stop the pain."

"It might. It might not. It might set up a bloody infection and trigger a heart attack." He started to get out of bed.

"John," she said.

He looked back at her, raised her to her feet, wrapped his arms around her.

"You've got to do something," she whispered. "Not just . . . nothing."

He pressed his face against her, the sweet smell of her, lowered his head, and pressed his lips to her shoulder.

"Promise me," she whispered.

He lifted his face and held her at arm's length.

"I'll tell you where we will go," he said. "We'll go to Segura de la Sierra."

He smiled; she was staring at him, puzzled, frowning, shaking her head. He put his arms around her waist, kissed her, drew back, and gazed into her face. "We'll drive up there one morning," he said quietly. "Before the sun is up. Before it gets too hot. We'll drive up through the mountains. There's a village there, and a little castle. You have to ask for the keys in the village, and you let yourself in, as if it were your own house. And you can stand and look down, all the way down to the valley."

"John," she said. "Don't."

"Or Cazorla," he murmured. "It looks just like *The Crooked Path*. Did I ever tell you? There's a fortress right on the peak."

He could see them there, perfectly clearly, as sharp as a memory: he could see them driving the long spectacular road through Cazorla, Segura, La Villas; through the thick woodland where he had once seen ibex; he could see himself and Catherine at Ubeda, in the beautiful churches, and at Baeza, the Renaissance town, Moorish and full of medieval splendor, in the white and gold cathedral, in the Plaza Santa Maria.

He could see them in absolute clarity and detail; he could feel Catherine's arm linked in his, and their shadows ink black against the harshness of noon, and he could feel her. He could feel her lying in a white room heavy with heat, naked, the full length of her pressed to him, feel her mouth and touch. The image blasted through him, incredibly vivid, a drench of intoxication, and he knew in that same second that they would never be there.

And that light was rushing outward, and leaving the soft ensnaring waves around his feet, and the inexorable pull of the sea; and that it was inevitable, and part of the world, a moment passing in the world that would take him with it. Just as everything in the paintings had passed out of the canvas and lived. He would exchange that experience. He would pass through the paintings and into the whispering ocean, into nothingness. It was just a movement, a necessary passage. Just like the figures in the painting had turned toward him and began to rush from their places.

And he could see something else, too.

He could see that he had lived.

And that this had been truly living, and that this was what it meant: that he had been more than alive, to be with her.

They went downstairs and the house felt stifling, even so early. They opened all the windows and the doors, grateful that finally a small breeze began to blow through.

"I've never known it to be so warm at this time of year," Catherine said. She walked on, turning her head to smile briefly and anxiously back at him, as she went into the kitchen.

Standing by the stairs, he heard the car coming.

He waited, listening to the speed as it made its way up the drive between the trees. He walked to the open door and stood leaning one shoulder against it, shading his eyes. He saw a car come into view; saw Helen's expression; knew before the car even stopped, before she even got out, what had happened.

She came striding toward him across the gravel and he had time to think: *No, not yet, not today*, before she spoke. The words, the idea, came straight into his head, without thought, without prompting. He pushed himself away from the door and walked toward her.

Helen glanced briefly at the two cars in the drive alongside hers.

"Is she here?" she asked.

He didn't ask the obvious question. "Yes," he told her.

"Have you given them to her?"

"Helen," he said, "come inside. Come and talk to me."

"No," she said. "Make her go."

He paused, shook his head.

"Tell her to go away," Helen repeated. "I'm not speaking to you with her in that house."

They looked at each other. Her gaze, the violent electricity in it, frightened him. But she wasn't trembling, and she wasn't rushing her words. He had never seen her quite this way.

"I'm not telling Catherine to go," he said. He extended his hand. "Come inside."

She stayed where she was. "Where are they?" she asked.

He dropped his hand, knowing what she meant. "In the house."

She gazed at the open door, then back at him. "You've shown them to her."

"Yes."

"Oh, my God," she murmured. She looked at the ground, passed a hand over her forehead. "I knew it would happen one day," she said. "You always behaved as if they were yours. Now you've taken them."

"You can see them," he said. "Come inside and look at them. They're safe."

"Safe from me," she murmured.

"Helen," he said. "You never wanted them. You always wanted to sell them. As for being mine . . . they were left to me. I made you co-trustee."

"And you always wanted to hoard them," she retorted.

"That was the instruction."

"Not to hoard them. To look after them."

"I've kept them safe all these years."

"And what changed?" she demanded.

He walked to her side and took her gently by the arm. "Helen," he said, "how did you find they were gone?"

"I went to the bank, of course."

"To do what?" he asked.

She stared at him.

"You were going to take them," he said.

She wrenched her hand away from him.

At that moment, Catherine came to the door; seeing them, she walked over. "Helen," she said. "How are you?" Helen merely stared at her. Catherine's gaze shifted to John, and back again to his sister.

"I've come for the paintings," Helen said. "I want my half. You divide them up however you like. You can give me the ones you like least."

"Helen," John said. "I can't do that."

"You can even get her to decide a fair division," Helen said.

"Helen," John repeated. "It can't be done. It's not going to happen."

Helen at last dropped her gaze from Catherine and rounded on her brother. "This is the only thing I ever asked you for," she said.

John tried to hold her hand. She pulled away from him.

"Please come inside," Catherine said.

Helen glared back at her. "I don't want to talk to you, don't you understand?" she snapped. "I want to talk to my brother."

Catherine glanced at John. "I'll be in the kitchen," she murmured, and walked back to the door.

"That was rude," John said.

"The lady of the manor," Helen retorted. "Already."

John caught his breath. The familiar pinprick, the needle searching the muscle. He shifted his weight, as if that would distribute the pain.

"I can lend you money. If that's what you need."

"I don't want a loan. I just want what is mine."

"They aren't yours," John told her. "They don't belong to us. They're just in our care."

"Oh, for Christ's sake," Helen said. "Why are you so bloody precious about them? Let them go! They're just daubs. Why let them sit in a box somewhere? They could be doing us some good."

John had been watching her narrowly. "Where has all your money gone?" he asked.

Color came to her face. "That's none of your business. And anyway, I never had any money."

"Your salary . . ."

"Spent."

"The money Dad left you."

She began to laugh. "Five thousand pounds?" she said. "There's thousands upon thousands in those paintings. You could let me have at least some of them!"

John rubbed a finger across his brow, torn, frowning hard. "We were talking about it . . ."

"You've discussed this with her?" Helen asked, furious now. "What was it, 'Give Helen one of them. Which one shall we choose? One of the little ones. The one even she couldn't recognize when it was put under her nose!' "

"It wasn't like that at all," John protested.

"You superior bastards! I want a house," Helen said. "I want a place to make a home. Is it so very much to ask?"

"But you can't just snap your fingers and make that happen overnight," John pointed out. He paused, looked at her more closely. "You're strung out. Have you seen a doctor? Did you come down here without seeing anyone?"

Fury darkened her expression. "Why can't I have what I want?" she said. "Why can't I have it now? You've set up with her overnight, it seems to me. Look at her in this place. You'd think she'd been here for years."

"You don't understand," John said.

"Oh, I do," Helen replied. "I understand that you can have whatever you want."

He searched her face, worried. He had heard this kind of repetitive reasoning before. She looked disheveled, he realized. Her hair hadn't been combed; her clothes were creased.

"I worked for what I have," John said. "It didn't just fall into my lap. I built up a business. And you've got every opportunity for a decent life," he added.

As quickly as the anger and impatience had crossed her face, now they were replaced with a grimace of utmost grief. "You don't understand what my life is," she murmured. "What it's been."

Then, before John could stop her, Helen was running for the house. He set off after her. She wrenched open the front door and plunged down the hallway, opening doors as she went, unfamiliar with the rooms. At the end of the corridor, she found the kitchen. Catherine was sitting at the table, a cup of coffee in front of her.

"What did you say to him?" Helen said.

Catherine stared at her. In the next moment, John appeared in the doorway behind his sister. "Say to who?" Catherine asked.

"My brother."

Helen leaned on the table. It seemed to Catherine that the other woman was going to hit her; she recoiled, scraping back the chair, half rising to her feet.

"You can't have these things," Helen said, in a low voice.

Catherine met her gaze. "I don't want anything," she replied. "Only John."

There was a moment; a perfectly still, silent moment.

Then Helen walked past Catherine's chair. John and Catherine looked at each other, with the same puzzled, regretful expression. Then everything happened at once. Catherine felt the chair tugged backward. Helen grabbed a handful of her hair, pulling her bodily off the chair with a cry of pain and surprise.

"No!" John said.

Catherine was half crouching. She felt how ludicrous it was. Helen was shorter than she was. It was impossible. She swung her body to the side in an attempt to dislodge Helen's grip.

"Catherine!" John shouted.

Helen had taken the bread knife from the draining board; the pressure of the blade against her throat stopped Catherine's struggle instantly. John stepped toward them both. "Put it down," he said softly. Catherine couldn't see Helen's face; she hardly dared breathe. But she saw John's look of absolute terror. "Helen," he murmured. "We'll help you. Listen to me. We'll help you."

The blade pressed harder.

"I know how you feel," John whispered. "I know what it does. Let go of Catherine. It'll be OK," he continued. Catherine saw him edging toward them both, inch by inch. His gaze never left his sister's face. "I can help," he repeated. "Let me help."

Then Helen's voice came as if from a distance; thready, plaintive, a high-pitched whisper.

"You can't help me," she said. A pause; a flutter of breath in Helen's voice.

Catherine saw John's foot hesitate on the floor; she raised her eyes back to his face. His hand was outstretched to Helen, palm upward, a gesture that she should give him the knife; then his hand turned. He suddenly glanced down at Catherine. Something like surprise was in his expression. His color altered. He lost his footing entirely and staggered backward, clutching at a chair and missing it.

He fell to the floor.

"John!" Catherine cried.

Helen stepped back; the knife dropped.

"John, John," Catherine said, scrambling across the floor. She had almost fallen to her knees in Helen's grip; now she reached John's side on hands and knees. He was lying on his back, staring at the ceiling.

"John," Catherine said.

He looked at her.

The light was behind her, streaming through the open window.

He thought he caught a scent of rose, but it passed. He thought he saw her turning more than once through the green glass, raising her head to look at him. He realized that he had never quite finished the window on the stairs, and the portrait in the glass there.

He opened his mouth to tell her to be careful. To be careful how the cracked frames of glass should be handled. That the color should be matched. He had always wanted to match the stained-glass color to the original.

It was a difficult tone, a particular tone.

It was the color of the first leaves and the color of the water below the cress beds by the weir gates. It was slightly darker than the summer grass. It was the color of dozens of thinly painted brushstrokes of yellow-tinged watercolor, caught in a mirror where a face was reflected.

It was a shade of green, a shade of green . . .

Postscript

The front steps of the Tate were crowded; the queue stretched all the way toward the river and snaked westward along Millbank.

It was a winter day and there were snow flurries in the air. But the crowds remained with an atmosphere of good humor. Every now and again the vast main doors were opened; ticket holders were admitted for half-hour passes only.

In the two days since the new gallery had been opened, six thousand people had seen the paintings.

Catherine Sergeant stood now in the center of the room.

She had been there for the whole two days, watching the faces of people as they entered the gallery, each one carrying the program that had the words "Donated to the Nation: The Brigham Collection" emblazoned across its cover.

The Fairy Feller's Master-Stroke, which the Tate already owned, had been rehung in center stage, with a broad strip of empty space around it. Leaflets and guides had been printed to show the detail that even a close inspection of the painting might miss: the tiny pale centaur in the bank of clover, the face of Richard Dadd's father in the top right-hand corner of the canvas; the belts, buckles, and lacing of shoes; the deep folds of material; the faint edge of a woman's face reflected in the mirror; and Richard Dadd himself to the right-hand side of the raised axe.

On either side of the painting were all the others, *Songe de la Fantasie*, brought from the Fitzwilliam Museum in Cambridge; and the copy of *The Master-Stroke* that John and Helen had owned. *Contradiction*, loaned from a private collection; and *Sketch to Illustrate Melancholy*. One after the other the newly discovered portraits from Bedlam, each one full of terrible poignancy, faces of muddled hope and misguided obsessions, sealed forever in their cages of the 1840s; the *Sketch to Illustrate Jealousy*, brought from Connecticut; *The Crooked Path* from the British Museum.

On the opposite wall, *Devon Bridge* and *Tlos in Lycia*, and the dozens of notebook sketches of Syria that John had also owned. And, in the center of these, *The Child's Problem*, which inevitably stopped each member of the crowd in his tracks. In the glass cabinets on the other side were the miniatures, again with the tiny replicas of *Port Stragglin*, *Marius in Carthage*, *Flight of Medea*.

Catherine closed her eyes briefly now.

The opening night had almost been too much; she had missed John so acutely, so physically, on seeing the completed exhibition. Even Amanda and Mark's presence by her side had failed to help. She had felt, bizarrely, irrationally, that she had allowed Dadd to be inspected and exposed.

None of the compliments had moved her; none of the enthusiasm of other collectors, whose own paintings were also here for the first time under one roof. Everything became jumbled; the noise of the guests, the questions of the press. She had had to leave and stand outside, breathing in the icy air, watching the tourist boats plowing the choppy tide down to the National and Cherry Garden Pier, their lights fragmented on the water.

It was two and a half years now since John had died.

Two and a half years since the ambulance had come to the door of Bridle Lodge. They had told her that he had died almost instantly, but she doubted it. Something of him stayed in that room for a long time, some part of him that had never left her.

Helen had spent the next year in care. Catherine saw her sometimes, if she ever needed to come to London; where Helen would be the same as ever, sometimes high, sometimes haunted. They never spoke of the paintings. During her year in care, Helen had relinquished her trusteeship of the Dadds. And they never spoke of John, who had altered his will to leave Bridle Lodge to Catherine, and stipulated his wish that the paintings be left to the nation. Robert had worked abroad, in Germany, for the last two years. There had been no contact between them at all.

She walked through Derry Woods every day. It saved her sanity.

Catherine had seen two years of seasons come and go; sat by herself with Frith in the dark sometimes in summer, listening to the deer that still passed along the same route through the valley in the dark. Walked in the last weeks of winter, waiting for the spring. Walked down to the village by the bridge, and back up again to the weirs below the house.

Peter Luckham had come only last week and told her that the water beds must be cleared again. The cress had grown as thickly as he had predicted. But the whitebeam were lovely when the spring did eventually come; John had been right to plant them. Their images were in the stream all the way down to the water meadows.

John had given her that: made the world different. She couldn't name it, or quantify it. But it was there, changed forever, a vibrant thing, of joy and significance, that he had shown to her. Even without him, even in the depths of grief, she didn't merely exist. She lived.

It was made for love, he had told her. To be alive in the world.

She opened her eyes.

It was enough.

She wanted to go home now, to go back.

She took a long last look at the paintings and the crowds, then left and went through the reception, passing the waiting queues.

On the steps of the gallery, catching her breath in the cold wind, she stopped a moment, closing her hand around the miniature that she always carried in the locket around her neck. It was *The Child's Problem*.

A piece of John that she could not let go, the only Dadd painting that she had not told them about.

She walked down the steps, her hand still closed tightly around it.

Author's Note

Richard Dadd's feelings and beliefs were never actually recorded, other than brief observations by doctors at Bedlam and Broadmoor; my creation of them is supposition. It is a fact, however, that many of Dadd's paintings are either actually, or presumed, lost, and the story of *The Girl in the Green Glass Mirror* is built around a fictional hypothesis of what might have happened to them. *The Fairy Feller's Master-Stroke* is kept by Tate Britain in London; so is *The Child's Problem*.